Adranabar

S L K Sharp

Published in 2009 by New Generation Publishing

First Edition

Published by New Generation Publishing

*For my parents, grandmother, Crystal, Clive, Mary, Harry
and the family of cats – Tiger, Disa and Monsieur,
my companions on the road*

ACKNOWLEDGEMENTS

Bernard, Diane J, Diane W, and Ian, for their help and support – Adranabar would not have come to fruition without you. George, Marjorie, Carlisle Writers, Jo Reed, YWO, Jim Eldridge and all who have been kind.

Many thanks to K, for help and inspired creation of the cover design, Turbot the Fish for interpreting the geography of the world and masterminding the map. Pamela for kindly taking time and trouble to proof read the final draft and make helpful suggestions.

And Caedec, my hero – here's to more adventures in the worlds.

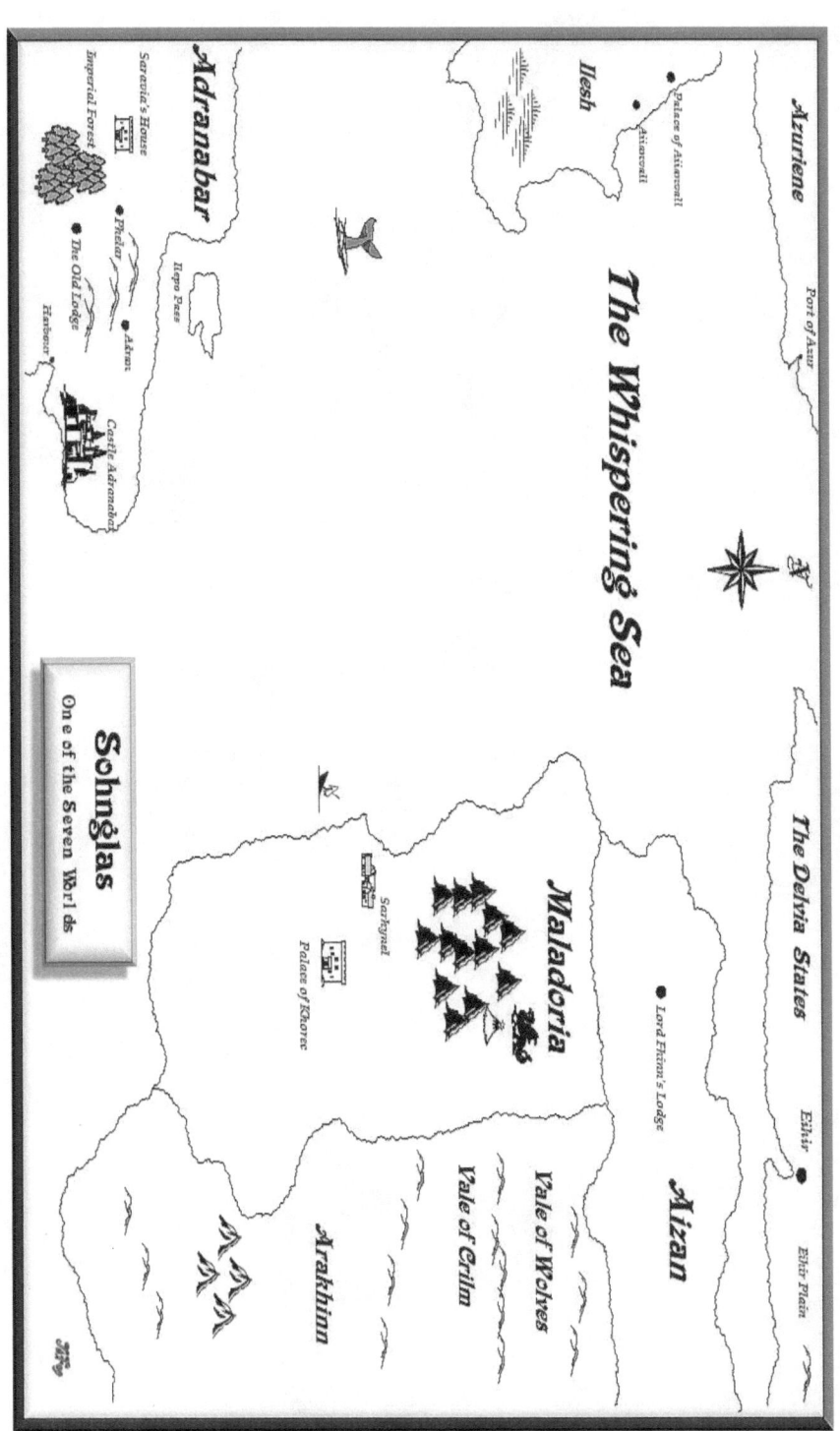

The Whispering Sea

Azuriene

Port of Azur

Ilesh

Palace of Aziarouli
• Aziarouli

Adranabar

Saravia's House
Imperial Forest
• Phelas
• Adran
• The Old Lodge
Harbour
Castle Adranabar
Ilepo Pass

The Delvia States

Eihir
• Eihir Plain

Sohnglas
One of the Seven Worlds

Maladoria

• Lord Fhinn's Lodge

Palace of Rhorvc
Sarkgnel

Aizan

Vale of Wolves
Vale of Crilm

Arakhinn

7

List of Characters

Adranus	Seer to King Caedec and the Royal Household.
Andas	Ship's Carpenter on Azenia.
Aramintha	Salmir's daughter.
Arawena	Caius's childhood sweetheart.
Arraw Sen Miean	Arawena's father.
Arrkir	An adviser to The Crown Prince of Ilesh.
Arunsar	Prince Orthon's Physician.
Atheil	Lord Griann's Manservant.
Aylvian	Caedec's grey war horse.
Bhelus	Adviser to The Crown Prince of Ilesh.
Caius Peregrinus	King Caedec's Master of Horse and ward of Adranus, the seer.
Captain Lhimm Oxghar	Captain of Azenia and famous poet, later Admiral Oxghar.
Cook	Known simply as Cook. She looks after Erarunde's household.
Crilm	Prophet of the Gods of Light in the seven worlds.
Darthus	Master of Horse and father of Janus.
Dhannan, the Black	Prince Orthon's favourite horse - given to Sapphire by the Prince.
Dharvian	Darthus's horse.

9

Duke Marial of Azur	Queen Tsabani's adviser at court.
Egrinar	Sorrel's father and adviser to The Crown Prince of Ilesh.
Elisha	Sapphire's mother (died - plague).
Eloise, The Card Reader of Delvia.	Prince Orthon's favourite fortune teller.
Elthann	Court Jeweller (Adranabar).
Enrhin	Keeper of the Old Lodge near Phelar.
Erarunde	Guardian of the Imperial Forest and Saravia's father.
Erussah, The Learned One	King Caedec's adviser on Law and other matters.
Gai	Wizard, close friend and adviser to the Caedec, The Red King.
Gainen	Gai's brother.
Gille	Lord Caton's manservant.
Gracia	Gai's mother (deceased).
Grey Shadowman	Princess Varcia's companion in the Vale of Wolves.
Griann	Lord Griann Dechevil, Elder of the Adranabar Lords.
Heziale	A sage and friend of Gai's family in Ilesh.
Hhannon	The King's Physician
Hhariann	A War Kotroi – larger cat-like creatures, akin to the size of a leopard, native to Maladoria.

Janus	Darthus's son.
Jhils	Member of Azenia's crew.
Jhinn	Son of Mararuss and Princess Oriahh, Prince Orthon's nephew.
Khinart	Usurper of King Caedec's throne and his sworn enemy.
King Caedec I	Caedec, the Red, also known as the Red King, the rightful King of Maladoria.
Kotroi	Cat-like winged creatures native to Maladoria.
Laderine of Gyle	The Crown Prince's cousin and Mistress of the Royal Household in Ilesh.
Liviaa	An orphan girl Caedec rescues in Ilesh.
Loranda	Darthus's late wife and mother of Janus (died in childbirth).
Lord Caton	Queen Tsabani's ambassador.
Lord Fhinn of Aizan	Ruler of the shipbuilding nation of Aizan.
Lucha	Sapphire's maid after the death of The Lady Annas.
Mai the Golden One	Guardian of the Dragons of Sarhynel.
Maranth	A bay mare Sapphire rides in Adranabar.
Mararuss	Prince Orthon's enemy, Princess Oriahh's widower and father of Jhinn.
Mathuen, son of Ethuen	A young squire in Adranabar.
Merrick	Master of King Caedec's household.

Mhiria	Daughter of Sar-Mhirian, the holy man and Nheve's betrothed. Their wedding is attended by King Caedec's retinue.
Moramus of Gyle	Husband of Laderine and The Crown Prince's ambassador.
Mordain	Khinart's brother.
Nheve	Brother of The Crown Prince of Ilesh.
Niaa	Also called the Black Witch. Niaa uses sorcery to help Khinart's cause.
Prince Orthon	Caedec's cousin and ruler of Adranabar.
Princess Oriahh	Prince Orthon's late sister, wife of Mararuss and mother of Jhinn.
Princess Ormiahh	Prince Orthon's daughter (deceased).
Princess Varcia	Prince Orthon's wife (deceased).
Queen Ahrisa	Sister to Queen Tsabani of Azuriene and King Caedec's wife.
Queen Irmardia	The Queen of the Whispering Sea and Lhimm Oxghar's beloved.
Queen Tsabani	The Queen of Azuriene and Sapphire's aunt.
Rharll	Leader of the Acelphidi, a notorious gang of pirates.
Rulf	Lord Fhinn's adviser.
Salmir	Prince Orthon's favourite adviser.
Sapphire	Known as the Blue Witch. She is Queen Tsabani of Azuriene's niece and last of the Witches of Azuriene.

Saravia	Daughter of Erarunde, Guardian of the Imperial Forest.
Sar-Mhirian	Follower and friend of the prophet, Crilm and his seven sisters.
Sigamus	Saravia's cat.
Sir Atalamir Iboreal	A supporter of King Caedec and discoverer of the Alphus Berry.
Sorrel, Knight of the Order of the Median	Egrinar's son.
The Lady Annas	Sapphire's devoted companion.
The Marshall of Askengarr Castle and his son	Darthus's brother and nephew.
The Seven Sisters of Crilm	Annas, Delvia, Marhn, Phinnia, Helicia, Addria and Vheshia.
Thoro	Second in Command on Azenia.
Varmarah	One of the finest horses in the worlds stabled in Adranabar.
Vinaii, The Crown Prince of Ilesh	Ruler of the land of Ilesh.

Caedec the Red sat reading his diary by the dying light of day. He paused, studying his hands. They were as dry as parchment and peppered with spots of black ink. Brushing his greying hair from his shoulders he adjusted the circlet on his head.

Cinders spattered the hearth as a bell rang, heralding the approaching dusk and the beginning of night.

Caedec was staring at the flames as Gai entered the chamber, leaving a trail of wet footprints as he made to warm his hands. A band of yellow metal wound like a serpent around a thin, bloodless finger, caught the firelight, making the incised lettering dance.

"What tidings, Gai? Castle Adranabar seems quiet to my ears. I have not heard a mouse squeak."

Gai scratched his head, pushing back a lock of gold hair from his forehead. "There are several ships in the harbour, and the courtyard is full of people setting up camp for the Festival, despite this foul weather."

Caedec raised his bushy eyebrows. "My cousin is indulging his passion for fortune telling no doubt. I hope the readings do not displease him, or I fear he'll plunge into a depression and I will have to coax him from the abyss."

Gai nodded. "Yes, a familiar scenario where Prince Orthon's concerned."

Merrick, Master of the King's Household, entered carrying a tray and poured them both wine.

"Punctual as usual, Merrick," Caedec commented.

"Shall I light the candles and draw the hangings, sire?"

Caedec nodded. Merrick lit a taper and toured the chamber, his ruddy complexion was bathed in candlelight as he heaved the hangings across the window, blocking out the icy draught.

"What shall I write? Once I was known as Caedec, the Red King, I had a country to govern, a wife and a son. They were my purpose, my reason for life. Now, I have nothing save this," he said taking the crown from his head and holding it for a moment. He studied the lions engraved upon it - their eyes of blood red garnet sparkled amidst the burnished gold. "Such a fine object, at least it brings me some comfort and reminds me of home on yet another long night in this interminable exile," he said placing it on a table beside his chair.

Caedec's attention turned to the fire, as a log burned, turning to ash. In his lap the diary lay open, its red cover blending in with the folds of his cloak. "You're quiet, Gai. How goes the alchemical quest?"

"Not well. Disappointing is a term I would use," he said studying his rain soaked boots and feeling embarrassed at the wet footprints he had made on the floor. He leaned down, pulling the faded rug over them. He glanced at Caedec, hoping he would not notice it had moved.

Caedec took a sip of wine from his goblet, his feet sliding over the footstool, its embroidered cover worn where they were used to resting. "Come now, you're a powerful wizard. We are old friends and I will speak with candour, do not despair, have faith in yourself."

Gai nodded. "I'll try, yet I'm filled with doubt on occasion and this is but one."

Caedec studied Gai's expression. "It will pass as all things do. How long has it rained? I am weary of it."

Gai frowned, deep lines appearing on his brow. "I can't remember when it started. Adranabar is sodden – the rain sweeps remorselessly over the land and shows no sign of stopping. My horse hates the soft ground."

Caedec nodded. "Then I'll write - another wet day in the land of Adranabar," he said taking up a quill and dipping it in a pot of ink.

Gai smiled, revealing a set of straight, white teeth. "Perhaps it's not the most interesting of entries - but nevertheless an accurate one."

Caedec raised his goblet "Let's drink to that, rain and yet more rain," he said laughing, his crimson eyes sparkling in the candlelight.

Gai wore a serious expression as he sipped his wine. "Caedec, I've heard rumours, the corridors are rife with speculation. It seems The Crown Prince of Ilesh, seeks a new ally. Apparently, Khinart's thirst for power grows and Maladoria may no longer be enough for him. He casts his ambition further afield."

Caedec hesitated, the goblet pressed to his lips. "Vinaii must be concerned," he said sinking into his chair, as if crushed by a heavy weight. "So, Khinart is not satisfied with my throne and seeks another. I wonder if he thinks the same of my wife?" he said gripping the stem of his goblet.

"Sadly, I've heard nothing of Queen Ahrisa. But if Vinaii wants rid of Khinart and the threat he poses, it could be a chance for us."

Caedec raised an eyebrow. "It may, but what can we offer? Our war chest is hardly brimming with gold ducins."

"Perhaps not, but a powerful ally and a rebellion from within Maladoria could sway the balance and secure our victory."

"Seriously," said Caedec straightening himself up.

"Why not? You are loved by your people. Surely the fates will be kind and our fortunes will change."

"Keep me informed, Gai. I await developments with interest."

Queen Tsabani sat in a Loakwood chair with her hand resting lightly on its arm, her fingers clenched around a crystal globe. She gazed at her reflection and found it pleasing. Her breathing slowed as she studied the worlds reflected in the crystal. A light tap on the door announced a visitor.

"Enter," she commanded, hiding the globe under several scrolls.

Sapphire curtsied. "Aunt Tsabani ...Your Majesty. As you are aware, I am expected at the Festival of a Thousand Suns, in Adranabar. A ship sails on the tide and the time has come for me to leave Azuriene - if it pleases Your Majesty."

Queen Tsabani studied her niece for a moment, thinking how lovely she looked. "Sapphire, I was once as young and impetuous as you are. Be careful, there are many dangers in the worlds. The Festival attracts those who practice the magic of darkness as well as light. Your mother, Crilm rest her soul, isn't here to guide you so I must do my best. Now, I'll say no more. Go, with my blessing."

"Thank you," said Sapphire as she curtsied and withdrew.

Queen Tsabani stood by the mullioned window of her chamber. She noticed several birds settling on the palace roof, gazing at them until she saw Sapphire in the courtyard below. Queen Tsabani watched as Sapphire made her way to a carriage drawn by four white horses. A footman opened the door and she disappeared from view. "Safe journey, you're more precious than you'll ever know," whispered Queen Tsabani.

Sapphire noticed the port was busy as the carriage drew on to the quayside. She saw a pennant of black and gold fluttering atop the *The Marial*. Dusk was settling on the water and the tide was high as she alighted from the carriage. She fastened her cloak and pulled up the hood to stop the cold wind biting her face. She watched as people scuttled along like crabs towards the ship. She noticed Lord Caton,

17

her aunt's fashionably attired ambassador, sauntering along the quayside towards her.

"Lady Sapphire, Her Majesty commands I escort you on board,"he said bowing low.

Sapphire smiled. "Why thank you, Lord Caton - that is very thoughtful."

Sapphire felt herself guided towards *The Marial*. "Make way for The Lady Sapphire of Azuriene," he said as he ploughed through the mass of people, ensuring her swift progress.

Once safely on board he introduced her to the captain and made to withdraw. "My Lady Sapphire, please extend my good wishes to the Red King," said Lord Caton smiling. Sapphire felt his fingernails catch her skin as he touched her hand. He held her gaze for a moment, and then he was gone.

Sapphire was shown to her cabin and immediately began searching through the contents of several coffers. At last she found what she was looking for - a gown of blue velvet encrusted with pearls from the Whispering Sea. "A new gown to please my love," she said aloud, as she laid it on the coverlet and placed a pouch containing an amulet beside it. She admired the gown for a moment then surveyed the cabin. A letter placed on a writing table caught her attention. She noticed it bore an ornate seal and picked it up, feeling the paper as she scrutinized it.

Caedec strolled across the courtyard of Castle Adranabar, inhaling the aroma of spices drifting up to the battlements of the fortress palace, with its vast cobbled courtyard, curtain wall and cylindrical towers.

A sea eagle circled as he strode along the uneven path to the harbour. He knew every stone underfoot and soon the stretch of water surrounded by walls came into view. Taking deep breaths of salty air he stopped to admire several vessels, and then resumed his progress to the shore.

Caedec stared at the view over the Whispering Sea as if bewitched by sirens.

A wave raced towards him swirling in eddies at his feet, the hem of his cloak darkening with the water's weight. He stepped back almost treading on a black cat sitting on the shore. He stared, fascinated by the creature. As he followed its gaze he noticed a vessel heading towards the harbour. His heart pounded when he saw a sail of silver and gold.

"Surely this vessel brings tidings from The Crown Prince," he said turning to the black cat, but it had vanished leaving him on the shore alone.

Gai noticed the door of his chamber was slightly ajar, letting a stream of candlelight escape. Someone, or something, was already there. Waiting. He squeezed through the opening glancing at the anteroom and saw nothing had been disturbed. All was as he had left it. A heady scent hung in the air as he stood listening for intruders. "Sapphire!" he said barging in and tripping over several books in his haste to greet the elfin figure of a woman sitting inside a circle of burning candles. He jumped over them, pulled her close and kissed her. "My love you're here at last," he whispered.

Sapphire pulled away, brushing hair like captured sunlight from her porcelain complexion.

"Let me look upon you, Sapphire I've missed you and your attire is magnificent," said Gai studying her gown.

"I hoped you would like it," she replied with an adoring glance. "I wanted to see my husband and help the King."

"Sapphire - be discreet there are spies everywhere, our marriage must remain secret," Gai faltered, noticing her expression.

"It's not my fault I'm admired by The Crown Prince."

Gai's body stiffened. "I'm sorry - I didn't mean to offend you. Forgive me, I possess a jealous nature."

Sapphire's expression softened. "I accept your apology."

"Is the amulet safe?"

Gai's eyes glittered as Sapphire produced a silk pouch from the folds of her gown, and placed the jewel in her palm.

"I'll guard it for you," he said, his fingers hovering above the magical object.

Sapphire clenched her fist and stepped back. "I think not - it was entrusted to me. I am the last of the witches of Azuriene."

"As your husband I could ..."

A scathing look crossed her features silencing him in mid sentence. "You should go. I've an audience with Prince Orthon," she said turning away.

Caedec retraced his steps to the harbour hoping to find the ship moored there. He stood at the wall resting his hands on the coarse stone. He watched men and boys unloading coffers from merchant vessels, lining them up on the quayside and looking to the captains for a gold coin for their trouble. Witches, wizards and their familiars disembarked making their way up to the castle. Their hats, decorated with mystical symbols fascinated him.

Caedec gazed at the clear waters of the Whispering Sea lapping against the dock. A galleon, with the silver head of an Ileshian leopard emblazoned on the main sail, caught the sunlight. His attention turned to the vessel as it was towed into the harbour and dropped anchor. He watched as a rowing boat approached the ship and a young knight, lean and long limbed with hair of flame was rowed to the quayside.

Caedec's eyes cast reflections of red on the knight's surcoat. He studied the young man with curiosity as he approached.

"Sire, may I speak with you?"

"Certainly, your countenance looks familiar."

"I'm Sorrel, Knight of the Order of the Median. I don't think we've met before this day."

"No, perhaps not but you remind me of … my son, Greylan. I have not seen him since the Battle of Eihir Plain," said Caedec, the light fading from his eyes.

Sorrel stood with head bowed remembering the strange disappearance of the King's warrior son on the battlefield.

"Come lad, walk with me awhile."

Caedec and Sorrel strolled from the harbour towards Castle Adranabar. They wandered across the courtyard picking their way through the gatherings of mystical folk. From the folds of a blood red tent Azuniel, the necromancer's hooded eyes followed them as they entered the castle. Once inside they climbed a staircase leading to a gallery. Caedec stopped, drawing the young knight's attention to the portraits of his ancestors. After several moments of reflection they continued up another flight.

Sorrel was fascinated by the bloodstained flags hanging from the vaulted ceiling.

Caedec approached a red flag embossed with a unicorn. He whispered several magical words and it moved, revealing a doorway. They walked along a passage to a door peppered with iron. Sorrel followed the King into the chamber beyond. He gazed at the tapestries as Caedec seated himself. Caedec indicated a chair and Sorrel sat down, grateful for the opportunity of resting his aching limbs.

Caedec smiled. "Now, Sorrel what tidings do you bring?"

Sorrel's brow furrowed. "His Majesty, The Crown Prince, has received reports from reliable sources in Maladoria. It seems Khinart is negotiating an alliance with the Emperor of The Delvia States. He believes such an alliance would be disastrous for the lands of Ilesh, Adranabar, Aizan and perhaps even Azuriene. So, The Crown Prince offers his support should you decide to regain what is rightfully yours. He desires unity, sire. The Crown Prince believes war is coming. Will you sail to Ilesh?"

Caedec's expression was thoughtful. "Please thank The Crown Prince for his kind invitation. I will prepare for the voyage."

Sorrel bowed. "The Crown Prince will be pleased to receive your favourable reply."

Caedec smiled. "I hope we meet again young man – I wish you safe passage."

"Thank you, sire. I'm sure we will. I have other matters to attend to elsewhere in Adranabar and then I return to Ilesh. Perhaps I will be there to welcome you to our country."

Caedec nodded. "I look forward to that."

Caedec stared at the leaves caught in the breeze. Suddenly, the trees stirred as a creature, dark as night, leapt off a branch and flew across the sky. "Come, look at this."

Gai made to the window just in time to see a black cat-like animal land on a branch and wash its fur.

"A Kotroi, I believe this one has flown from Maladoria. It is an auspicious sign."

"Indeed," Gai replied in a disinterested tone as he returned to the dining table. He stared at his plate then pushed it to one side.

"Gai is anything troubling you? Perhaps a walk in the gardens will brighten your mood."

Gai attempted a smile. "No, nothing I can speak of," he said pouring water into a goblet and pressing the cold glass to his lips. "Perhaps a breath of air would clear my mind."

As Gai and Caedec strolled, the weather changed.

"There's a storm brewing," said Gai as a bolt of lightning shot through the gunpowder sky.

"We should return, Gai … at once," said Caedec turning quickly as he felt something brush the back of his neck. "Well, I could have sworn I felt fur or something …"

Darkness was falling as they entered the courtyard. Gai watched as Caedec disappeared into the labyrinths of Castle Adranabar. He pulled his cloak tightly around him as he was drenched by a torrent of rain. Gai hesitated, watching a cloaked figure emerge from a tent. He was convinced it was Sapphire and set off in pursuit. He struggled for breath, his wet cloak weighty on his tall, thin frame. As he gained pace the figure vanished into the Rose Garden. He looked in dismay at the dirt covering his apparel. "Damn!" he muttered.

As Gai and Caedec strolled through the courtyard a scream shattered the tranquil afternoon, stopping them in their tracks. Caedec's face was full of tension.

Gai was alarmed as he watched Prince Orthon's guards run towards the stables.

"What in the worlds is going on?" said Caedec as Darthus, the Prince's Master of Horse, drew level with him.

"Sire, there's a disturbance at the harbour," he replied reining in his skittish mount.

Gai and Caedec exchanged glances and quickened their pace. Caedec's cloak trailed on the cobbles impeding his progress. He heard several voices reach a crescendo as he strode towards a mob with Gai following, uttering incantations.

Chaos reigned over the harbour - broken coffers and fruit covered the ground. Caedec's fingers were poised in readiness on the hilt of his sword as a cry pierced the air. "Maladorians out!" He saw several courtiers had been cornered by a crowd brandishing weapons of every description. He noticed knives, swords and even pitchforks were in evidence. Caedec noticed a bearded man holding a dagger to a boy's throat and was consumed by fury. "Leave them alone!" he bellowed. As his sword emerged from its scabbard the silver blade, wrought by the sisters of Crilm, sparkled and Caedec's grip tightened on the hilt set with seven jewels. He held it aloft and the gathering hesitated, frightened as the emeralds' hue dazzled them. "We didn't mean any harm - we're loyal to our Prince," said a voice from the heart of the crowd. Suddenly, the mob parted to let the bearded man pass. He eyed Caedec with disdain. "I say Maladorians out! We don't want you here. Our taxes have been raised to pay for the Prince's pleasures and yours. This is our land, why don't you go back to where you belong," he said as the crowd applauded him.

Caedec scowled, feeling the blood pumping furiously around his body. "Prince Orthon will not tolerate this - go home and you will escape punishment," he said as they whispered amongst themselves.

"We've come to see the Prince, so let him answer for himself. Who rules Adranabar is it you or him?" replied the bearded man.

"Prince Orthon will not be held to ransom. You may seek an audience using the proper channels."

"Hah - tell him Mararuss Laboute wants him. I know what he'll say."

Cries of laughter rose from the crowd as they edged forward.

Darthus and his men had rounded up a group of miscreants making off with a ship's cargo. As he glanced over the water he realized Caedec was in danger and rallied several horsemen. A sound of thundering hooves scattered the mob.

Darthus leapt from his horse, pouncing on Mararuss Laboute and knocking him to the ground. They struggled violently, their swords clashing as they fought a deadly duel - but Darthus's knightly stature was more than a match for the hefty frame of Mararuss Laboute. A dance of death continued until Darthus gained an advantage over his opponent. He flung Mararuss against the wall, pinning him to the stone with the full weight of his body. "I ought to run you through, but the Prince will have your hide this time," Darthus hissed.

Janus tried to move his young limbs, without success. His body felt as if it was petrified. "I will have my vengeance, Mararuss Laboute. I swear it on my mother's tomb. You'll never put a knife to my throat again, nor will any other. I will be a great warrior and nothing will frighten me."

As Caedec sheathed his sword he watched the rebels cut down like sheafs of wheat, or captured and hauled off to the dungeons. He clasped Gai's arm. "I trust you are unharmed. What a dreadful business, Gai. I believe the time has come for us to leave Adranabar. I pray I am spared to return to the land of my forbears," he said.

Caedec took Janus in his arms. He saw the boy's tears trickle down his cloak.

As they walked in silence a black cat, Caedec's secret guardian, slipped into their footsteps as the cold rain of the Western Peninsula began to fall. Castle Adranabar loomed and Darthus greeted Gai and Caedec, taking his son gratefully in his arms and lovingly stroking his face.

"Janus is distressed, but unhurt," said Caedec.

"Thank you. We've had our share of trouble this day."

Caedec nodded. "There may be more to come."

Prince Orthon surveyed the Great Hall with the gaze of a wolf stalking prey. His hair shone like a raven's wing in the candlelight. Gai was surprised to see Sapphire at the Prince's side. His face clouded with darkness. Jealousy stirred in his soul.

Prince Orthon had spared no expense. The Great Hall of the Unicorn was full of tables covered with food and goblets. Conversation and laughter filled the hall. As the music began Caedec stepped forward flanked by Gai and Caius, his Master of Horse. Caius wore a cloak embroidered with dragons. A cascade of red hair covered his shoulders. An enormous cheer resounded as they took their places at the Prince's table.

Dancing and merriment followed. A trumpet sounded and Prince Orthon rose as a chill air crept in and the atmosphere changed. Silence descended and the Great Hall was a mass of bowed heads as he spoke.

"I remember *The Gain Well* dropping anchor here. I still recall the drawn faces I saw that stormy night - escape from Maladoria had taken its toll. Now, we are gathered to wish all a safe journey home. I'm sure you've heard tidings of Mararuss Laboute's arrest. At this very moment he is imprisoned, charged with treason. I ask for your support at this troubled time and request you tarry for the trial."

Glances were exchanged and the impending hearing cast a pall over the proceedings. Once his speech had ended, Prince Orthon immersed himself in conversation with Sapphire. Something was afoot. Caedec could feel it.

"I had not anticipated this. Darthus, I must have an audience with Prince Orthon," Caedec whispered.

"Yes, sire - I'll see to it."

Gai and Caedec, accompanied by a guard of Maladorian nobles, left the Great Hall of the Unicorn. Strolling across the courtyard they heard chants of "Free Mararuss!" from without the castle walls.

"Caius, what do you know of Mararuss Laboute?" said Caedec as they entered the south wing.

"I know very little, sire. Only that he hates Prince Orthon and wants revolution."

Caedec grimaced. "My cousin has a deadly enemy."

Thankful to reach the sanctity of his chamber, Caedec sank into a chair and as if by magic Merrick appeared bearing a goblet of warmed Adras.

"How were the festivities?" Merrick enquired hovering, hoping for some gossip.

Caedec hesitated. "There was good food, wine an enjoyable evening . . . Orthon's speech was rather surprising."

"How so?"

"My cousin requests we tarry for the trial of Mararuss Laboute and I have promised to prepare for a voyage to Ilesh."

Merrick scratched his head. "I hope they hang the blackguard, threatening that poor lad and causing a riot, it isn't right and proper."

"His fate will be decided soon enough. I had hoped our voyage would not be delayed, but perhaps the fates decree we remain for some reason," said Caedec.

Merrick's features clouded. "Prince Orthon has grasped an opportunity to rid himself of this man."

"Quite so, yet I believe our presence may antagonize an already delicate situation. That is my concern."

Winter elementals swept over the sea. Ice would soon form slender webs across the castle's windows, heralding the Claws of Winter. Caedec sighed and lay down on the four-poster haunted by ghosts - his sleep was troubled. Tired of tossing and turning he got up and sat in a chair by the fire. As he studied the sky a dog barked, the sound carried on the wind as shutters rattled. A light mist was settling on the battlements, as a golden moon bathed the ancient fortress. Statues of Wolves, guardians of the soul and symbols of the Union of the Wolf, the fellowship of the seven worlds, cast shadows on the walls.

Caedec was transfixed as tiny stars formed the shape of a Kotroi, a winged cat.

Stars shifted as the Kotroi's wings beat and it flew towards Ilesh. Caedec was astonished, believing the fates were guiding him. He rose and made to the ante-chamber, poured water into a bowl and studied his reflection in the sparkling liquid. A face with a halo of golden hair smiled back at him. "Ahrisa," he said as the jug slipped from his grasp, exploding into fragments as it hit the floor.

"Caedec, my husband, come home," said Ahrisa and the vision vanished.

Caedec was astounded, it was so long since he had seen his wife, or heard her sweet voice. He was saddened the vision had been so fleeting. He shed a tear as a searing pain consumed him, plunging him into darkness.

Merrick was woken by a noise. He rushed to Caedec's chamber and finding no answer entered to find the bed empty. Noticing the door of the ante-chamber ajar, he ventured in to find Caedec unconscious and bolted in panic.

Gai dressed hastily and went to investigate the commotion outside his chamber. "By the Lords of the Realms, what's the matter, Merrick?"

"Lord Gai, come quickly… the King."

Gai felt a cold sliver of ice pierce his heart as he looked upon the King. "Merrick, help me carry him to the bed."

Sapphire still half-asleep was drawn by the disturbance. Standing at the door to the ante-chamber she struggled to comprehend what had happened. "What's the matter?"

"Caedec is unwell," Gai replied.

"May I look upon him?" said Sapphire, her face full of concern.

"Of course, come hither."

Sapphire stared at Caedec's ashen pallor - touching his brow she felt the skin waxen. Her fingers closed around his wrist as she recited a healing mantra. A golden mist covered his inert body, whirling about his limbs. Caedec came round to find Sapphire, Gai and Merrick peering at him. "Why are you staring at me in this morbid fashion?"

Gai breathed deeply, feeling a sense of impending loss, his features clouded with concern.

Caedec attempted a smile. "I saw Ahrisa. I felt a searing pain in my chest and woke to find you staring at me. Is it day or night?"

Sapphire and Gai exchanged glances. "Darkness is still upon us," she replied.

Caedec was troubled. I am worried about Orthon, Gai. I believe Mararuss and his followers will cause him distress."

Gai pulled the coverlet over Caedec. "Prince Orthon can manage his own affairs."

"Yes, of course …" Caedec's voice trailed off.

"I agree Prince Orthon's life has been blighted by tragedy. I've heard rumours of foul play concerning his late wife and daughter. I believe unrest in Adranabar will try his constitution further, but you must not worry, it isn't good for your health," said Gai.

"Orthon was born under a dark star. He has much to bear," replied Caedec.

Prince Orthon beamed as the card reader approached. She was dressed in a flowing gown of black velvet with a jewelled ruff around her neck. "Good of you to come, Eloise. How was your journey?" he said taking her hand and leading her to a chair.

"My journey passed well enough, sire, though at times the seas were stormy."

"How are things in The Delvia States?" said Prince Orthon.

"At home, dear Emperor Illavian values my art. I'm summoned to the palace on more occasions than would be good mannered to mention, but I wouldn't miss the Festival of a Thousand Suns for any amount of gold coin. I must keep abreast of gossip."

Prince Orthon grinned. "Then we are honoured with your presence."

The card reader blushed, seating herself with a graceful movement. Prince Orthon studied her hair of burnished copper. She returned his gaze with black, piercing eyes.

"Shall I begin?"

Prince Orthon shifted in his chair taking a sip from his goblet, his fingers curled around the stem as the cards were dealt.

The Card Reader of Delvia placed several cards on the table, studying each in turn. She paused, concentrating on the pattern they made. "I sense love around you - a secret love - one who is unattainable or a person of a lower rank than yourself. Alas, they also tell of someone who wishes you ill. There are troubled times ahead and you will need all the strength you possess to overcome them. Be careful - danger lurks in the shadows and all is not as it seems. Remember these words and keep this with you," she said taking the Prince's hand and placing a charm wrought in gold and set with jewels into his palm. "It will protect you."

Prince Orthon said nothing as he put a bag of coins on the table. "Thank you for the charm. I hope I won't need its protection."

"I'm afraid you will."

Prince Orthon shivered.

The card reader took the bag feeling its weight for a moment. "Thank you, I will of course, answer any questions."

"You have given me much to ponder. Thank you," he said.

"My pleasure."

"Stay for supper, I insist, Eloise. You and I are friends of old and I would be glad of the company."

"How could I refuse?"

"Splendid!"

Merrick was making breakfasts. As he prowled the kitchen in search of herbs and spices he was startled by a loud knock. He opened the door to find a burly man with an ungainly scar on his face standing on the threshold. "What can I do for you?"

"I'm looking for Merrick?"

"You've found him," said Merrick, cheerfully offering his hand in greeting.

"I'm pleased to make your acquaintance. Prince Orthon commanded me to give this scroll to you. It's for King Caedec," he said withdrawing the paper fastened with Prince Orthon's seal from his belt with plump bejewelled hands.

"Certainly, I will see to it." Merrick replied taking the scroll, studying the messenger with curiosity. "If you'll excuse me I will deliver this at once."

Merrick handed the scroll to Caedec. He watched as the parchment unfurled, intrigued by the elaborate script.

"I am summoned to the High Court. A date has been set for the trial of Mararuss Laboute," said Caedec flinging it down on the writing table. "I believe Orthon is courting trouble, Mararuss is popular. Alive he may fade away - dead he might not. Orthon has ordered the High Court to convene and commanded the Adranabar Lords attend the hearing. I am called as witness for the prosecution."

Merrick was distressed to see the Caedec angry. "Shall I help you don your attire?"

"Yes, I must be ready for the day ahead," said Caedec composing himself as he was dressed in a woollen tunic, with breeches tucked into long boots. Merrick was pleased with his work.

"Merrick summon Gai for me, he must hear these tidings."

"Of course," he said bowing as he withdrew.

Gai retrieved the parchment, the silver particles in his eyes shone as he scoured the document. "Prince Orthon has acted with haste."

Caedec nodded. "He has and it grieves me, I have been unable to speak to him about the matter and now the Lords are summoned. Why in the worlds has he involved them? They would depose him given the opportunity and yet he cannot see them for what they are."

Gai frowned. "Prince Orthon has made up his mind to execute Mararuss Laboute. As for the Lords, I know Sapphire cares nothing for them – but Griann is a good fellow and loyal. He does not forget his love for the Prince's daughter. If Oriahh had lived, he would've made a good husband and son in law – Prince Orthon would not have been troubled on either count. He will keep the Lords in order. I'm sure of it."

"Then let us thank the Gods Orthon has his support," said Caedec.

Gai returned to his chambers. Sapphire was lying on the bed eating fruit. "Where have you been?"

"With Caedec – why do you ask?"

Sapphire looked at her husband with expectation. "Curious that's all. Tell me more."

"Prince Orthon intends to bring Mararuss Laboute to trial. He has summoned the Lords and means to use Caedec as his witness."

"The Lords of the Northern Isles are on their way as we speak? I've no wish to encounter that rabble again, flaunting their riches and vulgar manners, why it's nauseating. The revenue they reap from the Adras is obscene. I feel sorry for their tenants gathering the ingredients and getting little payment in return."

Gai smiled. "You aren't enamoured of them?"

Sapphire laughed. "I'll be happy when we sail to Ilesh. The Crown Prince has asked for my help. His lands are plagued by strong winds and he's concerned about the destruction they cause. He thinks it might be the work of a witch."

Gai's cheerful expression vanished. "I see - I'm sure The Crown Prince will enjoy your company."

Sapphire was hurt by his tone. "I believe it would be unwise to refuse."

Gai struggled to hide his jealousy. He could barely bring himself to look at her as she swept out of the chamber, without a second glance. A cold breeze drifted through a half-opened shutter and Gai felt the chill. "What have I done, Sapphire?" He whispered.

Caedec opened the lid of a silver box, studying several scrolls and letters. "I must reply to these," he said as Merrick entered carrying a tray.

"Sire, I've spoken to Darthus. An audience has been arranged with Prince Orthon. He'll see you after you've finished your meditation, before Crilm's bell strikes noon," said Merrick.

Caedec nodded, pausing as he ate a chunk of spiced fruit with a slice of moulded bread, a speciality unique to Adranabar.

It was a pleasant walk to the Prince's apartments with birds singing and flowers in bloom. Caedec faltered - convinced he heard the sound of laughter. He shook himself, trying to shed his reverie, feeling the presence of Princess Varcia's ghost. He saw her face reflected in the puddles dotted around the courtyard, as he had in the river long ago, then she was gone, as quickly as a moon at midnight.

Caedec approached the royal apartments with a heavy heart. "How in the worlds am I to dissuade Orthon?" he said aloud. Prince Orthon's guards stood to attention. Their cloaks, tunics and breeches were clean and pressed. He noticed the blades of their swords glinting in the sunlight. Darthus was astride Varmarah, Caedec watched with admiration as she trotted towards him. "My word, Darthus, the guards are well turned out and Varmarah looks well. Her coat is like liquid sylverine. She's certainly one of the finest horses in the worlds."

"Thank you, sire. Do you know she has a new foal? I believe he has the makings of a good war horse. I see you're alone. May I escort you?"

"Yes, indeed. I am delighted to hear of the new foal. I expect it has pleased my cousin," Caedec replied.

Darthus opened the door and they stepped in to a passage. As they walked its length, Caedec glanced at the paintings of Princes of Adranabar hung opposite those of the Kings of Maladoria. Caedec studied his likeness facing that of Prince Orthon.

"I wonder, Darthus. Will there be more portraits to hang on these walls? Greylan has gone and Orthon lost his wife and daughter to the Vale of Wolves. In future our alliance may not exist. I have learnt nothing is certain in the worlds, but everything is as it should be or it would be otherwise."

Darthus nodded, not quite knowing how to reply. "I'll announce you." After a few moments he returned. "Prince Orthon will receive you," he said ushering Caedec towards the inner sanctum.

"Cousin - good of you to come at this hour," said Prince Orthon in greeting.

"My pleasure, it is kind of you to receive me."

"Leave us, Darthus," commanded Prince Orthon.

Prince Orthon was standing by a window of stained glass. He gestured Caedec to a chair beside a fireplace piled with logs. Caedec noticed a smell of burnt spices in the air as Prince Orthon seated himself.

Caedec studied his surroundings. "This was Varcia's favourite chamber."

"You have a good memory, cousin. I use it mostly for that reason, I feel my late wife's presence strongly here – it comforts me."

"Alas, you and I are not good at keeping our loved ones safe," replied Caedec staring into the distance.

"No, we are not, much to the detriment of our dynasties," Prince Orthon wore an expression of one who has accepted the fates. He rose resting his hand on the mantel. "I have given this much thought of late."

"We are older and these things become important with the passing of time," said Caedec noticing his cousin becoming distracted, tapping his fingers lightly on the stone.

"Did you want to speak of anything in particular?" said Prince Orthon.

"Yes, the trial of Mararuss troubles me."

"Why's that cousin?"

Caedec shifted uneasily. "I hear Mararuss Laboute and his ideas of revolution enjoy a degree of popularity. I believe the trial will draw attention to his cause and I am reluctant to play out my role as witness for the prosecution. There's another reason, The Crown Prince has invited me to Ilesh, to discuss a matter of importance."

Prince Orthon's face flushed with anger. "Caedec, it is out of respect for you that I order this trial. Mararuss must be punished."

"Orthon, I believe there's more to this."

Prince Orthon hesitated. "Perhaps there is something you should know. This may come as a shock but Mararuss married my sister – in secret of course. If I had known about the wedding, I would have put a stop to it."

Caedec's face was ashen. "I am astounded to hear such tidings."

Sadness clouded Prince Orthon's features. "In truth, I tried to keep the marriage quiet, in part because I did not approve of the match and the life of a soldier, as he was then, was not compatible with my sister's delicate constitution. It was apparent to me, if not to others. But Mararuss did not take kindly to my views and my sister was bewitched by him. I can think of no other explanation - she wouldn't listen to me and it caused something of a rift between us. Thankfully, we were reconciled before she died and I believe she saw her husband in his true guise. Even then Oriahh would hear no ill said of Mararuss and you see there was the child she longed for – Jhinn, he's a young man now. I believe you've met."

"Jhinn … yes, I believe we have. Cousin, let the matter rest - for the lad's sake. Wouldn't his father's execution drive him away? "

Prince Orthon waved his hand dismissively. "I have considered the matter. I cannot uphold treason. I would lose face if I were to alter course now."

"Orthon for your own sake have mercy. There must be a way round this."

"I remember you showed mercy to one who did not deserve it. A grave error on your part and one you have paid a heavy price for. I don't intend to follow your example, Caedec."

"You are referring to Khinart."

Prince Orthon nodded. "Khinart took your country and your wife. He left you to live this shadow of a life in exile, far from everything you love."

Caedec felt hot and uncomfortable. "Khinart was my friend, he betrayed me. Have you not trusted a friend and found your judgement wanting?"

Prince Orthon fell silent. "The trial begins soon. This conversation displeases me."

"Very well cousin, as you wish, I will let the matter rest. I bid you good day."

Janus gazed through the window of his bedchamber. He felt a cold draught creep through the crevices making him shiver. The view over the harbour and the sea beyond was bleak. Night was drawing near and the lanterns were being lit.

"Shipwreck! Shipwreck!" Janus heard the cry echo over the Whispering Sea.

A ship with rent sails and rigging awry, limped into port. Some of the masts were splintered, as if snapped by a giant. He stood transfixed as the cargo was brought ashore. He saw bodies wrapped in black linen laid on the ground. Janus gazed at the rippled glass hoping to catch sight of its name.

"*Maid of Ilesh*," he read aloud as the shipwreck settled on the water. His curiosity satisfied he climbed into bed, pulled up the coverlet and wondered what the morrow would bring.

Darthus could tell things had not gone well. Caedec's usual good humour had evaporated. He was a man draped in darkness. Darthus felt sad for him, he thought the fates had not been kind to the King.

As they strolled along the passage to the main door and out into the courtyard, the sun was breaking through cloud.

Caedec paused. "Darthus, it lifts my spirits to see the sun on an otherwise dreary day. I will return to my chambers to prepare for the trial," he said his shoulders drooping at the mention of impending legal proceedings.

"Very good, sire," said Darthus bowing.

Merrick saw Caedec cross the courtyard.

"Oh dear - the King looks troubled," said Merrick aloud.

As Caedec entered his chamber he threw off his cloak and called. "Merrick! Merrick!

Merrick came running out of the kitchen, thinking something was amiss.

"Bring me some wine."

"Of course, I'll fetch it at once."

Merrick returned with a goblet filled to the brim. As he handed it to Caedec, several red drops spilled onto the stone flags. Caedec studied the stain. "I hope that's not a bad omen."

Merrick studied the red marks and feeling troubled withdrew.

As Caedec drained the goblet he drifted into a sound sleep.

Merrick was startled by the sound of footsteps, looking round he saw Gai approach. "What news, my lord?"

"None, Merrick, I called to see how the King fares."

"He's had his audience with Prince Orthon. I don't think it went well by the look on his face when he returned, demanding a goblet of wine. He's sleeping now. I wouldn't disturb him if I were you."

"Then it wasn't a success," said Gai.

"Doesn't look like it to me."

Gai let out a long sigh. "Then I expect the trial begins on the morrow."

"I've heard nothing to the contrary, my lord."

Gai's face was drained of colour.

"Don't worry my lord - all will be well. You'll see."

"I hope you're right,"

"Of course I am," replied Merrick with a broad smile.

Caedec woke with a pounding headache. "That dratted wine does me no good. I wish I could leave it well alone. How long have I slept?"

"It's 8 of the clock - well into the evening and darkness is creeping in. You've slept a good while. It'll have done you no harm."

Caedec shook his head. "Far too long, you should not have let me. I have much to attend to before the trial begins on the morrow."

Merrick nodded. "I thought that might be the case. Lord Gai called - he wanted to ask how your audience with Prince Orthon went."

"Where is he now?"

"He retired to his chambers. I told him you were asleep and didn't want to be disturbed."

Caedec gave a shrug of his shoulders. "Oh well, no matter, I will speak to him anon. Summon Erussah for me. I seek his counsel on this matter," he commanded.

"Of course, sire - I'll send for him at once."

"Good man - I'll receive him the moment he arrives."

Caedec drank a goblet of water. Surveying the chamber, his gaze settled on the window. He noticed the sky was dotted with stars and watched as day turned into night - his thoughts turning to his homeland. His reverie was interrupted by a loud knock.

"Sire, may I announce Erussah, the Learned One?"

Caedec cleared his mind, focussing his attention on the towering frame ambling towards him. He studied Erussah's mass of silver hair and felt the weight of his vibrant blue eyes. Caedec thought his grey cloak made him look like a large drifting cloud. Indicating a chair, he watched as Erussah seated himself, arranging the books dangling from several chains attached to a belt fastened around his waist. Caedec waited until he was comfortable before starting the conversation. "Erussah, it is good of you to come. How are you?"

Erussah folded his hands in his lap. "Well enough, I suffer from aches and pains here and there. But I'm fortunate, my mind is clear and my memory is good despite my age," he said and laughed.

"Well, that is indeed fortunate for us all," replied Caedec smiling. I expect you have heard tidings of the impending trial."

Erussah's head tilted. "Yes, it would be hard not to - there's certainly gossip and speculation about it."

Caedec frowned and shifted in his chair. "I believe there is. I have summoned you here at this late hour to ask your advice on the matter. I believe you have studied the laws of Adranabar."

"I have, I thought it might be useful to do so."

"How wise you are, Erussah. I would be interested to hear your thoughts on the matter."

After a lengthy discussion Erussah left the King's Chambers as dawn was breaking over the battlements of Castle Adranabar. Caedec felt weary and did not bother to undress - he lay down on the coverlet fully clothed and slept.

"Order!" said the guard as the gathering crowd attempted to storm the courtroom.

Maladorian courtiers were already seated behind the jury. Eventually, the crowd quietened and filed in to the courtroom in an orderly fashion.

The jury took their seats - several yawned, their faces pale and pinched. Their eyes were rimmed with red from reading papers, as it was customary under Adranabar law to study all the evidence before proceedings commenced.

There was a gloomy atmosphere in the courtroom. The panelling on the wall was plain and black stone, quarried in Azuriene, covered the floor making the chamber austere.

Time moved slowly as the Adrabanar courtiers entered to the beat of a drum. Richly clothed in velvet and jewelled silks, they brought a rainbow of colours in to the building. The gentlemen of the prosecution rose and the drum beats stopped as the courtiers seated themselves.

After a period of silence the drum resumed its slow beat and a trumpet sounded. Everyone rose as Caedec, Gai and Erussah took their seats. A hush descended as a trumpet sounded again. Prince Orthon made his entrance in full ceremonial attire - his cloak was trimmed with stones of blue sapphire and grey aermian. A crown of intertwined lions and unicorns set with precious stones, sat firmly on his head.

Lord Griann, Elder of the Lords of Adranabar, and Darthus accompanied him to his chair. Prince Orthon seated himself flanked by Griann and Darthus. Lord Griann's sandy hair and fresh complexion contrasted with Prince Orthon and Darthus's dark brooding looks.

"We now receive the prisoner, Mararuss, to be tried in this court by the grace of our sovereign, Prince Orthon of Adranabar," announced a disembodied voice.

Mararuss made towards the chair in the centre of the floor. His attire was sombre - he looked subdued staring into the distance.

"You are accused of high treason. How do you plead?" said the prosecutor.

"I plead not guilty to the charge of high treason."

"Call the witnesses for the prosecution."

The first witnesses were bystanders, a man and his wife visiting the castle. Their testimonies placed Mararuss at the quayside at the appropriate time on the day in question. The defence questioned the couple and refuted their statements as insubstantial evidence. The prosecution asked that the court be adjourned before further testimonies were heard, but the defence would not agree and the hearing continued.

A witness for the defence was called. A young man from the gallery stood before the court. He was composed and recounted his version of events without lifting his gaze. He stated that Mararuss had not threatened anyone and had been demonstrating with a few friends against the raising of taxes. He believed Mararuss was opposed to this.

Caedec leaned towards Erussah. "The boy has been primed well," he whispered. "Indeed, he gives as fine a performance as any player in a tragedy."

Erussah nodded in agreement.

Caedec exchanged glances with Gai.

"I call Janus as witness for the prosecution," announced the prosecutor.

Darthus was anxious as he gazed at his son's ashen countenance. After a slight pause the defence began their questioning.

"Were you threatened by the defendant, Mararuss?" enquired Mararuss's adviser.

Janus was tearful and said nothing. Mararuss's adviser repeated the question. Janus still did not reply. He stared at Mararuss and began sobbing. Darthus became distressed.

Caedec wore a look of disapproval. "Janus is too upset, Erussah. This cannot continue. This is not the way to conduct matters."

Erussah left his seat to confer with the gentlemen of the defence and prosecution. Darthus was summoned and after giving his

37

son a reassuring hug, picked him up, carrying him out of the courtroom.

Several grooms wandered the length of the stables tending to the horses.

"Janus, the foal is coming to you," said Darthus.

Janus patted the foal, thinking it looked like a thundercloud on legs. He noticed a cluster of white hairs in the shape of a star on its forehead, as it nuzzled his hand. Tears welled up inside him and he tried to hide his face in its mane.

Darthus watched his son unaware of Prince Orthon's presence.

"How is he?" Prince Orthon enquired.

"Seeing Mararuss again has distressed him. He won't be able to return to the courtroom. He's a child and all this is too much for him to bear."

"There's no need. I've attended to the matter - the prosecution has another witness by special dispensation of the court."

"I'm relieved. Your kindness is appreciated."

Janus approached, trying not to appear upset.

"And how is Janus?" Prince Orthon enquired.

Janus sniffed and wiped his nose with the white handkerchief he held tightly in his small hand.

"I'm all right."

"I see you've taken to Varmarah's foal. You're a brave boy and as a reward I've decided to give him to you."

"Thank you, thank you," Janus replied.

"That is too generous, he cannot accept such a valuable gift," said Darthus.

Prince Orthon raised his hand. "My mind is made up Darthus - I believe those two will do well together."

Clouds full of rain scudded across the sky - the courtiers' cloaks soaked up the water from puddles in the courtyard as they made their way to the court.

"Call the next witness for the prosecution," said a voice from the gallery.

"I call His Majesty, King Caedec I," said the prosecutor.

Glances were exchanged in the public gallery as Caedec left his seat to stand before the gentlemen of the law. He was questioned by the prosecution and the defence. Mararuss sat staring at the King, watching him as he answered each question. Marauss's defender was last to speak. He circled Caedec like an eagle of the worlds.

"Sire, would you say this man intended to harm your courtiers?"

"Yes, I believe his actions were deliberate."

"Was Mararuss not simply voicing his opinions?" continued the defender.

"He made his views known, there's no doubt of it," said Caedec.

"Then we have a dilemma? Was Mararuss not part of a gathering that became a little rowdy," the defender said, pausing to study the jurors' expressions.

"I saw Mararuss threaten the boy."

Prince Orthon's face was full of concern as he whispered to Lord Griann.

Lord Griann rose from his seat to address the courtroom. "Ladies and gentlemen, the court will adjourn. The verdict will be announced on the morrow," he said, thankful the day was drawing to a close.

The courtroom was bursting at the seams on the second day of the trial. A call for order in the public gallery was announced as Lord Griann opened the proceedings. "By the power invested in me by His Majesty, Prince Orthon, the Schools of Law in Azuriene and this court, I pronounce verdict on the prisoner, Mararuss. Will the prisoner stand?"

Mararuss said nothing and remained seated.

Lord Griann wore a look of disdain. "Very well, I'll continue. The prisoner is found guilty of treason and will be taken from this court and imprisoned in the dungeons, awaiting execution."

A chorus of "Free Mararuss," came from the public gallery. A scuffle broke out and several people were forcibly removed. Caedec exchanged glances with Gai as two guards escorted Mararuss from the courtroom. The trial was over.

Jhinn followed the guards to an iron door. He waited as it was unlocked and passed through into the dungeon beyond. He heard the sound of the door slamming behind him.

"Where does time go?" said Mararuss.

"I don't know," replied Jhinn sitting on a narrow bench by the door.

"When I was your age I had so many dreams."

"Were your dreams full of death and glory?" enquired Jhinn staring at his father in the dim light.

"You remind me of your mother. You have the same freckled skin and red hair. Such beauty," said Mararuss.

"Good, I'm pleased. Does it make you uncomfortable?"

"Of course not, that's nonsense lad, I loved her."

"Is that why you broke her heart?"

Jhinn watched as Mararuss's face flushed.

"How can you say that?"

"You were always in the tavern drinking with other women and plotting rebellion."

Mararuss grabbed Jhinn by the throat, throwing his tall, wiry frame against the wall.

"Don't you question me, or by the Gods I'll make you sorry."

A contemptuous look crossed Jhinn's face.

"You broke my mother's heart and I hope you are damned sorry for it when they hang you."

Mararuss's grip slackened. "I fought for justice and for the people."

"You committed treason against the Prince and threatened a boy. Where's the glory in that? Prince Orthon is my uncle - he took an interest in me when you did not."

Mararuss released his grip and pushed Jhinn away.

"I'm sorry, lad."

Jhinn stared at his father. He turned away as tears streamed down his cheeks.

"May the Gods keep you - soon I will be no more and you will be alone in these worlds," said Mararuss, his voice breaking with emotion.

Jhinn's lips moved, but no words came. A lump had lodged in his throat. He knocked on the door, listening for the guard's footsteps. Father and son exchanged glances as it opened and Jhinn stepped into the darkness.

A mist descended over Castle Adranabar. As the stones were cast the old man knelt down, studying their pattern. His gnarled fingers traced the outlines of the inscriptions. A crowd had gathered, waiting for him to speak. Caius wrapped his cloak around himself.

Adranus the Seer's, thin frame rose from the ground. He turned his face to the sun. His pale flesh and high cheekbones framed by a mane of red hair, streaked with grey. The black cloak he wore was coated with dust. He looked around with unseeing eyes as the gathering murmured and shifted.

Caius wore a grave expression as he stared at the ship moored in the harbour, the water lapping gently against the sides.

"I will see the King now," said Adranus.

"I'll take you," Caius replied taking his arm as the crowd parted.

"Are the auspices good, Adranus?"

"Good enough, Caius. And this voyage...," Adranus stopped in mid sentence.

"Please, tell me more."

"We'll speak again in private. Now, I must see the King."

Caius looked disappointed as he guided him through the courtyard, making sure he didn't trip and fall on the uneven cobbles. "We're almost there."

"I must rest a moment. I don't want to meet my sovereign breathless and exhausted."

Caius led the old man to a wall. "Here - lean against this."

Adranus breathed deeply and clung to Caius's hand with bony fingers. Caius was silent, staring at the sea.

"You're anxious to return to our homeland," said Adranus.

"As always, you sense the truth. I'd like to go home."

"A young girl waits for you with hair the colour of raven and a smile like summer."

Caius stared at Adranus with a startled expression. "I mentioned Arawena to a living soul."

"No, and you shouldn't. You'll have to wait until she is of age. Her father would whip you if he knew your intentions. Old Arraw Sen Miean would be furious." replied Adranus laughing and patting him on the shoulder. Caius blushed and stared at the ground.

41

Adranus looked tired - his countenance was pale and drawn as they reached Castle Adranabar. Caius announced himself and the seer to the guard who let them pass.

Merrick was waiting to receive them. "Gentlemen, the King is anxious to see you, come hither," he said leading the way to the King's private chambers.

Caius and Adranus were ushered into the King's Chamber. Caedec was seated at a writing table awash with papers and scrolls. Maps were strewn everywhere. After a few moments he stopped reading, tossed some papers over his shoulder looked up and smiled.

"Welcome. Please sit down, if you can find some chairs under all this mess. Merrick will fetch some spiced wine and breads. I expect you are hungry."

Caius removed several piles of documents and maps from two chairs, one carved with unicorns running across meadows, the other carved with lions running up a mountain. Caius guided Adranus towards the unicorn chair.

"Sire, I'll leave you to speak with Adranus. I must attend to the horses."

"Thank you. We have much to discuss."

"I'll return later," said Caius touching the old man's arm.

"Thank you - you're a good boy."

Caius withdrew and Caedec knelt before the seer. Adranus reached out to him.

"My dear Caedec, if only I could see you," he said touching the King's lean face.

"And if you could what would you see Adranus? A weary, old man I fear."

"You haven't changed - I sense you're older, as we all are. Come now you're not King Ahrian's young son at court anymore, you're my King, and a King kneels to no one save his gods."

Caedec took the old man's hand and kissed it.

"Poor Caius, I feel I'm a burden to him. That terrible fire took his family, his home - everything from him," said Adranus.

"He is your ward and you are all he has. He was a child. If you had not travelled through the forest on your way to Sarhynel that day, he would not have been saved," said Caedec.

Yes, and I wouldn't have lost my sight," said Adranus brushing his hand over the marks on his cheek.

"You cannot see how he looks at you, but it is always with deep gratitude and affection. You are no burden to him."

"Please forgive the ramblings of an old man," said Adranus.

"There's nothing to forgive. Now tell me what the stones say about this voyage of ours."

"In truth the stones have told me very little, which is unusual. In all my days of casting them, I have not seen the signs I saw today. This puzzles me. For Caius, I sense the voyage will be a turning point for him, his life will be troubled, but he'll be happy despite this. But I cannot tell how the voyage will be. I'm sorry," he said shifting in his chair and fidgeting.

"You are withholding something from me Adranus. Is there magic abroad?"

Adranus hesitated. "Yes, magic of a most powerful kind. There's a veil across the seven worlds and I cannot see through it."

"What do you suggest?"

"I'm a seer. Alas, I'm not a wizard and I've no answers. Those are for others to find."

There was a loud knock and Merrick bounded in carrying a tray. He set it down, poured the wine and withdrew. Adranus picked up some bread and ate slowly while Caedec took a sip of wine. They sat in silence - neither quite knowing what to say.

Overcome by curiousity Merrick opened the door a fraction. He noticed the King and his seer had fallen asleep and the fire was dwindling. He went to fetch some logs, wondering whether a spell had been cast over them. As he approached the window to draw the hangings he noticed something on the ledge. He could see its silhouette caught in the light of the moons. Two violet eyes stared at him as the creature's whiskers brushed the window panes.

"Kotroi," he whispered.

Merrick was mesmerized as he stared at the outline of its wings and the tufts sprouting from its ears. Then it vanished amidst the night sky and he went to fetch several lengths of woollen cloth to keep Caedec and Adranus warm.

Merrick went in search of Caius and found him talking to Darthus outside the stables.

"Merrick, where is Adranus? Is he still with the King?" enquired Caius.

"Yes, they've fallen asleep. I haven't disturbed them - they look so tired I think they won't wake until morning."

"Thank you, I'll return to the King's chambers on the morrow. Sleep well, Merrick."

Caius and Darthus talked for a while then strolled into the stables, closing the doors behind them. Burning torches lined the walls and the grooms were giving the horses their last feed. Varmarah and her foal were eating some hay as Caius and Darthus passed their stall.

"That's a lovely looking foal, Darthus. I hear Prince Orthon has given him to your lad. Has he thought of a name yet?"

"Not yet, he still can't believe the foal is his," Darthus replied.

"He's a lucky lad."

Darthus was thoughtful.

"Does he still have nightmares?" Caius enquired.

"Aye - the poor lamb is exhausted by morning. His screams wake the household. We've tried everything. Sapphire has given me a potion for him - I'm hoping that will help the lad."

They watched the grooms finish tending the horses and went outside into the crisp night air. Darthus took a deep breath and studied the clear sky covered with stars.

Caius and Darthus wandered towards the harbour. They stopped to admire three ships from Ilesh and two Adranabar warships.

"I'm impressed - don't you think the Adranabar warships are much bigger than the Ileshian ships, Darthus? Look at their sails of red and gold emblazoned with lions and unicorns. I think the figures of lions adorning their prows are magnificent," said Caius staring at them in awe. "I believe more ships are sailing from the Port of Lhanara, further up the coast, they may be here by the morrow."

Darthus watched several guards patrolling the quayside. "These ships are precious. The Aizans build them well," he said gazing at the starlight reflected on the water.

"Are you joining us on the voyage, Darthus?"

"I haven't decided yet."

"King Caedec will be generous to those who help him. There will be rich rewards - property and land I'll warrant. Think carefully about it - Janus would be well provided for, if you were favoured by the King."

Darthus shook his head. "I'm older now and I've no desire to fight in a war again. Janus is young - I believe my place is here."

"Nonsense - it will be an adventure and your son will be a warrior one day. It would be good for him to learn the skills of battle."

"I don't want that sort of life for Janus. I would rather he studied at the Schools of Law in Azuriene."

Caius was aghast. "Surely, you don't contemplate such an existence for him, shut away shuffling scrolls for the rest of his life."

Darthus felt his blood rising. "I've ridden into battle and seen things so terrible I cannot bear to think of them. I wouldn't wish my son to suffer as I have done."

"You cannot choose a life for him - the Gods have already done so. Adranus has…" he fell silent as he watched Darthus's face flush with colour.

"We must return to the castle," said Darthus in a curt tone.

Caius said nothing, believing he'd said too much and caused offence.

Silence hung heavily upon them. Darthus's expression was akin to an impending storm and Caius felt awkward in his presence. They walked to the castle, parting in silence.

Merrick heard stirrings from the King's Chamber. Adranus moved stiffly while Caedec yawned and stretched.

"Have you slept well?" Merrick enquired.

"Well enough. I think some breakfast might be in order, Merrick. We are hungry."

Adranus nodded in agreement and Merrick went to fetch some food.

"That was delicious," said Caedec licking his lips and pushing the plate into the centre of the table.

"I quite agree," Adranus replied finishing off the last piece of roasted fruit.

Merrick cleared the dishes away and asked if he should send for Caius. Caedec nodded and Merrick withdrew.

Caedec shifted in his chair. "If you wish you may remain here in Adranabar."

"Thank you, but my place is with my King. Wherever you go I'll follow."

"Very well, I respect your decision. I confess I hoped to hear those words," replied Caedec with a smile.

Merrick stood at the door and announced Caius.

"Forgive me - I have detained Adranus far too long."

Caius bowed, taking the seer by the arm and guiding him to the door.

Gai and Caedec watched the activity at the harbour. Coffers and crates stuffed full of provisions were carried on board the ships as grooms ferried hay and feed from the stables.

"I can scarcely believe we are almost ready to sail," said Caedec.

45

"Has Adranus determined what lies ahead on this voyage?" enquired Gai.

"Alas, he could not tell from casting the stones. He talked of a veil across the worlds. He believes there is powerful magic obscuring his sight."

"If we sail when the new moon rises we'll be protected and Sapphire has the amulet," said Gai pausing to stare at the sea. "We've a long journey ahead. May the Gods be with us."

Caedec nodded. "Adranus is coming. I asked him if he would like to remain, but he declined."

"I thought he would. I know in his heart he yearns for home, as we all do. Prince Orthon will miss you Caedec, you're his favourite cousin and he relies on you, but he wouldn't like you to know it," said Gai.

"And I will miss him. Indeed, it grieves me to leave at such a time. There's unrest in this country. Deep in my heart I fear for him, if his subjects revolt, what will become of him?"

Gai gave a shrug of his shoulders. "He will have Lord Griann's support. Our time has come – we cannot tarry."

Gai and Caedec watched as another Adranabar warship sailed into the harbour, a lion roaring on its prow, heralding the start of the journey home.

Branches clothed in green leaves shifted in the breeze. A glimmer of light filtered through the trees as Sapphire rode out of Castle Adranabar. She followed a winding track along a river reaching into the countryside. Sapphire stopped at a clearing, dismounted and tethered Maranth, a bay mare. She watched as a rider astride a black horse thundered into the clearing. Prince Orthon dismounted and strode towards her.

"Forgive me, Sapphire, I've kept you waiting. It wasn't easy leaving the castle,"said Prince Orthon as he unwound the cloth covering his head and most of his face.

"I accept your apology. I appreciate how difficult it must be for you, Orthon."

"What of Gai?"

"I'm sure he suspects nothing."

Prince Orthon took Sapphire's hand in his as they walked into the forest. Sitting on the trunk of a fallen tree he studied her features. Sunlight flickered through the trees casting patterns on the forest floor. A flock of small black birds fluttered around the tree tops singing.

"Have you seen Azuniel?" said Prince Orthon.

"Yes, I've done as you wished, I saw him at The Festival of a Thousand Suns. I think Gai saw me leaving his tent in the courtyard. After that I was more careful and we met at the sign of the Attine Mouse on the old road leading eastward."

"Can he help me?"

"Yes, he's visited the Vale of Wolves," she replied.

Prince Orthon gripped her hand. "You don't know what this means to me," he whispered. Sapphire smiled but said nothing.

Prince Orthon breathed deeply pulling her close and burying his face in her hair.

"Orthon, I must leave now."

"Must you, so soon?"

"Yes, I cannot tarry," she said wondering whether to continue the conversation. After a period of deliberation she spoke again. "Orthon, Ormia has gone from the worlds and it may be that she cannot return. Varcia dwells in the Vale of Wolves - she has yet to leave. Azuniel said he could bring her back, but his price for doing so is high."

Prince Orthon looked devastated. "What is his price?"

47

"It's extortionate. Orthon, please leave the fates as they are. Don't interfere with the will of the Gods."

"Tell me what it is."

"Very well, Azuniel wants the Crown of Adranabar."

Prince Orthon grimaced.

"I implore you - don't give your country to a necromancer like him. Think of your subjects."

"They're tired of me - why should I think of them?"

Sapphire paused. "Stay in the light, keep away from the darkness. Accept the fates and let go, that's my counsel on the matter."

Prince Orthon stared at the ground deep in contemplation.

"I must leave. Think on my words," she said.

"Please don't go, why not tarry here and marry me. Leave Gai - he doesn't love you as I do. We'll rule Adranabar together and all will be well."

A confused expression crossed Sapphire's face. "I can't – I'm sorry. I'm needed in Ilesh and the King needs my help."

Prince Orthon was bereft. "If that's what you want."

Sapphire stood up and walked away. As she untethered Maranth she hesitated wondering whether to retrace her steps and reconsider her decision, but thinking better of it mounted and rode off.

As Prince Orthon patted his horse and prepared to mount he heard a twig snap underfoot. A man with dark hair, dressed in green, emerged from the forest carrying a silver axe. Prince Orthon studied the short, plump form of the woodman striding towards him.

"That's a grand horse you have there. I haven't seen any like that round here. Merchant are you?"

"Yes, that's right. Well I'll be on my way, good day to you," replied Prince Orthon putting his foot into the stirrup and swinging himself into the saddle.

The woodman looked puzzled, thinking the stranger seemed familiar, but said nothing as he watched him ride into the forest.

As Prince Orthon followed a worn path through the trees, he heard a girl's laughter, stopping for a moment he watched her collecting fallen branches, noticing she was accompanied by a red haired young man holding a basket.

"Well I'll be damned, I'm sure that's my nephew," said Prince Orthon nudging Dhannan the Black forward. He gasped as he caught sight of her face. "Why she's the image of my sister, Oriahh and my wife come to that. Dear Crilm, is this a ghost I see before me - have the dead come back to life? No, it cannot be - but the likeness is uncanny. This girl has the same red hair and vivid green eyes. I wonder who this pretty maid is. It seems there's another tryst in the forest today," he whispered in Dhannan the Black's ear.

Prince Orthon entered Castle Adranabar through the sally-port. He left Dhannan the Black with a stable lad, buying his silence with a gold coin. Prince Orthon slipped into his bedchamber, taking off his boots and discarding the shirt, breeches, riding cloak and scarf he was wearing – the attire of a travelling merchant he'd used to disguise himself. He put on his nightshirt and had just pulled the coverlet over himself when he heard a knock, followed by shuffling footsteps.

"My Prince has slept late this morning – there is news of Lord Griann - he arrives at noon."

Prince Orthon pulled himself up. "Why is he returning so soon?"

"I believe he comes to say his farewells to King Caedec."

"Of course, he's fond of my cousin."

"What is the matter?" enquired The Lady Annas, searching Sapphire's face, moistened with tears.

Sapphire turned away, staring at her reflection in the looking glass. "I don't know what to do."

Lady Annas was puzzled. She smoothed several strands of hair, the hue of water darkened by a tree's shadow, from her high forehead. "Sapphire, what troubles you? I've cared for you since your poor mother, Elisha, succumbed to the plague. I'm your kinswoman - you can confide in me."

Sapphire's composure dissolved as she covered her face with her slender hands. The Lady Annas moved to comfort her. "Why are you so sad? Does Gai make you so unhappy?"

"He's my husband and yet he is indifferent to me," replied Sapphire. "What can I do?"

"I don't know. I fear there's nothing to be done. Gai's heart is his own - he'll never change. A man cannot change his nature. It is written in the stars and alchemy is his mistress. Don't be sad - there are other men who admire you and would make you happy, if you would open your heart."

"Are we going with them?" Janus enquired studying the scar on his father's hand.

"I think not. Our place is here. We have Prince Orthon's horses to care for," Darthus replied as admired the vessels moored hull to hull in the water. Two Aizan warships had just arrived. He noticed

49

their white sails, painted with the masks of grey wolves, billowing in the sea breeze.

Janus was disappointed. He stared at the Aizan warships in awe - thinking them magnificent as he caught sight of the carvings of leaping wolves adorning their prows. He longed to be aboard, enjoying high adventure on the sea.

Gai and Prince Orthon stood on the battlements of Castle Adranabar. Gai was staring at the harbour and the Whispering Sea beyond.

"Are the amulets for the horses ready, Gai?"

"Yes, I cast the last one as the new moon rose. They'll be safe – we haven't lost an animal wearing one yet."

"Varmarah and her foal will remain here. Naturally, you shall have the best war horses – all the greys and blacks I can spare. Caedec will have Aylvian. I give Dharvian to you and Dhannan, the Black is for Sapphire," stated Prince Orthon.

"I'm surprised you are giving up Dhannan, the Black. You're most generous," said Gai.

Prince Orthon shivered. "I've spent too much time inside the castle and feel the cold more than I used to. I'll return to my chambers."

"Of course, by all means," said Gai watching a sea eagle circle over the Whispering Sea.

Caedec sat alone in the Great Temple. He listened to the bell as it rang out, breaking the silence, its shrill note echoing through the temple. He did not move until silence returned like a welcome friend. He knelt before the altar, his head lowered.

A statue of Crilm seemed to smile at Caedec as he stood up and bowed. As he walked along the aisle towards the entrance he stopped to admire the embroidered hangings of Crilm's sisters: Annas, Delvia, Marhn, Phinnia, Helicia, Addria and Vheshia.

"Lovely aren't they?"

Caedec stopped gazing at the embroidered panels. "Sar-Mhirian how wonderful to see you - how are you and what brings you here?" he said clasping the holy man's shoulders and studying his once familiar features.

"I've sailed here on *Azenia* an Aizan warship, under Captain Lhimm Oxghar's command. I expect you've heard of him – he's a famous poet as well as a Master Mariner."

Caedec smiled at the tall man with golden skin and black hair tied in a knot, wearing a robe of gold silk fastened with a broad sash of scarlet standing before him.

"What a coincidence, I believe I will be travelling to Ilesh on the very same vessel."

Sar-Mhirian smiled. "I'm pleased Caedec, you've been in exile too long, it's time you took your place in the world Crilm named Sohnglas, again."

Caedec nodded. "Thank you for your kind words - how is Crilm?"

"Caedec, I have travelled here from the Vale of Crilm and he's remarkable - he hasn't tired of immortality. His desire to help the sentient beings of the seven worlds is boundless. I'm in awe of him."

"Good tidings, indeed. Are you staying in Adranabar for a while?"

"Sadly no, I'm sailing to Ilesh for the wedding of my daughter, Mhiria to Nheve, brother of The Crown Prince. I'm looking forward to it - you know what lavish occasions weddings are in Ilesh," said Sar-Mhirian.

"I do indeed."

Caedec and Sar-Mhirian conversed at length as they strolled towards the castle.

Caedec slept little and felt the night passed slowly like the flight of an eagle in the worlds. He was wracked with doubt, and tortured by thoughts of war and death. Since he was a child, Caedec had dreaded the coming of night.

Merrick rose early to ensure the King's retinue was ready for the voyage. He opened a window and listened to the noise outside – the castle was coming alive. It would soon be time for the procession to the harbour and the ceremonial blessing of the horses as they went aboard ship.

Darthus noticed a crowd gathering as the procession wound its way to the quayside. He watched Janus fasten amulets of wrought silver around the horses' necks and listened to Sar-Mhirian recite a blessing as the amulets were fastened.

Gai and Caedec gazed at the horses boarding the ships. Caedec noticed Prince Orthon's sad expression as Sapphire and The Lady Annas said their farewells. Prince Orthon held Sapphire's hand longer than necessary, gazing at her longingly as she boarded the warship, *Azenia*.

Lord Griann stepped forward to embrace Caedec and say his farewells. As he moved away, Prince Orthon approached. "May you return to Adranabar one day with Ahrisa, your Queen."

"When I have regained my throne I will return with her by my side. Until then farewell, dearest cousin – my heartfelt thanks to you," said Caedec as he waved to the gathering for the last time.

Captain Lhimm Oxghar welcomed Caedec aboard. "Sire, welcome to *Azenia*. I hope your quarters meet with your approval."

"I am pleased to make your acquaintance, Captain Oxghar. I have enjoyed reading your poems."

"Thank you. I'm deeply flattered."

Caedec smiled studying the captain's pale countenance framed by a mop of thick, black hair. He could see why Irmardia, Queen of the Whispering Sea, was entranced by him.

Merrick approached and the captain withdrew.

"Sire, may I show you to your quarters?"

"Yes, by all means, lead on Merrick," said Caedec following him along a gangway.

Merrick felt relieved thinking the King seemed impressed as he surveyed the sumptuously furnished rooms and large bed with blue silk coverlet embroidered with dragons.

"I believe I will be most comfortable. What say you?"

Merrick nodded in agreement.

Darthus was frantic, Janus had disappeared. "Where can that lad be? I should've kept a tigher hold on him at the harbour," he said aloud with a sickening feeling in the pit of his stomach. He searched Castle Adranabar to no avail - the boy had simply vanished into thin air.

As the ship rocked and pitched, Janus began to feel sea sick. He was starting to regret sneaking aboard *Azenia* while his father was distracted, saying his farewells to the King. As he crouched beside Dhannan the Black, he felt homesick.

Captain Oxghar was at his writing table studying charts and maps. He sighed as he rose from his chair to look through the panes of clear, indestructible Azuriene crystal in the stern. Sunlight filtered through the sparkling mineral, warming his face and bathing the cabin with light. As *Azenia* ploughed through the Whispering Sea he saw a dolphin swimming alongside and realized Queen Irmardia was following the ship.

Caedec stood on deck watching as the brightness of day faded into twilight. A mist descended over the sea and a breeze drifted over the water, nipping his face with icy claws. Alone with his thoughts he fastened his cloak to keep out the cold. He heard someone sobbing below deck and decided to investigate. As he approached Dhannan the Black's stall, the sound grew louder. He stroked the stallion's warm nose and noticed the straw moving. "When I was a lad I ran away to sea but alas, the seafaring life was not what I thought it would be."

Caedec noticed the straw was still. "Are you hungry?"

"Yes, very."

Caedec recognized the voice. "Come out Janus. Dhannan has little enough space as it is."

Janus emerged wearing a sheepish expression and brushing the straw off his sleeves. Caedec felt sorry for him. He looked so sad and dishevelled.

"Merrick will make up a bed for you and make you a little supper."

Captain Oxghar put his papers to one side, rising from his chair to greet the King.

"There is a matter I wish to discuss with you," said Caedec.

"By all means - may I ask what troubles you?"

"We have a stowaway – Janus, son of Darthus, my cousin's Master of Horse."

"Is he all right?"

"Yes, he's tired and hungry, but other than that he is unharmed. He seems rather disappointed with the seafaring life."

"His father will want to know his son is safe," said the captain rubbing his forehead.

"Indeed, I expect Darthus will be distraught by now."

Captain Oxghar frowned. "I'm sure we can send a message confirming the boy's whereabouts. However, I suspect his father has realized there's a connection between the ships' departure and his son's disappearance."

"I expect so, captain. Darthus will be lost without that young lad. Shall we send him home when we reach Ilesh?"

"I'm sure it can be arranged."

"I was like him when I was his age, always dreaming of adventures. I stowed away on one of my father's ships and got as far as The Delvia States before I was discovered," said Caedec with a wistful look on his face.

Captain Oxghar smiled. "Sire, you astound me. Might I make a suggestion?"

"By all means, captain."

"I have a wonderful bottle of vintage Adras and I believe this might be the time to open it. I've received reports of War Kotroi gathering, I believe they'll soon join our fleet."

"That is good news and I am partial to vintage Adras."

Captain Oxghar opened the bottle and poured the sparkling liquid into two goblets.

"Let's make a toast, captain – here's to friendship as long as life itself."

As Prince Orthon sauntered across the courtyard he noticed the scaffold, the sight of it made him shiver. He saw Jhinn hurry past and called to him. "My dear nephew, how are you?"

Jhinn's face was flushed. "I am well, sire," he said bowing.

"I was on my way to visit your mother's grave. Will you accompany me?"

Jhinn nodded. "I'd be honoured."

Prince Orthon and Jhinn made towards the Great Temple. They entered the building, cloaked in silence. Prince Orthon unlocked a door leading from the vault into a garden, hidden by high walls.

Jhinn saw three tombs and as he read the script on the stones, realized they belonged to the late Princesses Varcia, Ormia and his mother, Oriahh. A tree, covered in white blossom, stooped over the graves, as if protecting them.

"Trees flowering in winter - how can that be?" said Jhinn looking at them with a wondrous expression.

"An enchantment cast by a dear friend. Never underestimate the power of magic, Jhinn. I come here to this garden, always in bloom, to be with my family. It's a great comfort to me," said Prince Orthon, his voice tinged with sadness.

"I can't remember visiting my mother's grave."

"Your father thought it best you didn't. I'm afraid he has little time for sentiment, as you'll have gathered. Do you miss your mother?"

"Yes, I do, very much."

"As I, she was a beautiful, cultured woman and yet there was something tragic in her soul. Was that not so?"

Jhinn nodded his head in agreement. "I believe her life was touched by a darkness no-one could dispel. Not even those who loved her most."

"Of late I've thought a lot about the future. Adranabar needs an heir to give it stability and a sense of continuity," said Prince Orthon.

Jhinn was puzzled pondering the meaning of his uncle's words.

"I mean to name you as my heir. Of course, the position brings responsibility – your conduct, friends, and the woman you marry, must all be beyond reproach. In fact, you may not be able to marry whom you please. An arranged marriage to a princess from another realm is likely, perhaps inevitable," he said studying his nephew's expression.

Jhinn felt as if a heavy weight had fallen on his shoulders.

"Under our laws of succession, you're the rightful heir to the throne of Adranabar. However, the pursuit of power is not without sacrifice," Prince Orthon continued.

Jhinn was troubled, but said nothing.

"I sense you're not interested in my view of statecraft," Prince Orthon stated - an element of steel creeping in to his voice.

Jhinn remained silent, his feet shifted and he felt uncomfortable.

"Do you wish to stay for your father's execution on the morrow?"

"I don't know, perhaps not."

"There's an old lodge in the hills by Phelar, it belonged to your mother and she entrusted it to me until you were of age to inherit it. I believe that time has come – why not tarry there awhile and think about what I've said. If you leave soon you could be there by nightfall."

Jhinn was thoughtful. "Very well uncle - I'll consider your proposal."

"Good lad. We'll speak again on your return."

Prince Orthon returned to his chambers to find Darthus waiting for him.

"Sire, I must speak to you about Janus."

"Of course, I have a few moments."

"Thank you."

"Have you received any news about the lad, Darthus?"

"No, not yet, but I believe he stowed away on one of the ships bound for Ilesh. I can think of no other explanation."

"I expect he'll be safe enough with my cousin's people. When they reach Ilesh they'll send him back."

"I've heard a ship from Aizan will be here soon. I gather it's bound for Ilesh. May I join the vessel, sire?"

Prince Orthon hesitated. "All right, you have my permission - may the Gods be with you."

A wind gained momentum over the Whispering Sea. *Azenia's* crew stopped to listen to the whispering folk, their voices rising from beneath the water, creating a rushing sound on the surface of the sea. *Azenia's* crew could not understand their language, but the words had a melodic, enchanting quality they found hard to ignore.

Caedec stood on deck with Captain Oxghar.

"There's a storm brewing. Can you hear the whispering folk?" enquired Captain Oxghar.

"Indeed, I can, captain."

A sudden gust of wind jolted the ship and Caedec stumbled. Captain Oxghar caught him as he fell.

"I think you should go below deck, sire. A storm will be upon us, before much longer."

Caedec nodded, steadying himself.

"We're not far from Ilesh," said Captain Oxghar as another gust of wind whipped across the Whispering Sea - forcing a wave over the deck of *Azenia,* making the ship reel with its force.

Captain Oxghar saw the raging storm reflected in Caedec's eyes as the waves crashed against *Azenia's* side. Captain Oxghar barked orders to the crew as the warship was driven towards several jagged rocks.

Sapphire rushed to the door as The Lady Annas screamed, "No Sapphire. Stay here. You know what'll happen if you're swept overboard."

"But I want to help – I must."

"If you're drawn down to the worlds beneath the Whispering Sea, you'll lose your powers and won't be able to help anyone."

"Don't worry - I'll be all right."

Sapphire scrambled on to the deck noticing the sails and rigging were rent by the merciless wind. A sheer rock loomed through a fountain of white spray. She looked for the other ships, but saw no sign of them. "I pray the rest of the fleet are out of harm's way," she said as the full force of the storm was unleashed.

Sapphire fought to keep her balance as the ship pitched violently in the water. She saw the captain giving orders to the helmsman, while the crew manoeuvred the sails. She breathed salty air as a wave lashed the ship. Sapphire noticed *Azenia* was perilously close to the rocks. She felt the warship judder as she heard a sound of splintering timber.

"Such madness," she whispered holding the amulet. As spray leapt over the side Sapphire read the inscription on the jewel and began to recite an incantation. "I hope the Gods hear my words."

Captain Oxghar was exhausted - water ran in rivulets down his face and neck. His hands were raw and bloody. "Damn these treacherous waters," he said as the spray drenched him and he slid across the deck banging his head on the ship's side.

"Let's get this water bailed out, lads," Thoro commanded watching a torrent of sea water gush through a rent in the hull. "Plug the smaller holes with tar and oakum, jump to it lads!"

"Merrick!" called Gai as he carried Caedec below.

With Merrick's help Gai was able to guide Caedec to his quarters. His breathing was laboured as he took shuffling steps. Merrick helped him lie down on the bed.

"Fetch the physician, Merrick," said Gai, his face wet with sweat and sea water.

"Jhils find the captain and see he's all right," commanded Thoro.
"Yes sir," replied the young lad sprinting away like a fawn.
Jhils saw Captain Oxghar slumped on deck. "Sir, are you hurt bad?" he said kneeling down and trying to stem the blood oozing from a gash on his forehead with a rag.
"I'm all right, really I am - it's just a scratch."

Sapphire studied the cloudless sky and thought the signs auspicious. She was confident the incantation had been heard as she gazed at the calm waters.
Sapphire screamed as a War Kotroi flew into a mast. She winced at its cry, staring in horror as the creature's tail lost its grip and it hurtled towards the deck. She climbed the rigging followed by several members of the crew. Sapphire gasped as the War Kotroi's muscular tail caught on the rigging, staying its descent. She could see it was injured – one of its wings was torn and clotted with blood. Without warning, the rigging gave way and the War Kotroi's body plummeted. Sapphire's fingers fumbled for the amulet in the pocket of her gown. She could feel her heart pounding as she held it and began reciting a mantra.
"Hhariann!" said Gai running towards the War Kotroi lying on the deck. He gazed at the wounded creature, stroking the rough, dry fur on its paw. "I'm so pleased you're alive," he said feeling the weight of Hhariann's stare as its spirit communed with his and the War Kotroi's story unfurled.
Sapphire was mesmerised as Gai continued stroking Hhariann's paw. Tears streamed down his face as the War Kotroi withdrew it, laying his head on the deck.
"Will he be all right?" Sapphire enquired.
"Yes, he's suffered but he's safe now and his wing will heal," replied Gai. "I've asked Merrick to fetch the physician. I believe Caedec is very ill."
Sapphire's eyes widened. "Then I must go to him."

Sapphire found Caedec sleeping peacefully, holding the amulet over his body she recited a healing mantra, as Merrick snoozed in a chair. She had just finished when Hhannon, the King's Physician, entered the bedchamber. Sapphire hid the amulet in the folds of her velvet cloak. She studied the physician's flawless skin and glossy black hair as he

59

approached. His black tunic and trousers clung to his slight frame. His feet were clad in slippers of red silk.

"What's the matter with the King?" asked Hhannon.

Merrick woke, shaking himself. "He collapsed on deck as the storm raged," he replied rubbing the sleep away.

"Ah, I see he's very pale. Has he any pain?"

"I don't know – he hasn't spoken," said Merrick.

Hhannon placed a manicured hand on Caedec's forehead. "There's no sign of fever or disease," he said to no one in particular. "Sapphire, have you given him any potions?"

"No, Hhannon I have not."

Hhannon raised a thin black eyebrow. "I'll administer my needles, now leave us!"

"I don't trust him and those needles of his," said Merrick.

"He's a possessive sort. I'm not sure I trust him either," she added.

Captain Oxghar was seated at his writing table, reflecting on the state of his ship. A loud knock shattered his contemplation and Thoro, his second in command, ambled into the cabin like a bear.

"Captain, an injured War Kotroi has flown into one of the masts and King Caedec has been taken ill, his physician attends him as we speak."

Captain Oxghar sighed. "I trust the War Kotroi and the King are comfortable. Tell me, is the hull repaired?"

"Not yet, but we're doing our best, captain," said Thoro smoothing a lock of wet hair from his forehead, his soaking uniform clinging to his burly frame.

As Thoro withdrew Captain Oxghar felt his eyelids grow heavy. Eventually, he stirred realizing he'd fallen asleep slumped over the maps on the writing table. He noticed Queen Irmardia was seated on a chair watching him.

"I see you've hurt yourself - you look tired, Lhimm."

"Oh, the cut on my forehead's nothing. I slipped on deck, that's all."

Queen Irmardia sighed. "Give up this life, Lhimm and come with me."

Captain Oxghar nodded pausing before he replied. "I want to Irmardia but I cannot, at least not yet. I have a duty to my Lord Fhinn of Aizan and those aboard my ship."

Queen Irmardia sighed again as she perched herself on the corner of the writing table.

Captain Oxghar stared at her tall, slim body and longed for the touch of her skin. He noticed her blue gown was adorned with tiny seed pearls with several tears, where it had caught on the rocks under the Whispering Sea. He studied her long, wavy hair, the colour of a pale moon and kept in place by a tiara of mother of pearl, hung with crystals. Strips of pearls adorned her arms and neck. He was fascinated by her bare feet and the tiny fins on her ankles.

Queen Irmardia's voice was nearly a whisper. "Our cities are beautiful. I want you to see them. Fall overboard Lhimm, I need you and I can't wait forever."

Captain Oxghar was in the grip of a dilemma. He shifted uneasily in his chair. "According to your lore if I fall into the Whispering Sea, I can't return to these worlds. I must dwell in your realm forever."

Queen Irmardia arranged a strip of pearls wound around her arm. "Yes, that is so."

"Then I must be sure the time is right. That's all I can say."

Blue sparks of fury flew from the Queen's eyes and her tiara wobbled almost falling from her head.

"Irmardia, please be reasonable."

Captain Oxghar was taken aback. "Irmardia, please…"

Queen Irmardia vanished into the depths of the Whispering Sea and the captain was left on his ship, wondering.

Captain Oxghar's mood was sinking faster than an anchor into the seabed as his thoughts turned to Queen Irmardia. He began to regret refusing her and wondered whether he would see her again. As he dipped a quill into a pot of blue ink he wrote the title of a new poem – 'My Lost Love – Will She Return to Me?'

"Land Ho!"

Captain Oxghar listened as the cry echoed through the ship. "It must be Ilesh," he said aloud, resuming his writing until he was interrupted by a knock and Thoro's swift entrance. "Captain, land has been sighted."

Captain Oxghar stopped to study the map. "I'm aware of that. According to my calculations we're on course, Thoro."

"Very good," said Thoro alarmed by the captain's appearance. His face was drawn and empty of life - like a man whose spirit had been stolen by emissaries of the Gods.

Sapphire maintained a vigil by Caedec's bed, guarding him from evil spirits. He woke to find her sitting in a chair, her head drooping like a sleeping flower. Caedec was touched by her devotion.

"My dear Sapphire, how long have you been here?" he enquired as she pulled herself from the frontier of sleep.

"Not long, how are you?"

Caedec smiled. "I feel weary."

Sapphire's face was full of concern. "I'll send for the physician."

"As you wish my dear, but promise me you'll retire to your bedchamber, it's obvious you are in need of rest."

As Sapphire withdrew Caedec pulled the coverlet up to his chin. Deep lines of worry were drawn on his face. He was plagued by memories of the storm, believing it had rent the fabric of the worlds. These thoughts haunted him, like a wraith in the night – stealing his peace of mind.

Sapphire was pleased to return to the sanctuary of her quarters, reciting the incantation at the peak of the storm had taken its toll. The Lady Annas greeted her warmly. "My dear child, how pleased I am to see you. How's Caedec? I heard he was ill."

"He's well enough," said Sapphire noticing The Lady Annas was unusually pale herself.

"Good, I'm pleased to hear it. I've been worried about you, up on deck in that storm," she said embracing Sapphire.

Jhinn arrived at the old lodge before nightfall. It was tucked away in an ancient forest - constructed from blocks of stone with a square middle section, flanked on either side by towers with conical roofs.

As Jhinn walked up the steps to the main entrance the door opened revealing a man dressed in black, with hair of glistening silver and eyes of emerald set in an equine face. He noticed the man's crooked fingers and knotted knuckles.

"I've been expecting you, My Lord Jhinn. Welcome to Viarra," said the old man bowing. "My name is Enrhin."

Jhinn was intrigued. "How long have you lived here?" he enquired.

"Well, now then there's a question - far longer than I care to remember. Viarra is an old house, built by Orte Viarra, founder of the House of Viarran, when Phelar was the capital of Adranabar. Prince Orthon is his direct descendent. But perhaps you are already aware of its history, my lord?"

Jhinn shook his head. "That's interesting. You are well informed, Enrhin."

"I trust you had a good journey, my Lord Jhinn?"

"It was pleasant enough. I've brought my companion, Saravia with me. She's taking a stroll in the gardens – would you prepare a chamber for her and make sure she's comfortable."

"Of course, I'll see to it. Nothing is too much trouble. I'm here to serve you," he said guiding Jhinn into the house.

Jhinn wandered down the hall. He gazed at the shields and paintings of battles and horses hung on the walls, wondering if they had once belonged to Orte Viarra. He noticed two doors at the end of the corridor and made towards one bearing a lion's mask. He touched its metal whiskers then rubbed its nose, intrigued by the finely worked metal.

Turning the handle, the door gave on to a chamber with several arched windows running from floor to ceiling along one wall. He studied the view of the garden and forest beyond. He surveyed the chamber, noticing several chairs, shelves stuffed with books, a circular table with lion paw feet and an imposing fireplace with a standing lion at each end. A portrait of a young woman above it caught his attention.

Jhinn stood gazing at the painting for a moment. He recognized the subject immediately - it was his mother, Princess Oriahh. He marvelled at its lifelike quality, feeling as if her essence was sealed into the canvas. He was startled by the striking resemblance Saravia bore to his mother and was unnerved by it.

A clock chimed and questions clouded his mind.

"Why did you have to die by your own hand?" he said aloud.

"I didn't mean to leave you. Darkness wrapped itself around me, obscuring my vision and corrupting my soul. I was lost to the Dark Gods. Won't you forgive me, Jhinn," his mother's voice resounded in his mind.

Jhinn was distressed and turned away from the painting, wondering if he was losing his mind. He stood by a window gazing at Saravia picking flowers, the colour of her gown casting a pink hue on the glass.

"Radiant isn't she? Rather like me."

Jhinn turned to look at the painting.

"Saravia was meant for you. With her you will feel complete. If you give her up, as my dear brother may suggest, or a rival steals her away, you will suffer. All the riches the throne of Adranabar will bring won't make you happy. Listen to your heart, Jhinn and its counsel will serve you well."

Jhinn felt strangely calm as if a golden cloud had burst above his head showering him with peace and tranquillity.

A drum beat accompanied Mararuss Laboute to the scaffold. Dark clouds full of rain covered the sky and cries of "Free Mararuss" rode the wind. An atmosphere of unease permeated the scene as he climbed the steps to the platform and silently awaited his fate.

A dozen men, clad in black and armed with daggers broke through the crowd. They set upon the castle guards with a savage vengeance, knocking several unconscious to the ground and mortally wounding others. They collapsed, blood pouring from their wounds, agonizing cries rising from their throats. In the confusion Mararuss Laboute was spirited away. Several guards clustered around Prince Orthon, shielding him from the mob baying for his blood.

Castle Adranabar's cavalry thundered into the courtyard, with Darthus at the fore. In the noise and confusion the crowd dispersed making towards the gate like a flock of sheep. Prince Orthon was bundled into the castle, unharmed but deeply shocked, while the castle guards searched in vain for Mararuss.

Prince Orthon was furious the execution had dissolved into chaos. "Damn those rebels! I'll have their heads!" he spat out the words as if they were poisonous venom.

Darthus caught a young rebel and handed him over to the guards. He felt pity as he watched the terror stricken wretch marched off to the dungeons as he made his way to the Great Hall of the Unicorn where he joined Prince Orthon and his closest advisers seated around a table. Prince Orthon wore an intense look of concentration as Darthus gave his account of events.

"You've done well in catching that rebel - see you extract everything he knows by whatever means you think fit. But leave him alive, he may be useful to us," Prince Orthon commanded.

Sapphire woke to find everything on *Azenia* bathed in sunshine. She watched bright slivers of light dancing on the coverlet, as she listened to the crew calling to each other as they carried out their duties. Sapphire looked at the porthole, noticing a line of white rock rising from the sea.

"Ilesh," she whispered.

Janus was standing beside Merrick on the deck of *Azenia* as it sailed into the harbour. His eyes widened when he saw the towering walls, glistening like snow. He watched the guards patrolling them, noticing two immense doors, their hinges inlaid with silver and gold, realizing it must be the city gate.

Captain Oxghar joined them. "Behold the walls of Aiianvall are shining in the sun," he said with a flourish.

Merrick and Janus were puzzled.

"It's the first line of one of my poems. You've heard it?" enquired the captain.

Merrick and Janus exchanged glances then Merrick spoke. "Of course *'The Walls of Aiianvall'* one of your most celebrated poems. I've heard the King quote it many times."

Captain Oxghar was reassured, his vanity restored.

Aiianvall's gates remained closed as *Azenia* approached the other ships moored in the harbour. Captain Oxghar recognized several vessels from the Maladorian fleet and was pleased they appeared undamaged by the storm at sea.

Below deck Hhannon was fussing over the King.

"Damn it! I don't need any more treatment. I'm all right I tell you!" said Caedec waving him away. Hhannon bowed his head respectfully and said nothing.

Caedec breathed deeply before he spoke again. "Truthfully, I am much better – you may go. I must prepare to meet The Crown Prince. I'm sure you understand."

Hhannon bowed again. "I see you are under great stress – it is not good for your health and I'm concerned."

"I appreciate that - I am sorry if my outburst offended you."

Hhannon withdrew from the King's bedchamber without a word.

Merrick returned with Janus, encountering Hhannon in the passageway. He was worried when he saw the look on his face.

"I am full of concern for the King – but he will not heed my advice," he muttered brushing past them.

"Why is the physician worried about the King? Is he going to die?" enquired Janus.

"No, lad – he's feeling better. Take no heed, the physician's usually worried about something or other," replied Merrick, trying to sound cheerful.

Merrick entered the bedchamber to find Caedec sitting quietly in a chair. He noticed Caedec's hand was shaking as he reached for a book.

Caedec felt the weight of Merrick's stare and quickly hid his hands under the folds of his cloak.

Merrick recalled the physician's words as he combed the King's hair, placing the circlet of burnished gold engraved with lions on his head. As Merrick finished adjusting it he noticed Gai enter.

"Sire, the city gates are still closed. We await the arrival of The Crown Prince to welcome us. Most of the horses have been unloaded onto the quayside. Caius tells me they are in good health, despite the stormy voyage," said Gai studying Caedec's countenance.

Caedec nodded. "More waiting," he replied in an agitated tone.

"I've been assured The Crown Prince has left the palace. Aylvian is saddled and ready for your ride into the city. When the gates open the wait will be over," said Gai.

Captain Oxghar stared at a blank piece of parchment lying on his writing table. There was no sign of Queen Irmardia and he felt abandoned by her. He turned to gaze at the window in the stern. Nothing stirred beneath the calm surface of the Whispering Sea. He heard a light tap and Thoro entered.

"Captain - it's time."

Captain Oxghar nodded. "I pray all goes well for the King."

"Sorrel, we meet again," said Caedec shaking the young knight's hand.

"Your Majesty is very kind. I'm flattered you remember me."

"Why would I not and how well you look."

67

"Thank you," said Sorrel his face flushed. "His Majesty, The Crown Prince, is nearing the gate. He asks if you're ready to ride through the city to the palace."

"Tell him I am ready to accompany him."

A fanfare sounded as the gate opened and The Crown Prince, riding a white horse with bridle of gold, galloped onto the quayside. His white cloak billowed - the golden hilt of his sword caught the sunlight. His sharp eyes fixed briefly on Caedec, settling on Sapphire for a moment as he steadied his horse. "Caedec, welcome to Ilesh, come ride with me to the palace," he said in greeting.

Caedec smiled. "Vinaii you haven't changed, you're still the lissom youth I recall, with the same dark hair and handsome features."

Aylvian trotted alongside The Crown Prince's white stallion into the city of Aiianvall. They were engaged in conversation as Gai and Sapphire followed in their wake.

King Caedec's retinue made their way into the capital of Ilesh, flanked by the The Crown Prince's bodyguards.

Aiianvall's streets were clogged with people. Flags hung from the windows of buildings with grand facades. White flags painted with the mask of an Ileshian Leopard, contrasted with the Maladorian flags of red, emblazoned with a circle of seven gold lions.

Another fanfare sounded as the procession reached the end of one street and turned into the next. Caedec's courtiers were heartened by the crowd's cheers and Caedec was elated.

Aylvian whinnied and sidled. Alarmed, The Crown Prince's bodyguard shielded the two monarchs. A girl with hair the colour of rain drenched corn had fallen in front of Caedec's horse. Blue meadow flowers were strewn over the cobbles. Aylvian nudged the child as she lay on the ground. Caedec dismounted, helping her up he noticed her grazed knees. "That was quite a fall young lady," he said smiling.

The girl began to sob.

"Where is the child's family?"

Several bodyguards emerged from the crowd and made towards The Crown Prince. After several moments and much whispering he dismounted and strode towards Caedec. "From what I can gather her name is Liviaa – she's an orphan living on the streets of the city."

"Then she must come with us. We can't leave the child hurt and without family or protection. Sapphire will attend to her," said Caedec.

The Crown Prince was aghast. "Caedec, she's a street child – we know nothing about her. Is this wise?"

Sapphire made her way through the throng of bodyguards to comfort the girl. The Crown Prince's expression softened and he raised no objections as Caedec placed her in the saddle and began leading Aylvian towards the palace. As the crowd surged forward, the guards tried to stem the tide of people calling out to Caedec and offering their hands. Eventually, the procession came to a halt and those on horseback dismounted. Maladorians mingled with the Ileshians as Sar-Mhirian gave blessings and brought tidings from Crilm. Sar-Mhirian was overjoyed when he saw his daughter, Mhiria with her betrothed, embracing them both in turn.

Lord Griann stared at the clock. Night was falling over Castle Adranabar like a cloud of black feathers. Prince Orthon had retired to his bedchamber, against the counsel of his advisers, who felt he should make himself more visible to his subjects in such time of crisis. Lord Griann had heard reports of uprisings throughout the land.

Darthus returned from a foray into the countryside confident there was no threat to the castle, but now Mararuss had escaped he believed danger lurked everywhere. Darthus knew Prince Orthon's advisers feared for their safety. He had overheard their hushed conversations in the darkened passageways of Castle Adranabar. *"Prince Orthon is impossible, there's no reasoning with him these days"* was one remark he pondered at length.

Jhinn stared at a red glow in the night sky. He was curious, opening the window with a degree of caution. Smoke wafted into the chamber and he sensed something was amiss. He turned from the window, surprised to find Enrhin standing by the bed.

"My lord, please forgive this intrusion. I've heard Mararuss Laboute has escaped and there are uprisings all over Adranabar. Rebel soldiers have set fire to towns and villages and The Lords' armies have been sent to keep order."

Jhinn's face was ashen - his expression one of deep shock.
"There have been alarming developments since I left Castle Adranabar," he said gazing at Saravia as she lay sleeping. "Will we be safe here?"

"Difficult to say, my lord, Viarra is hidden by the forest and the rebel army may not pass this way - I pray they do not. I trust you weren't followed here by your father's men?"

Jhinn's brow was creased. "No, I believe not. Thank you, Enrhin - you may leave us. I will ponder this news," he said wondering where his father was hiding.

"Behold the Palace of Aiianvall!" said The Crown Prince as a stone structure with square paned windows came into view. The palace comprised myriad towers of differing heights - protected by an outer wall set in a landscape of rolling green. An avenue of trees lined the arrow straight road leading to an arched gate in the outer wall.

Caedec smiled at Captain Oxghar who looked ill at ease on horseback.

The Crown Prince and several of his bodyguards cantered through the arched gate with Caedec and his entourage following.

The Crown Prince noticed three of his closest advisers huddled on the palace steps watching the Maladorian courtiers. He glanced at Arrkir, thinking his smile suggested mischief and Bhelus, with his lined face and grey hair. Egrinar towered over them, his red hair and pale countenance commanding attention. The Crown Prince studied their handsome attire for several moments.

Arrkir leaned towards Bhelus, his dark hair falling across his face, and whispered in his ear. "I see Sapphire, the Blue Witch, rides Dhannan the Black."

Bhelus looked surprised. "Are you sure? Is that not Prince Orthon's favourite horse? By Crilm it is! It's Dhannan the Black," he said holding a glass, hanging from a long gold chain around his neck, up to his eye.

Arrkir gave him a cold look. "Could you be more discreet?"

Bhelus's face flushed and he stared at the ground. "Why is she called the Blue Witch?"

"Her eyes you fool, surely you've noticed them," replied Arrkir with a look of exasperation. "What does this mean, gentlemen? Why is Sapphire riding Prince Orthon's favourite horse?" he said rubbing his hands, as his fellow advisers exchanged knowing glances.

Lord Griann and his men saw Viarra rise out of the mist, like a spectre from a tomb, as they approached the forest. Lord Griann breathed the air, heavy with the scent of roses and Phinus trees. He pushed their spindly branches out of his way as he rode along the forest track.

Enrhin heard the sound of horses' hooves and felt afraid - he stepped outside fearing the worst. Lord Griann saw him and waved.

"Enrhin, 'tis I, Griann, don't you recognize me?"

"My word, so it is, what brings you to these parts?"

"I've come to fetch Lord Jhinn - his uncle commands he return to Castle Adranabar," he said brushing a leaf from his riding cloak.

Enhrin nodded. "That's understandable – have you encountered any rebels?"

Lord Griann shook his head. "None – the road was deserted."

Enrhin's breathing was laboured as he entered the bedchamber. In his haste he had forgotten to announce his presence. "My Lord Griann has arrived. He brings tidings from Prince Orthon. He wishes to see you, my lord."

Jhinn woke with a start, pulling himself up and resting on several pillows. "What? At this unearthly…?"

Enhrin looked apologetic. "Lord Griann and his men have ridden most of the night."

"I see - then it must be important."

Lord Griann wandered through the house while his men breakfasted in the kitchens. He came upon the chamber overlooking the garden and stopping to admire the fireplace, noticed the portrait of Oriahh. He stared at it spellbound. He heard the door open and Jhinn entered his face drawn. "I'm sorry to prevail upon you, but I thought it better to travel with cover of darkness. I expect you've already heard about the rebellion," he said studying his untidy host.

Jhinn nodded. "How is my uncle?"

Lord Griann hesitated. "Upset - he feels betrayed by his subjects. The mob was baying for his blood – it was not a pretty sight, Jhinn believe me it wasn't. Your father's escape has angered him to a great extent. He will want vengeance for this insult. He commands you return to the castle. He believes the lodge is vulnerable and could easily be taken by rebel forces."

Jhinn nodded his head in agreement. "Perhaps I ought to return?"

"It might be wise under the circumstances."

As Saravia entered the chamber, Lord Griann's jaw slackened, almost dropping with surprise.

Jhinn noticed his reaction as he introduced Saravia.

Lord Griann bowed taking her hand, brushing her warm flesh with his lips.

"I'm pleased to make your acquaintance, Lord Griann," said Saravia blushing.

A jealous look crossed Jhinn's face. "My uncle commands my return to Castle Adranabar. It seems I am needed there."

"Then you must go. Shall I inform Enrhin? " enquired Saravia, a note of sadness in her voice.

Jhinn nodded. "Please do."

Saravia curtsied and withdrew.

Lord Griann was astounded. "By the will of Crilm, she's the image of your late mother."

"Yes, I suppose she is."

"My word you're a dark one, a secret lover. I gather Prince Orthon is unaware of your … companion."

"As far as I can say, he is and I prefer to keep it that way," replied Jhinn.

"Then you're not bringing her to the castle. Where will she go? You can't leave her here on her own with a rebel army on the rampage – anything could happen to her – she's very pretty."

Jhinn flushed. "Saravia will return to her father's house and you're taking far too much interest in her welfare – I don't care for it."

Lord Griann wore a broad grin as he strolled through the gardens, stopping to smell the flowers now and again. He noticed his men were preparing for the journey back to Castle Adranabar. He listened to them laughing and telling jokes as they tended the horses. Recalling his meeting with Saravia, Lord Griann felt the worlds were a much brighter place.

Chapter 12 – A Wedding

Sunlight streaked the palace lawns as a legion of gardeners tended the grounds and fresh-faced young maids picked as many flowers as they could carry. Preparations for the wedding of Sar-Mhirian's daughter to The Crown Prince's brother were underway. In a quadrangle between the quarters of the Knights belonging to the Order of the Median and Crilm's Temple, a huge tent of rose red silk sat on the lawn like a vast unopened flower.

Flowers covered the temple roof, while inside amidst a blaze of gold and silver, Sar-Mhirian was seated on a silver chair wrought in the shape of a dragon - its face forming a canopy over his head. Sar-Mhirian looked serene as he recited the mantra of Crilm.

'Blessings of the worlds walk with thee and never leave thee. Let it be so.'
He recited the mantra until the temple was filled with golden vapour.

Mhiria was dressed in her wedding gown of silver silk, beaded with Azuriene crystals, sparkling like tiny stars. Her gown was fitted at the waist with puff sleeves and a train like a silken cobweb. Mhiria's hair dark and lustrous was piled high on her head and held with clips of pearl. Her feet were clad in silk slippers embroidered with dragons. Mhiria's maids smiled as she studied her reflection.

"Mistress looks lovely," they said in unison.

Mhiria smiled and the chamber came to life.

Nheve was attired in a grey silk tunic and breeches. His sword's hilt fashioned like a dragon's head was tucked into a belt slung low on his hips. The Crown Prince wore purple, the gold dragon hilt of his own sword shone in the light.

From his window, Nheve watched as guests made their way to the temple, escorted by Knights of the Order of the Median, their helmets styled like leopard-heads, catching the sunlight.

"Vinaii, there's the Blue Witch," he said, his nose almost touching the glass.

The Crown Prince rushed to the window, hoping to catch a glimpse of her. "Where is she? Who's she with?"

"Ah! So it's true, you are enamoured of her."

"What! Don't be ridiculous."

"Dear brother, you're keeping secrets from me," said Nheve smiling.

"I wouldn't be the first Crown Prince to marry a witch."

"Well, well, it's more serious than I imagined. A word of warning Vinaii, Arkirr tells me she rides Prince Orthon's favourite horse. And I've heard rumours of a secret marriage to Gai."

The Crown Prince tried his best to look nonchalant. "Gai cares too much for alchemy to take a wife and what can Orthon mean to Sapphire?"

"Exactly, or what does Sapphire mean to Orthon? That's the question on the lips of many courtiers in the palace."

"Orthon is generous with his horses. He's given many to his cousin. I saw them on the quayside," said The Crown Prince.

"Maybe it's just gossip. Anyway, it's high time you thought about marriage. It might be good for you," Nheve replied and laughed.

The Crown Prince's expression had a determined quality about it as he spoke. "I'm serious, Nheve, I mean to take Sapphire as my wife."

"Then I wish you luck, though I doubt you'll need it. You've always got everything you wanted," Nheve replied his voice tinged with envy.

The Crown Prince looked uncomfortable as he glanced at the clock. "It's almost time for the ceremony."

Nheve and Mhiria entered the temple to a great cheer. All the guests rose from their seats as the couple walked past. Sar-Mhirian stood at the front underneath an arch of leaping dragons, one silver - the other gold. As the guests were seated the ceremony began. Sar-Mhirian spoke and time seemed to alter its usual pattern as the holy man talked of love and loss in the worlds. After a period of silence he joined Nheve and Mhiria's hands in readiness for the Summoning of the Blessings.

"By the power of Crilm, our friend and protector in the worlds, I summon the blessings."

Two columns of white light formed on either side of the couple and Sar-Mhirian repeated the mantra of Crilm several times.

'Blessings of the worlds walk with thee and never leave thee. Let it be so.'

As the columns of light began to swirl around the couple like summer rain, they embraced. A sound of tinkling bells filled the temple as the happy couple, followed by their guests emerged from the temple into the sunlight. Flowers slid off the roof showering the wedding party with their scent. There was laughter and a general air of hilarity as they entered the rose red tent for the wedding celebrations.

Sar-Mhirian embraced his daughter. "I hope you will be happy. I know your mother would be proud of you today. How I wish she could be here. You look lovely, my dear."

"Thank you father – I'm so happy."

"Then I'm pleased. My life has been worthwhile."

Mhiria was overcome with emotion.

Caedec, Gai, Sapphire and Captain Oxghar were enjoying themselves as Liviaa and Janus played on the lawn.

"A lovely wedding and a most pleasant afternoon, don't you think, Gai?" said Caedec helping himself to another goblet of Adras.

Gai was distracted. His gaze firmly fixed on The Crown Prince, who was paying Sapphire a considerable amount of attention. Arrkir was also watching The Crown Prince. Caedec gave up waiting for a reply and wandered off in search of Captain Oxghar, who was also fond of a goblet or two of Adras.

"Do you think they make a handsome couple?" Egrinar whispered to Arrkir.

Arrkir's expression changed to one of disgust. "Don't be absurd - she's a witch!" he said spitting out the words as if they were burning his throat.

Egrinar was perplexed. "That is so - she is a witch and a rather beautiful one I must say. She also belongs to the Royal House of Azuriene. An alliance forged between our two countries would certainly be advantageous – don't you think?"

Arrkir's face was like thunder. "I will not allow The Crown Prince to marry a witch and that is my last word on the matter," he said sweeping out of the tent.

As daylight waned, the guests drifted back towards the palace to prepare themselves for the evening's entertainment.

Entering the ballroom, Queen Tsabani was resplendent in a flowing gown. Her neck and arms were adorned with jewellery fabled throughout the worlds. She gave Caedec a cold look as he approached.

"My dear sister-in-law how lovely to see you," he said in greeting.

"And you. May I present my ambassador, Lord Caton?"

Lord Caton bowed.

"How you've changed, you were a boy when we last met and now you are a young man – handsome too."

"Sire, you flatter me," he replied in a purring tone.

"Ah those were the days, before Greylan was taken from us," said Caedec reminiscing.

"Sire, his loss is great," replied Lord Caton.

Caedec nodded in agreement.

Nheve and Mhiria led several couples into the centre of the ballroom. They stepped across a black and white floor flooded with the light of a thousand candles. Guests admired themselves in gilded looking glasses as the music started and the dance began. The Crown Prince danced with Sapphire to the annoyance of the ladies of the court. They looked enviously at her silk gown and golden hair set in waves, adorned with sapphires of every hue. The Crown Prince gazed at her with admiration. As the dance ended he held on to her hand.

Captain Oxghar entered the ballroom to a round of applause and soon found himself encircled by adoring ladies.

"Captain, pray read us some verse," they entreated.

"It will be an honour," he said gazing at their beautiful faces.

Several silver buttons on the captain's tunic jangled and as if by magic he produced a slim, red book from his pocket and began to read a poem.

The walls of Aiianvall

Behold the walls of Aiianvall are shining in the sun
as white as death and as cold and long

The walls of Aiianvall speak to me
of fame and fortune, strength and gain
as fair as the eagle of the worlds
they are like pearls from the Whispering Sea
the sea that brings my love to me

The court ladies swooned as Captain Oxghar closed his book and bowed to thunderous applause. Nheve and Mhiria rushed towards him uttering words of thanks for the marvellous rendition of their favourite verse.

Arrkir noticed that The Crown Prince was nowhere to be seen and wearing a dark expression, strode across the lawns in search of him. "He's with that witch, I'll wager," he muttered.

Sapphire and The Crown Prince sat in silence admiring a moon's reflection on the surface of the lake.

After a lengthy silence and much fidgeting The Crown Prince spoke. "Sapphire, there's something I want to ask."

Sapphire gazed at him with expectation.

Arrkir struggled to contain his fury when he saw The Crown Prince with Sapphire. He approached the arbour trying his best to feign a pleasant disposition. "Ah! There you are, Your Majesty."

The Crown Prince groaned as he was interrupted.

"Sire, you left the ballroom without a guard. I fear for your safety in these dangerous times."

The Crown Prince felt his temper snap. "I'm not a child! Don't question my judgement. Get out of my sight, Arkkir. By Crilm, if your father had not held sway with mine and smoothed your passage at court you would not be here now," he said shaking with anger.

Arrkir's expression of surprise betrayed his thoughts – he had not anticipated such a reaction. He withdrew murmuring apologies, the colour draining from his face with each step.

The Crown Prince turned to Sapphire. "Now, where was I?"

Sapphire shivered, feeling awkward about the exchange she had witnessed. "I'm cold – let's go inside."

"Of course," he said a note of disappointment in his voice.

An uneasy silence settled between them as they left the arbour.

"Will you ride with me on the morrow? We can go up into the hills where the scenery is beautiful and no-one will bother us. And you can see the damage the winds have wrought over the land."

"Vinaii, are you ever really alone? You're surrounded by courtiers, guards or advisers. "

The Crown Prince frowned. "When we leave the palace behind it will be different. I promise you there will be no courtiers, guards or advisers to bother us. Say you will."

Sapphire hesitated. "All right 'til the morrow then."

As Jhinn and Griann's party approached the forest they saw no sign of rebel activity. The trees were as still and silent as the grave.

"I'll leave you now. I know a safe route," said Saravia.

"No, wait a moment, I'll see you safely home," replied Jhinn.

"There's no need. You must make haste, I'm sure your uncle will be anxious for your return."

Saravia rode off not waiting for a reply. Lord Griann's heart was heavy as he watched her vanish into the forest.

As she approached her father's house coils of smoke were rising from the chimney. Saravia was puzzled. A fire was rarely lit until winter's claw held the forest in its iron grip and snow lay on the ground. She ran up the steps and opening the door heard strange voices coming from within. Saravia felt uneasy as her feet trod the worn flagstones in the hall. She glanced at the familiar wood panelling and clocks of differing shape and height, standing like soldiers in a line. A shrill chime startled her and she crept along the passage as if she was walking on ice. Noticing a door slightly ajar, she peered through the crack, catching a glimpse of a dark haired man lolling in a chair by the fire. "Mararuss Laboute, what in Crilm's name are you doing here?" she whispered.

A draught crept through the meeting chamber as Caedec stared at the table full of papers and scrolls. He noticed Arrkir examining his fingernails.

Erussah's brow was lined with worry. "The Crown Prince demands a sizeable portion of Maladoria and Sapphire's hand in marriage, with King Caedec and Queen Tsabani's blessing as her legal guardians, in return for his support."

A stunned silence settled over the chamber. Arrkir smirked and Gai shifted in his chair.

"I see that the treaty is exact in its requirements and stipulations. I would speak with The Crown Prince about this," said Caedec making to withdraw.

"As you wish, sire. I will convey your thoughts to His Majesty, The Crown Prince," said Arrkir lacing his hands.

"Well, gentlemen we have much to discuss," said Caedec seating himself by the fireplace, thankful for the refuge of his chamber. Gai and Erussah followed suit staring at the flames.

"I must confess I too am saddened by the terms of the treaty," said Erussah.

Caedec studied his fingers. "I will try to negotiate with Vinaii. What is your advice, Erussah?"

"The Crown Prince is entitled to ask for what he wishes. We cannot attack Khinart without his support. We haven't enough gold ducins to wage war on the scale needed to oust your enemy. Perhaps we could offer him a share of the spoils, rather than tracts of our country. As for Sapphire, well it's not our custom to dictate the ways of the heart. But, an alliance with The Crown Prince is crucial," said Erussah, smoothing the folds of his cloak.

"Gai, pray tell me your thoughts," said Caedec.

"I am, as you are, greatly saddened by the terms of the treaty. I can say no more. I have nothing to add."

Merrick entered and began piling logs on the fire.

"Where's Sapphire? I haven't seen her today," enquired Caedec.

"She's riding in the mountains with The Crown Prince. Said she was going to look at the damage caused by the winds he'd told her about," replied Merrick.

Gai returned to his apartment, a storm raged in his heart when he thought of Sapphire riding with The Crown Prince. He was torn - feeling part of him was prepared to give her up while the other was not. Deep in his heart he knew there was no alternative. Caedec needed The Crown Prince's support, the battle for Maladoria depended on it and he could not bear to see him spend the rest of his days in exile, never to see his beloved wife or country again. If Sapphire was the price he had to pay – then so be it. As he made his decision he felt his heart break.

As Sapphire and The Crown Prince approached the log cabin, she marvelled at the view. Green pastures gave on to hills and snow capped mountains. A biting wind blew through the valley like the breath of a dark god, as they hurried towards it. As the wind gained speed, she felt relieved to be safely ensconced in the cabin. Through the window she could see how it had devastated the landscape - trees lay uprooted like an army of fallen soldiers.

Sapphire fell in love with the cabin's rustic charm and comfortable furnishings. She thought The Crown Prince was happier - the strain had lifted from his features. "I love it here," she said.

The Crown Prince smiled. "My grandfather built it. He hated all the protocol and intrigue at court and longed for a simpler life in the country," he said putting logs on the fire and warming his hands as they burned. "That's better."

Sapphire sat in a well-worn chair. The Crown Prince picked up a book leafing through its pages.

"Sapphire, I know I asked for your help with these wretched winds. But there's more to it than that. We've met several times now and the fact is, I'm in love with you – will you be my wife?"

An awkward silence followed as he studied her expression.

"I'm not expecting an immediate answer, but I hope you'll consider my proposal. You're not surprised are you?"

Sapphire gazed at the firelight as he continued leafing through the volume. "I'm honoured, Vinaii, but … will you give me time to think about it?"

"Is there someone else?"

Sapphire felt her heartbeat quicken when she thought of Gai. "I cannot say."

"I see. Captain Oxghar writes excellent poetry," he said changing the subject.

"Yes and he's a good captain. We're fortunate Lord Fhinn of Aizan could spare him. We may not have survived the storm without his good seamanship and that of his crew," replied Sapphire, her face damp and flushed.

"I'll see he's handsomely rewarded. I understand *Azenia* sustained some damage and is being repaired."

"Yes, we'll be on our way once the ship is seaworthy."

"Sapphire, why not remain here in Ilesh. Soon the Claws of Winter will grip the worlds and the battle for Maladoria will be dangerous. There will be many casualties. It will be dangerous for you – I fear for your safety."

Sapphire listened to The Crown Prince her head tilted slightly, pausing before she replied. "I know you have my interests at heart, but the King has need of me. Only when the war is won can I return."

"Very well - I'll take up the King's cause and join you. I won't let you go easily."

Sapphire had not anticipated this turn of events and was lost for words.

Captain Oxghar boarded *Azenia*. He noticed Hhariann seemed better - his fur gleamed in the sunlight as the crew fed him several shiny fish. He entered his cabin and seated himself at the writing table. "It's good to be back," he said aloud. Sorting through a pile of documents he came across a letter fastened with a blue seal, embossed with the figure of a dolphin. Captain Oxghar's heartbeat quickened as he broke it in two. A ring fashioned in the shape of a dolphin, its tail sprinkled with Azuriene crystals, fell on to the table. He held it as he read the words written in strong, fluid letters, like a tiger marching across a desert. He noticed Queen Irmardia's signature – a capital letter I.

I trust you are well. I hope the ring pleases you.

"She loves me still," he whispered gazing at the sea through the window of bright crystal. He beamed as the ring jumped on to his slim finger, fastening itself securely around his flesh.

The Crown Prince was in a determined mood when he returned from his ride in the mountains. He summoned Egrinar, waiting impatiently for him.

Egrinar entered The Crown Prince's chamber, cautiously wondering why he had been sent for.

"I intend to join the King's voyage to Maladoria. I command you offer good counsel to my brother. He will rule while I am gone."

Egrinar listened to The Crown Prince's words with amazement. "Your Highness, I will be happy to advise your brother as you command. But this troubles me – I believe your presence is needed here. Nheve is young and recently married, he's not ready for responsibility of this nature and you're without an heir. I am concerned."

The Crown Prince made a dismissive gesture with his hand. "My mind is made up. I trust you will make all the necessary arrangements. If I don't return my brother will succeed."

Egrinar noted The Crown Prince's expression and decided to acquiesce. "Very well, Your Highness."

"Does Caedec want to speak to me about the Treaty?"

"Yes, he's expressed dissatisfaction with the terms."

"Send for him and we'll discuss it."

Egrinar bowed and withdrew.

Caedec was shown into the state apartments. He gazed at the walls covered in patterned silk, hung with paintings of The Crown Prince's richly attired ancestors - the House of Aiianvall was a wealthy lineage in the worlds.

Arrkir saw The Crown Prince leave his private chamber and decided to follow him. As he sauntered along the corridor towards the state apartments, Arrkir fell quietly into his footsteps. His curiosity aroused, knowing The Crown Prince held his most important meetings there. Arrkir was so absorbed in his thoughts he failed to notice his quarry's pace had slackened and almost trod on The Crown Prince.

The Crown Prince feeling he was not alone turned to find Arrkir at his heels. He glowered at him. "What are you doing? Are you following me?"

Arrkir took a step back. "Of course not, Your Majesty, I merely wish to be of service, please forgive my intrusion."

The Crown Prince's eyes narrowed. "You may go – I have no need of you."

Arrkir bowed as The Crown Prince entered the state apartments. As the door closed he lingered for a moment, hoping to see something of interest then strolled off down the corridor.

The Crown Prince greeted Caedec and they seated themselves, neither knowing how to start the conversation. After an awkward silence The Crown Prince decided to take the initiative. "Tell me your troubles."

Caedec shuffled his feet. "I would like to discuss the treaty. I confess I had not anticipated your terms."

The Crown Prince leaned back in his chair. "I see."

"I have a proposal, which I hope you will find agreeable," said Caedec.

"Then let me hear it."

Caedec took a long breath. "Dividing Maladoria will cause trouble - my subjects will resist this action strongly. In order to avoid these disruptive, not to mention expensive, complications, I will give you Arakhinn. When Khinart is driven out of Maladoria by our army – his reputation will suffer and his own people will be vulnerable. I believe we could acquire his lands with very little effort."

The Crown Prince nodded. "Possible."

"As for Sapphire, I cannot interfere with her choice of husband. Since her mother died Tsabani and I have been her guardians, under the terms of her will. But Sapphire has always done as she pleases. She is a powerful, young witch and you are a handsome man with a throne to offer. Why not let matters take their course – let the fates decide. I know Sapphire and she would not be well disposed to a match dictated by a treaty."

The Crown Prince was thoughtful. Several moments passed without a reply. He got up and paced. His body stiff with tension. Eventually, he spoke. "You are as wise as ever my good King. I believe it would be foolish to ignore your counsel. I'll have a new treaty drawn up. I also have a proposal for your consideration."

Caedec felt relieved, letting out a deep breath. "Very well," he replied, intrigued by the mention of a new proposal.

"I would like to join you in your quest."

Caedec raised an eyebrow. "You wish to leave Ilesh and fight with us?"

"Yes, I've given it some thought and spoken with Egrinar."

"Your mind is made up."

"It is."

"Then what can I say, other than you are most welcome to join us" said Caedec.

The Crown Prince grinned. "Now, let us drink to the spoils of war," he said pouring a flagon of Adras into two goblets and handing one to Caedec.

Queen Tsabani paced the length of the chamber like a caged animal. She felt the temperature dropping, as winter flexed its grip on Ilesh. Ice covered the palace windows and country folk made their way to Aiianvall in droves, the fields strewn with the frozen bodies of animals.

Queen Tsabani realized she was a prisoner of the elements as the Whispering Sea froze over and a barbarous wind plagued the land. She had heard the harbour was a wasteland of ice - a ghostly graveyard of ships. Both *Azenia* and her ship, *Azuronde,* were trapped, despite the sailors frantically stabbing the ice with poles and pouring cauldrons of boiling water on it to prevent it expanding and damaging the ships' hulls. Sheets of white crystal covered the vessels' bows. Icicles formed skeletal fingers around the masts and rigging, holding them in a death grip, like spectres trying to escape their tombs.

"I must return to Azuriene, everything may depend upon it," she said aloud.

Lord Caton knocked and entered. "I believe Your Majesty commands my presence."

"Indeed, this weather plagues my soul. I'm in need of company."

"Naturally, Your Majesty. How may I be of service?" Perhaps a game of cards would prove a distraction," said Lord Caton.

Queen Tsabani gave him a look as cold as the ice on the window panes. "That's not what I had in mind. I would speak with you, Lord Caton."

"Of course Your Majesty, does any particular subject interest you? Astronomy? I've always been fascinated by the stars."

Queen Tsabani shook her head. "No, Lord Caton, I wish to speak of Caedec. I want you to ingratiate yourself with him – gain his confidence. You were a friend to his son, were you not? And he is well disposed to you still?"

Lord Caton's lip trembled. "Well yes, I believe the King looks upon me favourably. I've no reason to think otherwise."

Queen Tsabani smiled. "Good, then that's settled. I will speak with him and ask you be attached to his court, as my ambassador."

"Your Majesty, am I to understand you wish me to spy on King Caedec and his courtiers?"

"Really, Lord Caton – are you questioning my motives? For your sake, I hope you are not," said Queen Tsabani.

Lord Caton felt threatened. "Of course not Your Majesty, I would not dream of it," he said bowing low.

"Good, I'm glad. Now, I will take a stroll," she said sweeping out of the chamber. "You will accompany me."

Queen Tsabani walked quickly through the palace colonnade. She felt the wind bite deep into her bones and gathered her heavy crimson cloak about her thin frame.

Lord Caton followed. He struggled to keep pace, finding his dainty steps were no match for her strides.

Gai and Caedec were also strolling in the colonnade and the two parties met by the entrance to the garden.

"Good morning! How nice to see you dear sister-in-law," said Caedec.

Queen Tsabani managed a smile. "And you, brother-in-law. May I speak with you?"

"Indeed – by all means."

"I wish to speak to you about my sister, Ahrisa. Have you any tidings?"

"Alas, no, I've heard nothing of my wife. In fact, I hear little of Maladoria these days. Since Khinart tightened his hold and secured the borders. A veil has been drawn over the country."

Queen Tsabani paused, gazing at the trees wrapped in snow. "Indeed, I'm sorry to hear it - a sad situation. I'm hoping to return to Azuriene, as soon as the weather permits. I wonder if you would grant a favour and allow Lord Caton to remain. I would rest easier if he were attached to your court, as my ambassador. You see I have great trust in him - I know he'll send me tidings of my dear sister – should there be any, without delay. I have no such faith in some courtiers I could mention."

Caedec wore an impassive expression, hiding his feelings of suspicion. "If it would please you, then so be it. I welcome the opportunity to renew my acquaintance with him."

Queen Tsabani gave a weak smile. "Thank you. I shall return to Azuriene with a lighter heart."

Gai noticed Caedec was strangely silent as they returned to the palace.

"Is there anything troubling you?" Gai enquired.

"Tsabani, I'm afraid. She asked if Lord Caton could remain with us. Apparently, she trusts him to send tidings of her dear sister."

Gai laughed. "Her dear sister, my word her feelings have changed."

"My thoughts entirely, her compassion is out of character and it concerns me. I believe she is toying with us and Lord Caton is a spy, or he is a fool caught in a trap."

"Lord Caton – that fop, a spy. That doesn't seem plausible to me. Perhaps Tsabani has made a secret alliance with The Crown Prince? They were betrothed at one time," said Gai.

"Indeed, or she has made an alliance of a worse nature," replied Caedec.

Lord Caton struggled to find any appeasing words as Queen Tsabani swept along the corridor in search of The Crown Prince. She was incensed, barging into the Library like a whirlwind. She hesitated surveying the room. Her eyes rested on Caedec seated in a chair by the window, reading. She marched up to him. "Have you seen Vinaii? I wish to speak with him."

Caedec looked up. "No, I have not. I expect he's locked away in his private chamber, busy with matters of state."

Queen Tsabani looked as if she was about to explode. "It's imperative I return to Azuriene. Why hasn't the ice melted? Can't he do something about it?"

"Tsabani, calm yourself. I sense your frustration. I am anxious to continue my journey home, but we must wait - there is nothing else for it. Be patient."

"Home! What do you know of home! You've been gone ten winters or more, leaving my sister to fend for herself – have you forgotten your enemy holds her prisoner," she said raising her voice and attracting the attention of several courtiers in the process.

Caedec closed his book. "I am sorry you cannot return to Azuriene."

"Is that all you can say?"

Caedec grimaced. "It is all I am prepared to. Now, if you will excuse me," he said rising from his chair and withdrawing as the courtiers bowed. Queen Tsabani watched him, a half smile on her lips, pleased The Claws of Winter had drawn blood.

Darthus stared at the icy patterns on the window panes. He saw the courtyard covered in a layer of snow. Castle Adranabar was cloaked in an eerie silence. Nothing stirred. Snow had brought its silent presence to the land.

Darthus had not encountered Prince Orthon for several days, not since they argued bitterly about Mararuss's escape. In a fit of pique Prince Orthon had revoked permission for him to sail to Ilesh to retrieve his errant son. But it was of no consequence - the Whispering Sea was frozen. He had heard the ships moored in Ilesh were trapped in the ice, prisoners of the sea.

Darthus was wrapped in gloom, he missed his son. Castle Adranabar's atmosphere had changed since the court in exile's departure. Prince Orthon was morose, spending his time shut up in his apartments, rarely granting his advisers an audience.

And there were rumours. Some said the Prince missed his cousin and his loss had driven him to the brink of insanity. Others said he was in love and his suit had been rejected, leaving him stricken by feelings of rejection, or he had fallen under the spell of an evil witch. Darthus was unsure what to believe, if anything. But Prince Orthon was a changed man, whatever the cause.

Darthus sighed, pondering whether life at the castle would improve when the Lords Jhinn and Griann returned. At least they were full of energy, while Prince Orthon's court had grown old overnight. There was nothing but grey haired, wizened men prowling the corridors speaking in hushed tones and whispers. Darthus wondered if he should have joined the exiled court on their voyage as Caius suggested many moons ago. A new life in another country in the company of good friends was tempting. He thought Janus had made a wise choice.

Saravia heard a pan hissing on the stove and went to investigate – she found the kitchen deserted. A trail of footprints led to the door - opening it she felt a blast of cold air as the Claws of Winter gripped her arm. She followed the trail as darkness approached with the stealth of a wolf. She saw her father cutting logs and piling them into a sack as she approached through the trees, her feet crunching in the snow. He heard the noise and stopped.

"Saravia, I wasn't expecting you 'til the morrow. I sent the servants to visit their families in the village. I daresay they'll be back by morning, but we've no help 'til then."

"I gather you have company, despite the lack of servants."

Saravia noticed a guilty look cross his face, but he said nothing.

"Father, how could you harbour such a person?"

"Saravia, there are things I can't tell you. How's your sister? Is she well - have you quarrelled again? Is that why you've come home?" he said avoiding the subject.

Saravia's face flushed as he gave her a knowing look. She made her way back to the house, buffeted by a bitter wind as she climbed the steps to the door. Icy fingers brushed her face and nipped her ears - she was thankful for the warmth of the kitchen. She had forgotten about the pan and now it was rattling and screeching like a banshee, as her father entered carrying a sack of logs.

"You left the pan on the stove again," said Saravia.

"Oh, don't fuss. It's all right. So I forget things now and again. I know I'm getting older. You don't have to remind me."

"Have you forgotten the most wanted man in Adranabar is sitting at our fireside, surrounded by his fawning followers?"

"No, I hadn't and that's enough Saravia. Mararuss is a good man, he may be a little misunderstood, but that's all."

"Misunderstood! He's poison, why his own son hates him...so I've heard."

"What do you know of him or his son?"

Saravia checked herself, worrying she had said too much.

"I've known Mararuss a while. He may not be a good father. But he cares about the people of this land and our struggle to pay the extortionate taxes Prince Orthon imposes upon us."

Saravia stared at him in disbelief, wondering how he could defend a man like Mararuss. "I'm going to my bedchamber."

"As you wish young lady, but I'll be serving dinner soon. Do you want any?"

"No, thank you. I've already eaten. Father, be careful. If the Prince should hear of this, things would go badly for us."

"Aye lass, you're right," he said touching her arm and drawing her to him. "Don't worry they won't stay long and maybe they won't come this way again," he whispered.

"Ah, my host is here at last. Come sit with us Erarunde, guardian of the forest," said Mararuss indicating a chair by the hearth. And where's this daughter of yours? We haven't seen her yet."

"She's just returned from visiting her married sister and the journey has wearied her. I'm afraid she'll not be joining us for dinner."

"Ah, shame, we could do with her company. These men are good companions, but alas they're not very pretty," said Mararuss laughing.

Erarunde smiled. "Well, I expect you'd like to eat and be on your way."

"There's no hurry, is there lads? It's not every day I meet a friend from the old days. You've done all right, Erarunde. Nice house, good position and two pretty daughters I hear."

"You have very good ears to have learned so much about me."

"What happened to your wife, Erarunde? You haven't mentioned her?"

Erarunde's expression clouded. "She died. My girls were very young at the time - she came down with a fever and didn't rally. Very sudden it was, very sudden."

"Oh, I'm sorry. It must have been hard for you – she was a good woman," said Mararuss.

"Yes – I haven't had an easy time of it, but there are others worse off than me. At least I've got my girls, they'll see me right, I'll wager."

"It's a long time since we were young soldiers fighting on the battlefields of The Delvia States and for what? Prince Orthon thought we could take the Emperor's lands and found we couldn't to our cost. How many lads were slain on those fields? If you ask me, the campaign was doomed, but he wouldn't listen to reason," said Mararuss.

"We saw terrible things, Mararuss. Things I wouldn't tell my daughters. I've no stomach for war."

Mararuss tapped his fingers on the arm of the chair. "We could be back on the trail of battle."

Erarunde was shocked.

"No-one wields an axe like you, Erarunde."

Erarunde stared into the flames remembering past battles. He recalled towns and villages burning, children crying for mercy, a smell of burning flesh, and the glittering head of his axe dripping with blood. He saw Mararuss's grinning face as he cut down his enemies. Visions of rape and murder followed by toasts to victory with goblets of blood filled his mind and he shivered, as if someone stood on his grave. "What good would I be? War is a young man's game."

"Shame," said Mararuss. "I was looking forward to your company."

A cat padded into the chamber, sat by the hearth and with long strokes of his pink tongue, meticulously washed a paw.

"Where have you been, Sigamus? Your mistress is home", said Erarunde stroking the cat's smooth fur.

Sigamus gazed at Erarunde then hissed at Mararuss.

"Cats, they always look at you with disdain, as if they can see your soul and the darkness within," said Mararuss.

Saravia heard a loud squeal. "Sigamus!" she cried as she ran down the stairs, bursting into the chamber to find a rebel dangling Sigamus over the fire, while Mararuss looked on with amusement. She snatched the terrified animal from the lad, studying the cat's singed tail. "How could you? Is this how you repay my father?"

Mararuss stared at her, the colour drained from his face, as if she were a ghost. He stood up moving towards her, as if he was sleepwalking.

Hearing his daughter's cries, Erarunde rushed in to find Mararuss leaning against against Saravia, who was still holding the terrified cat. She froze in terror as he touched her face.

"Oriahh," whispered Mararuss.

"What in Crilm's name is going on? Get off my daughter, or so help me I'll crush your skull with my axe!"

"I hope we meet again," he said drawing away. "A slight misunderstanding Erarunde. We'll have our dinner and be on our way."

"Go, and take your food with you."

"All right, my friend, I'll see you again."

Erarunde shook his head. "I'm sorry lass," he said comforting his daughter.

Mararuss left without a word, taking some food and gathering their horses, the rebels rode off into the night. Watching at the window, Saravia and her father listened to the horses' hooves fade away, as white flakes fluttered onto the ground.

Jhinn and Griann reached Castle Adranabar as snow began to fall. Steam rose from their horses' flanks as several guards, patrolling the walls, studied the riders. One of them recognized Jhinn and Griann and gestured to the others to open the gate. As the party entered the courtyard the lords dismounted and the grooms led the horses away.

"I hope you find your uncle well," said Lord Griann as Jhinn pushed past him, wearing a sullen expression.

Lord Griann threw himself into a chair. "That was a long ride, Atheil. I'm tired and frozen to the marrow" he said as his servant handed him a goblet.

"Aye, my lord, snow's falling and 'tis very cold," replied Atheil, pushing a lock of brown hair from his forehead as he removed his master's riding boots.

Lord Griann sighed. "I've a letter to write, pray bring me a quill and parchment."

Jhinn spent a restless night, shivering under the coverlet as the intense cold permeated his bedchamber. Knowing his uncle expected an answer to his proposal, Jhinn was gripped by a dilemma. As heir apparent to the throne of Adranabar he knew his life would change, yet to refuse would incur disfavour.

Saravia woke with fragments of the nightmare floating in her mind. She had dreamt the horses had bolted, galloping into the night, as flakes of swirling snow covered the land in a mantle of white. She watched Sigamus stir from his sleep and went to the window - drawing back the hangings she saw the stable door was ajar.

"Father, come quickly – the horses!" Saravia dressed hastily, covering herself with a riding cloak as she ran towards her father's bedchamber.

"What's the matter?"

"The stable door's open. We must make haste if we are to find them."

Saravia ran through the house. She was consumed with terror, hearing wolves howling in the forest. Stumbling into the kitchen she managed to light a taper at the stove. She lit a candle, noticing the larder was open. Several alphus berries were scattered across the floor. "Damn you, Mararuss, helping yourself to our winter store."

Erarunde stumbled in half-asleep. "Have you seen them? Are they out there?"

Saravia fumbled for the key, turning the lock while her father fetched a lantern.

"Looks like they've made into the forest, we'll have to wait until morning. We won't find them now."

"Father, there are wolves in the forest, I've heard them howling. What if…?"

"They'll have to take their chance, Saravia. It's not safe wandering about out there."

"But father – we can't let them die."

"I'm as sorry as you lass, but there's nothing we can do in the circumstances. Come now, we'll go back inside – it'll soon be light."

Saravia's shoulders slumped. The thought of losing her beloved horses was too much to bear. Reluctantly she returned to her bedchamber, feeling sick with anxiety she got into bed, tears streaming down her ashen face. Sigamus clawed at the coverlet, pulling it up he pushed himself under and lay purring beside her.

Erarunde lingered in the kitchen staring at shadows in the candlelight. He saw the larder door ajar and the alphus berries on the floor. "Poor Saravia, what a welcome for her," he said voicing his thoughts.

Lord Griann retired to the four-poster hung with tapestries. As Atheil removed the copper warming pan, Griann lay down on the linen sheets, grateful for some comfort and warmth. He pulled the coverlet over himself as Atheil arranged the tapestries. Lord Griann was glad of them, knowing they would keep out the icy draught, creeping through the crevices and gaps in the window panes. He breathed in the cold air until his throat felt as if it was frozen.

Jhinn was composing a letter to his uncle. He studied the blank parchment intently, reaching over the writing table for his favourite quill. He ran his finger over the tip. A drop of blood dripped on to the parchment as the candles guttered. Jhinn studied the cut it had made, struggling to quell the confusion in his mind.

The quill lay limp in his hand, the red plume shining in the candlelight. He pulled the inkwell towards him, opening the lid he stared at the black liquid. Gazing at the ink he felt drawn into a fathomless well of despair. His eyes closed and darkness lured him into the realm of the unknown. Candlelight danced as he slumped on the writing table. His grip loosened and the quill rolled across the surface. All was silent as the grave.

Saravia woke feeling the heat of a bright sun pouring through the window of her bedchamber. Sigamus sat on the rug, patterned with butterflies and hook nosed mice, washing his paws. Saravia entered the dressing room. She gazed at the carved, linen press and the tapestries sewn by her mother, shaking herself from her reverie she filled the bath with water and put on the warmest attire she possessed.

Erarunde offered his daughter a bowl of roasted berries, covered in a layer of honey with a slice of bread. Sigamus ran to his bowl, only to discover a few meagre pieces of fish.

"There'll be more for you when I've been to market, Sigamus," said Erarunde.

"Father, where will you find the money?"

"Mararuss and his men may have taken food from our winter store, but they didn't find the coins I've hidden away."

"I hope you have enough to buy new horses," replied Saravia.

"Ah, not quite," he said counting the coins in his broad palm.

Saravia looked at him shaking her head. "I'm going to look for them."

Saravia set off into the forest. She trudged through the snow, following a trail of hoof prints amongst the trees. Shivering as the cold bored into her bones, she lost sight of them. She walked until every bone in her body ached, stopping to rest by a frozen stream.

Snow began to fall, dressing the trees in ermine. In the midst of the snow storm she saw the outline of a horseman. She edged away from the stream, thinking Mararuss and his men might have set up camp in the forest. Watching the rider's progress, shielded by the trunk of an ancient Phinas tree, she gasped. The rider's mount was familiar with its massive build and distinctive coat, she likened to a pale sun shining on a winter meadow.

"Can it be Lord Griann?" she whispered.

As the rider drew nearer she moved away from the tree, hoping for better vantage point. When she saw the rider's face she felt her blood pump. "My Lord Griann?"

Lord Griann gazed at the huddled form standing in the snow. "Saravia?"

She blushed as he dismounted, striding towards her.

"Are you all right, Saravia?"

"Yes, thank you my lord. I came in search of our horses, three bay mares - they bolted from the stable during the night. Have you seen them?"

93

"Yes, they've followed Yarrow along this track," he said gesturing to the horses trotting towards them."

Saravia's expression brightened. "I'm overjoyed to see them safe and well."

"Then our meeting has been fortuitous, though I must confess I was hoping I'd see you again."

Saravia could hardly conceal her delight.

"I intended to write to you, but words failed me and I've longed to see you, before the ice thaws and I return home."

Saravia's expression changed and her features clouded with sadness.

"Of course you're welcome to visit my estates, if you'd like to. I'm sure it could be arranged. I would ask your father's permission of course."

"Thank you. I would like that very much," she replied, her countenance brightening.

Lord Griann mounted his stallion offering Saravia his hand. She took it, swinging herself easily into the high backed saddle.

"Walk on," he said patting Yarrow's neck.

Queen Tsabani put her face to the glass - the Palace of Aiianvall was wrapped in silence as a tear ran down her cheek. In her chamber, darkness prevailed. A solitary candle flickered, reflected in the looking glass. She wore her sadness like a court gown, a design of tragedy woven into the cloth.

Queen Tsabani reproached herself, wondering why she was consumed with hatred for Caedec. Her thoughts turned to her sister and she found herself gripped by jealously. "I've loved Caedec and I'm in love with Khinart and you, Ahrisa, have stolen their hearts just as you stole my father's when we were children," she said aloud looking at herself in the glass.

Longing for the night to end she pressed a white linen handkerchief to her face. She felt the cold material on her skin and closed her eyes, praying morning would come, filling the palace with light instead of gloom.

Captain Oxghar shivered. *Azenia* felt like a tomb. Sleep eluded him as he lay motionless in his bed. He tried not to think of the cold air devouring his skin and eating into his bones. He thought of Queen Irmadia and drifted into the realm of sleep.

He was woken by the sound of ice breaking apart. He stirred briefly as the door opened and a figure moved towards him. Captain Oxghar felt an icy finger touch his face, frosty breath lingered on his neck and the heady scent of the Whispering Sea hung in the air.

A yellow sun rose on a winter world. Beyond the Palace of Aiianvall the fields and forests glistened in the sunlight. The Crown Prince stared at the view, feeling the tense atmosphere in the palace had entered his study. He could find no escape from it. He recalled how Arrkir recounted Caedec's humiliation at the hands of Queen Tsabani with enthusiasm and was disgusted.

Shafts of light poured through the palace windows. Merrick entered the King's chamber with a heavy heart.

"What is it Merrick?"

"Sire, I've heard The Lady Annas is unwell. My Lady Sapphire is concerned. I thought you should know of this."

Caedec was in sombre mood as he tapped lightly on the door. A young maid curtsied and ushered him into the chamber.

"I'll fetch My Lady Sapphire."

Hushed voices emanated from the chamber. Caedec was saddened when he saw Sapphire's expression. "How does Annas fare, Sapphire?"

"I fear for her – she's so ill."

"I will summon my physician at once."

"Thank you, but there's no need – he's here. By Crilm's grace he was strolling through the collonade when she collapsed."

"That is fortunate. What does he say?"

Sapphire was downcast. "He's said nothing - only that her condition alarms him."

They entered the bedchamber.

"May I?" said Caedec approaching the bed.

"Of course," replied Sapphire moving aside.

Caedec was disturbed when he saw The Lady Annas. One eye was closed and her face was swollen beyond recognition.

"Annas, how sad I am to see you unwell."

She nodded but said nothing as her head nuzzled a pillow.

"She must rest," said Hhannon emerging from the shadows.

"Sapphire, the maid will sit with her. Promise me you will retire to your bedchamber," said Caedec his voice full of concern.

Sapphire nodded. Caedec withdrew, sadness settling on his features as he strolled the corridors in search of The Crown Prince.

The Crown Prince was returning from the stables, when he saw Caedec. "How are you this morning?"

"Well enough thank you. Have you a moment? I would like to speak with you about The Lady Annas."

The Crown Prince was puzzled. "Of course, is something the matter?"

"She is unwell. Is there anyone you can summon, Vinaii? Sapphire and my physician have been unable to help her."

The Crown Prince frowned. "I will look into it. What are Gai's thoughts on the matter?"

"I haven't seen him these past days. He has shut himself away in the Far Tower," said Caedec.

The Crown Prince nodded. "Of course, he seeks solitude."

Caedec was thoughtful. "We have need of him."

The Crown Prince nodded in agreement.

High in the Far Tower, Gai sat in quiet contemplation staring at an aperture in the blackened stone ceiling. He studied the light coming through it, a strip of parchment inscribed with alchemical symbols, rolled into a thin cylinder, resting in his hand. Passing it through the light three times then into a candle's flame, it burned quickly, a puff of fire leapt into the air. A plume of smoke rose through the aperture.

Gai studied a model of the worlds. Seven globes joined by a coil of golden Zerian, a metal mined in the mountains of Arakhinn, used in the making of alchemical instruments.

Caedec and The Crown Prince made to the Far Tower. They climbed the stairwell, arriving at the top, out of breath.

"Gai, open the door!"

Bolts were unfastened and Gai emerged from the shadows. He studied Caedec and The Crown Prince standing on the threshold. "What's the matter?"

"The Lady Annas is sick and we need your help," said Caedec, wheezing.

"Oh dear, I'll accompany you to her chamber," said Gai retrieving his cloak and locking the door.

Lady Annas was sleeping as Gai entered. A candle burned by the bed, casting yellow light on the white linen sheets. He approached quietly, gasping when he noticed her swollen face.

"My poor lady, what a cruel hand the fates have dealt you," he whispered.

Caedec and The Crown Prince could tell from Gai's expression that he feared the worst. Silence descended on them like a heavy cloud.

"Pray tell us, Gai, what ails The Lady Annas?" said Caedec.

"I don't know. I can't say I've seen its like until now, but I believe its hold is strong and beyond cure. I fear magic will have no effect. She is consumed by a deadly disease, a poison clouds her mind. I'll bring some incense to alleviate the symptoms. That's all I can offer I'm afraid," said Gai.

"Dear Crilm, what a blow. Poor Annas for this to happen now," said Caedec staring into the distance.

"Where's Sapphire?" enquired The Crown Prince.

"I insisted she retire to her bedchamber. She is weary," replied Caedec.

"Yes of course. It would do no good to disturb her with these tidings," said The Crown Prince.

As he entered the King's chamber, Merrick studied Caedec's expression. "How's The Lady Annas, sire?"

"Not well at all I'm sorry to say, Merrick."

Merrick fought back the tears welling up inside. "Are we to lose her?"

Caedec paused, wearing a thoughtful expression. "Fetch a flagon of Adras and two goblets - I believe we are in need of succour."

Sapphire was dreaming. She saw Adranus emerge from the shadows of the colonnade. He asked her a question.

"Sapphire, what do you wish for?"

"A more auspicious time," she replied without hesitation.

Sapphire woke with the phrase still in her mind and pondered the dream's meaning.

Caedec laughed as the fire flickered and the candles burned. He studied the glittering liquid in the crystal goblet. "A good vintage Merrick, is there any left in the flagon?

Merrick topped up the King's goblet and his own as his thoughts turned to the palace kitchens.

"Copper pans of such quality, I swear I've never seen the like before," he mused as Caedec dozed.

Gai felt the coldness of the palace corridors. He noticed the window panes were still covered in ice. He thought the day had passed quickly. Night approached with the stealth of a wolf as he tapped on the door of The Lady Annas's apartment. He gave the incense to the servant who answered, instructing her to place it by the bed and light it when a moon sat high in the firmament. "I will return later to see how she fares," he said leaving for the solitude of the Far Tower.

Sapphire entered The Lady Annas's bedchamber.

"My lady has slept well," said the maid, rising from her chair to greet Sapphire.

Sapphire smiled. "That is good news."

Annas opened an eye, gazing at Sapphire with kindness.

"How are you today?"

"Tired," she murmured. "Come sit by me."

Gai listened to the fire roaring in the grate and felt its warmth as he lit a taper and made to The Lady Annas's bedside. He produced several bundles of herbs from the folds of his cloak. He placed one on the coffer and lit it, inhaling the smoke drifting across the chamber. "I hope this will at least alleviate her symptoms," he said.

Sapphire was puzzled. "Won't it cure her?"

Gai wore a solemn expression. "There's dark magic at work in the worlds."

"Niaa," said Sapphire.

Gai looked uncomfortable.

"You've seen her, haven't you Gai?"

Gai nodded. "Last night I dreamt a dream of night. A bitter darkness I could almost taste. And yes, I saw Niaa."

Sapphire was afraid. "How I've dreaded this day, Gai and now it has dawned."

Gai gazed at her with compassion. "I know and I'm sorry. You must be strong for all our sakes."

Sapphire hid her face with her hands, struggling to keep her composure. "What is to be done? Should we tell the King?"

Gai's expression changed. "I don't know. Honestly, I don't know what's to be done."

Sapphire covered her face with her hands and murmured. "Then how can I?"

"Merrick, I believe my head will explode. I swear it's full of gunpowder," said Caedec with a groan.

"My body feels as if there's no blood left in it – a most peculiar feeling, I can tell you," said Merrick rubbing his hands to generate heat. He tended the fire, vowing he would never touch Adras again. His head was throbbing and he was cold.

Caedec strolled along the corridors of the palace. Standing at the entrance to The Lady Annas's apartment, he heard Arrkir's voice.

"Sire, how lovely to see you, I hear The Lady Annas ails."

Caedec eyed him with suspicion.

"My Lady Sapphire must be upset," said Arrkir.

"I'm sure all will be well," said Caedec tapping on the door, desperately hoping the maid would come quickly and rescue him.

"Of course – please convey my regards to The Lady Annas."

"Thank you."

Arrkir bowed and continued on his way.

Caedec let out a deep breath. "May Crilm save us from that character," he muttered crossing the threshold.

Caedec noticed Merrick was still ashen as he returned to his chamber. He sank into a chair by the fireplace grateful for the warmth, his thoughts turning to The Lady Annas.

"Sire, The Crown Prince is here," announced Merrick.

"Thank you. I will see him," said Caedec rising to greet his visitor.

The Crown Prince strode across the chamber. "How are you? And how is The Lady Annas this day?"

"I am well. The Lady Annas is about same."

The Crown Prince stared into the fire. "I've known her but a short time. Yet I've found her to be a charming, likeable soul."

"Yes, indeed, she is."

"Does Tsabani know of this?" enquired The Crown Prince.

"As far as I'm aware she does not, but she will have to be told. The Lady Annas is her kinswoman. Who will carry out the unenviable task?"

"Perhaps we should summon Lord Caton. He might be prepared to convey these tidings to Tsabani," said The Crown Prince with a wry smile.

"What a stroke of genius, I'm sure he will oblige."

"I expect so," said The Crown Prince leaning back in his chair.

In an ante-chamber of the state apartments, standing by a fireplace carved with wolves and snow falcons, Egrinar conferred with Bhelus. They paused, admiring the books lining the chamber, their spines colourful and lettered with archaic script. In the centre of the chamber stood a table with feet carved like a forest wolf's paw.

"My spies tell me there's unrest in the city. People are hungry and look for someone to blame for their plight. They believe The Crown Prince is the cause of their distress," said Bhelus.

"I feared as much. Nheve's wedding has not been received well in some quarters," replied Egrinar.

"There will always be those who resent displays of wealth," Bhelus added.

"How serious is this unrest?" Egrinar enquired.

"If the cold weather continues it will grow. If the thaw comes as it must, it will dissipate. Egrinar, you and I know the people well enough. They're not revolutionaries by nature. But we need to do something to maintain The Crown Prince's popularity, or things may go awry."

"What do you suggest?"

"That we empty the grain stores and bake as much bread, mixed with seed and alphus berries, as the kitchens can manage. It can be distributed in the city as a gift from The Crown Prince to his loyal subjects in recognition of their suffering and to alleviate the misery winter has brought to Aiianvall."

"Well done, Bhelus, what a good idea. Now to bring it to fruition," Egrinar mused. "I will speak to Laderine of Gyle about it."

"Careful, Arrkir will be jealous," said Bhelus laughing.

"My good friend Arrkir is jealous of anyone who speaks to Laderine, especially her husband."

Lord Caton made his way to the state apartments with light, quick steps. He felt carefree, waiting for his presence to be announced.

"Lord Caton, good of you to come so soon," said The Crown Prince in greeting.

"My pleasure Your Majesty, how can I be of assistance?"

"I'm afraid I have tidings of a distressing nature."

"Oh dear, a distressing nature," said Lord Caton raising his eyebrows.

"Yes, concerning The Lady Annas, I'm afraid she's very ill."

"Oh my, oh my dear Lady Annas, I'm shocked and dismayed," replied Lord Caton quite beside himself.

"I believe the Queen must be informed. I thought you, as her Ambassador, would be the very person to convey these sad tidings."

Lord Caton nodded in agreement. "Yes, of course, of course, I'll inform Her Majesty at once, if not sooner."

As Egrinar entered the kitchen he noticed Arrkir loitering.

"Laderine, I wondered if I might speak to you?" said Egrinar.

Arrkir glowered at him.

"In private, if I may?" Egrinar continued.

Arrkir grumbled something inaudible and grudgingly withdrew. Laderine, Countess of Gyle, was resplendent in a lilac gown with embroidered strapwork in gold and silver. Her long, red hair was plaited and interwoven with silver thread. She studied Egrinar with curiosity.

"Laderine, as mistress of The Crown Prince's household I felt I should speak to you."

"Pray what about? I trust my husband is well," she enquired.

"Oh yes, I've no reason to believe otherwise. I'm sure Moramus, is serving us well as our ambassador. I've heard nothing to the contrary."

"Thank Crilm," she replied breathing a sigh of relief.

"I believe there's some dissatisfaction in Aiianvall. Crops have failed and the people are cold and hungry. We, Bhelus and I that is, thought bread made here in the palace kitchens might serve as a gift to alleviate matters."

"We've enough grain here to make a substantial amount," Laderine replied.

"Have you enough seed and alphus berries?"

"I believe so. Does my cousin know of this? He hasn't spoken of it," said Laderine with a puzzled expression.

"I've yet to discuss the idea with The Crown Prince. I am pondering its feasibility at the moment. But I believe he'll be in favour of it."

Arrkir had his ear to the kitchen door. He was startled as it opened suddenly and he was confronted by Egrinar. He turned on his heel and sauntered off down the corridor, without a word.

Lord Caton wandered along the palace corridor studying his nails and wondering how to approach Queen Tsabani with tidings of The Lady Annas's illness. He struggled to find the right words. Queen Tsabani was becoming increasingly irritated with the weather and apt to give the sharp edge of her tongue to anyone who displeased her.

"No matter, I'll just have to tell her and be done with it," he said aloud.

"Tell her what and be done with it?"

Lord Caton blushed. He had been so engrossed in his thoughts he had been oblivious to the Queen's approaching footsteps. She stood with her arms folded and a look of intent on her face.

"Your Majesty, what a surprise – pleasant of course."

"Obviously, I thought I would take a stroll around the palace. Is there something you wanted to tell me?"

"Your Majesty, it's a private matter."

"I see. Then I'll send for you when I return to my apartments. You're dismissed, Lord Caton."

Caedec gazed at the countryside draped in twilight. A white eared owl flew past the window making him shudder at the sight of it. "A harbinger of misery and death is upon us," he said aloud, moving away.

Queen Tsabani called for her maid. "Adina, unfasten my cloak. My hands are numb."

A young girl with dark hair and a harassed expression entered the chamber. "Yes, of course Your Majesty," she replied unfastening the Queen's black cloak with her nimble fingers and gently removing it.

"Fetch Lord Caton, would you. And stop trailing that along the floor."

Adina curtsied and withdrew with it folded over her arm.

Adina showed Lord Caton into the sitting room. Queen Tsabani was standing at a window, with a view of the gardens.

"I'm so bored I have resorted to writing on the window pane," she remarked studying the diamond gracing her finger.

Lord Caton tried to read the words etched on the glass.

Roses lay dying in the snows of winter
My heart is still and lost to me
I entreat the worlds to save me
From my darkened soul

"Forgive me, I had no idea Your Majesty wrote such eloquent verse."

Queen Tsabani blushed. "It's an interest of mine, yes. I admire Captain Oxghar's poetry, but I fear I cannot hope to be as accomplished as he.

103

"Nonsense, Your Majesty. I fear the captain has a rival in his art."

"You flatter me, Lord Caton. I confess you do it very well."

Lord Caton smiled.

"You have something to tell me."

"Indeed, Your Majesty. It concerns The Lady Annas."

Queen Tsabani studied his expression. "What of my kinswoman?"

"She's gravely ill, Your Majesty."

Queen Tsabani turned her face from him. "Is she...?" the question faded from her lips like petals falling from a dying flower.

"Her illness is serious, Your Majesty, shall I arrange for you to visit her?"

"Yes, please do. She was good to me when I was a child."

In the fading light Lord Caton saw her reflection in the glass, and noticed a tear running down her cheek.

"I'll arrange it, Your Majesty," he said and withdrew.

As The Crown Prince entered the state apartments, Egrinar was waiting.

"You're early. I wasn't expecting you so soon."

"Your Majesty, I must speak to you – it's important that I do."

"Yes, of course," said The Crown Prince intrigued.

"Sire, your subjects have little food. This cold weather is causing hardship across the worlds. This also concerns me," he said handing a scroll to The Crown Prince, who glanced at it, handing it back with a look of disgust.

"I'm blamed for their plight? Is that correct?"

"I believe so," replied Egrinar.

"This scroll is extremely distasteful. Have you any idea who's responsible?" enquired The Crown Prince, his face flushed with anger.

"I have my suspicions, but unfortunately, no evidence."

"I suggest your spies find some."

"Your Majesty, I appreciate your distress. The drawing of Lady Sapphire is crude. I pray she doesn't see it. Your likeness is rather flattering."

The Crown Prince scowled pacing the floor. Egrinar watched as he paraded back and forth.

"Your Majesty, most have been removed."

The Crown Prince glowered. "Most have been removed! How many are still on display?"

Egrinar looked uncomfortable and mopped his brow with a handkerchief. "They'll be found and the perpetrator brought to justice."

The Crown Prince covered his forehead with his hand. "I trust this matter will be kept from Lady Sapphire."

"I will do my best to ensure that it is."

"Good."

"Your Majesty, I have an idea. I wondered if the grain store might be emptied and used to make bread for the citizens of Aiianvall. I've taken the liberty of speaking to Laderine of Gyle as to how this might be accomplished."

The Crown Prince was vexed. "Most of the grain we have was earmarked for the Red King's campaign. Victory may depend upon it."

"Your Majesty, I appreciate that, but I strongly believe we must do something to appease the people. We don't want a revolution on our hands."

"It grieves me to give anything when I see the filth on show in the city, but they're my subjects, I suppose I should help them. What's happening to this country?" said The Crown Prince frowning. "Have Arrkir watched. I would like to know whether he's involved in this."

The Lady Annas sat propped up on several pillows. She looked better and was able to speak a few words.

Lord Caton announced Queen Tsabani's arrival as she strode into the bedchamber. She greeted Sapphire as she approached The Lady Annas.

"My lady," said Queen Tsabani.

"Dear Tsabani," The Lady Annas replied.

Queen Tsabani sank to her knees dissolving into tears. Sapphire and Lord Caton looked on in disbelief. Displays of emotion were rare where Queen Tsabani was concerned.

"Leave us!" Queen Tsabani commanded in the midst of her tears.

Lord Caton and Sapphire exchanged glances as they withdrew.

Sapphire walked through the colonnade to the Far Tower. A bitter wind was blowing and snow lay all around. Sapphire was distraught as she climbed the stairs. She noticed the door was ajar and went inside to find Gai sitting reading a book by the fire at the end of the chamber.

"I was expecting you," he said.

She seated herself on the chair facing him feeling the fire's warmth on her cheek. After a long silence, when only the room seemed to breathe, he handed her a letter. She studied the folded paper for a while - opening it she studied its contents. "The High Priestess has granted our request. It seems we are free of each other."

"I believe it's for the best."

"I expect to hear of great progress in your work, now you're without distraction." Sapphire threw the letter on the floor. "Damn you and your alchemy!"

Gai was silent. As Sapphire marched out of the chamber, a cold wind blew in, upsetting alchemical instruments and scattering papers over the floor. "I pray Crilm will forgive me," he whispered.

Niaa stared at the crystal globe. "I'm so pleased when love dies," she said aloud, savouring the moment.

Her chamber was as dark as death with the scent of evil hanging in the air. She brushed the crystal with her bony fingers and the image faded leaving the globe empty. Niaa's face was reflected in the crystal. She admired her complexion, white as a shroud, her high forehead and aquiline nose. She compared her eyes to an eagle's and stroked her hair the colour of night. Niaa's lips were thin and red as blood. "How unhappy Sapphire will be. No matter, no-one seals Niaa in a well and gets away with it," she said in a poisonous tone.

Sapphire stood alone in the colonnade as a flurry of snow whirled about her. She stared at the flakes as they fell.

"Sapphire, are you all right?"

She turned to find The Crown Prince staring at her. She nodded. He moved closer as she managed a half smile.

"You look cold, Sapphire. Come into the palace. It's warmer there."

Her face was wet with tears, her lips moved but the words would not come. The Crown Prince took her in his arms, holding her tight. She did not resist as flurries of snow continued to fall, like slivers of whitened bone.

Footsteps crunched in the snow. Arrkir was aghast at the sight he beheld. His lips pursed as if he had tasted bitter fruit. "Your Majesty, forgive my intrusion," he said.

The Crown Prince released Sapphire.

Arrkir looked at her with contempt. "Your Majesty, may I have a word in private?"

"I'm afraid not. Sapphire is upset and I have promised to escort her," he replied guiding Sapphire into the palace.

Arrkir cursed under his breath.

Sapphire and The Crown Prince returned to The Lady Annas's apartment. Sar-Mhirian greeted them with a grave expression. "Your Majesty, Sapphire, I'm afraid the Lady Annas's health has deteriorated rather rapidly."

Sapphire gasped.

"Is she...?" The Crown Prince enquired.

"She has lost consciousness, though she still lives."

Caedec was reading, he looked up as Merrick approached.

"Sire, you have a visitor."

Caedec closed his book. "Countess, Laderine of Gyle. What an unexpected pleasure."

Laderine curtsied.

"Here, sit with me by the fire. My bones grow colder by the day."

Laderine sat down, arranging the folds of her gown. "I'm here to ask for your help."

"I am pleased to give it, if I can."

"Egrinar has advised Vinaii to distribute bread to the people of Aiianvall," she said.

"Have they not enough to eat?"

"It would seem they have not."

"Sire, may I speak with candour?"

"By all means, Laderine we will not be disturbed."

"There's discontentment in the capital. I've heard certain people want to bring about disruption in my cousin's realm, in order to further their own ambitions."

Caedec grimaced. "That is usually the case. We are living in turbulent times, Laderine. I will do all I can to help you but alas, where food is concerned, Merrick is your man."

Laderine smiled. "I thought he might be. I'd appreciate his counsel."

Merrick was overawed by the kitchens. Three, immense, interlinked chambers painted white with red tiled floors, with several tables and innumerable copper pans of every size imaginable hanging from the ceilings. Each kitchen had a fireplace with several brick ovens. One wall of the main kitchen was lined with books on the culinary arts. Merrick was in his element. Laderine smiled at the wondrous look on his face.

"The grain will arrive soon and then we can get to work," she said.

"Wonderful."

The Lady Annas's breathing slowed. Sapphire, The Crown Prince and Sar-Mhirian were at her bedside.

"I think we should inform the King and Queen Tsabani, I hope we're not too late," said Sar-Mhirian.

Hhannon nodded in agreement and the maid was instructed to send word to them.

Caedec, Queen Tsabani and Lord Caton approached the sleeping figure of The Lady Annas - the sound of her breathing filled the bedchamber. Sapphire held her hand as her breathing slowed and silence prevailed.

Sar-Mhirian placed his hand on her cold brow. "The Lady has gone – may Crilm protect her on her journey to The Vale of Wolves."

"I'll attend to her," said Hhannon.

The Crown Prince escorted Sapphire to her apartment. "I'm so very sorry Sapphire - I know how much she meant to you. I'll make arrangements for court mourning. I expect you will discuss other details with Caedec. Please rest and worry not. She is released from her pain and won't suffer any more. That is something to be grateful for."

"Thank you for your kindness. I'll rest now and gather my thoughts. I'll speak to Caedec on the morrow."

The Crown Prince made his way to the state apartments with a heavy heart. He composed himself and summoned Egrinar.

Egrinar was solemn as he conversed with The Crown Prince. "I'll see the court is informed of the death of The Lady Annas and the necessary protocol is observed. Under the circumstances, she may have to be buried here. If that is so, a suitable place will be found."

"We'll see what the King advises – The Lady may have left a Will of Wishes. We don't know yet," said The Crown Prince.

Queen Tsabani was furious. She stalked through her apartment like a tiger in a cage. "How dare they send for me so late?"

Lord Caton put his head in his hands and groaned.

"Did I hear you groan, Lord Caton?"

"Of course not Your Majesty. I was clearing my throat. I'm sure no offence was intended."

Queen Tsabani's eyes narrowed, glittering with venom. Lord Caton quickly averted his gaze.

"My dear Sapphire, what a sad time it is for us all. We have much to discuss," said Caedec taking her hand.

Sapphire nodded, seating herself. "Yes, I'd appreciate your counsel. There's so much to do at a time like this and the funeral ceremony is but one."

Caedec frowned. "I'll ask Lord Caton to relate details of the ceremony to Tsabani."

"Thank you."

"Tsabani can be volatile, especially if she feels excluded." Caedec's eyebrows arched. "These are troubled times, Sapphire, but they will make us stronger."

They sat deep in thought, until Merrick entered covered in white powder.

"Merrick, what in the worlds has happened?" enquired Caedec.

"There's been a slight accident in the kitchens, sire."

Chapter 17 – The Presence of White

Holes appeared in the ice. Captain Oxghar watched as the sun rose over the frozen waste that was the Whispering Sea. Hhariann stretched his wings and yawned, showing a set of white teeth. *Azenia* creaked and groaned. Captain Oxghar breathed the cold air. Change rode the wind. He could sense it. A thaw was coming.

Sar-Mhirian stood in the temple, where a short while ago he had blessed Nheve and Mhiria's union. He felt Crilm's presence and found himself longing to speak to him. "How much sadness there is across the worlds," he said aloud.

A breeze wafted into the building and Sar-Mhirian felt it warm on his face. He heard the sound of footsteps and saw Caedec striding towards him.

"Sar-Mhirian, may I speak with you?"

"Please do."

"I have thought long and hard about The Lady Annas and the manner of her death."

Sar-Mhirian listened, his head tilting slightly.

"I have a feeling something is not right."

"Sire, you're not suggesting she was murdered?"

Caedec was perplexed. "All I am sure of is a sense of foreboding. I believe all is not as it seems in the worlds. You have travelled more than I. Am I right to be so troubled?"

Sar-Mhirian's expression changed. "I've seen something of what is going on in the worlds, that's true and I've heard things of a worrying nature."

"Really, what sort of things?"

"I'll make sure we're alone," replied Sar-Mhirian closing the door and turning the key. "I trust we will not be disturbed."

They seated themselves comfortably on the dragon chairs.

"I will tell you all I know," said Sar-Mhirian in a conspiratorial tone.

Caedec leaned towards him.

"I've made my way in the worlds as an emissary for our Lord and Protector, Crilm. My journeys have taken me to The Delvia States, where I dwelt briefly, staying in Eihir. I heard something that disturbed me, I've not thought of it again, until now." Sar-Mhirian paused for breath. "The mistress of the house was a kind woman, though prone to gossip, as you can imagine."

110

"Yes, Delvia women are well known for their love of gossip," said Caedec with a broad grin.

"The mistress, her name escapes me for the moment. Forgive me - my memory is not as good as it once was. No matter, on this particular day she was speaking to her husband in hushed tones. I couldn't help overhearing a few words of their conversation. They were talking about a well and a broken seal."

"Niaa!" said Caedec.

Sapphire stared at the looking glass. A face haunted by sadness was reflected in the surface. "I am lost," she whispered.

Sitting with her head in her hands she sobbed until her body shook with a tremor of despair. The maid was drawn by the sound.

"Mistress, are you all right? Shall I send for someone?"

Sapphire shook her head and waved her away, crawling into bed she wished death would come and release her from pain and misery. But death did not come, only sleep and the realm of dream.

Sar-Mhirian received The Lady Annas's coffin into the temple. He recited a mantra for protection of the soul, as several knights of The Order of the Median lowered it onto a golden plinth. The coffin was black, imbued with the sheen of a wolf's eye and bound with three white silk ribbons, the Maladorian colour of mourning. Bowing respectfully, the knights withdrew, leaving Sar-Mhirian to recite prayers and mantras until the morrow, when the body of The Lady Annas would lie in state.

Arrkir skulked along the corridors in search of the young maid attending Sapphire. His patience was rewarded when he saw her approaching Sapphire's apartments, her arms full of laundered white linen. He quickly made to block her path. "Now pretty maid, how is my Lady Sapphire?"

Lucha studied his features and thought them rather like a falcon's. She felt uneasy in his presence. "My lady is well, sir," she replied after a long pause.

Arrkir gave her a forced smile. "I've something for Lady Sapphire, deliver it for me and I'll make it worth your trouble. If she asks who sent it, don't mention me, I prefer to remain anonymous," he said pulling a scroll and a purse full of coins from beneath his cloak.

Lucha eyed the gold coins as he pressed them into the palm of her hand, pushing the scroll into the folded linen he strode off, not bothering to wait for a reply.

Lucha made to the linen press and began sorting the sheets, studying the gold coins - she thought of her sick brother needing medicine from the apothecary and put them in her pocket. She unfurled the scroll. Her eyes widened and she rolled it up as fast as she could. "Poor Lady Sapphire, she doesn't deserve this, what am I to do with it?" she said aloud.

Lucha entered Sapphire's chamber and without thinking, threw the scroll into the fire, cursing Arrkir as she did so.

Erussah studied The Lady Annas's Will of Wishes. Caedec and The Crown Prince glanced at each other, speculating on the contents of the document. Erussah stopped reading and looked at them in turn. "The Lady's chattels and property in Maladoria, namely her house and lands to the east of Sarhynel, she bequeaths to Sapphire. The Lady Annas wanted to be buried in Maladoria, in the family vault, after a private ceremony."

"What are we to do? Does Sapphire know of this?" enquired The Crown Prince.

"She has made no mention of it. She has taken all this to heart I'm afraid. It's her nature, sensitive you see. Sapphire is unwell and I am concerned," replied Caedec.

The Crown Prince looked uncomfortable and shifted in his chair. "Egrinar was under the impression she may be buried here."

Erussah continued reading the parchment. "Gentlemen, it seems the Lady had given this some thought before embarking on the voyage. If I may I will read you this passage."

"Please do," said Caedec, leaning forward in his chair.

"I, Lady Annas, being of sound mind and limb, add to my Will of Wishes. If I should die on the voyage let me be cast adrift on the Whispering Sea and bid the white eagle devour me and set me free to travel to the Vale of Wolves and go where Crilm bids me."

Tears welled in Caedec's eyes. "Annas has provided us with an answer to our dilemma."

"Quite so," replied Erussah setting the parchment down on the writing table.

"She means to offer herself as a sacrifice to the dark gods," said The Crown Prince.

Sapphire was ashen as Caedec read the Will of Wishes to her. She said nothing, staring blankly at the paintings on the wall.

"I realize that her last wish may come as a surprise to you," said Caedec as he finished reading.

"She was excited about the voyage. She wants to appease the dark gods and help us on our way."

"I have heard ice is melting on the Whispering Sea. If that is so, the ceremony can take place soon," said Caedec.

"That is a good sign."

"Sapphire, I will inform Lord Caton. Tsabani will need time to prepare herself."

"Yes, yes of course."

"I am concerned, Sapphire, you are unwell."

Sapphire stared into the distance. "My heart is broken."

"Dear child, losing The Lady Annas has been a crushing blow, especially for you."

"It's not the only loss I suffer."

Caedec raised an eyebrow. "Your marriage to Gai has ended."

Sapphire nodded.

"I should have guessed before now. I am sorry to hear of it. You have suffered much since we left Adranabar," said Caedec his shoulders drooping.

Lord Caton approached Queen Tsabani and handed her a letter fastened with Caedec's seal.

"A communication from the Red King," said Tsabani reading the scroll. Once read, she threw it on the writing table, a look of disdain on her face.

"Damn," she uttered with contempt.

"Your Majesty is displeased?"

"Yes, I am most displeased."

Lord Caton thought it prudent to remain silent.

"Do you know what the arrangements are?"

"Certainly not, Your Majesty."

"Then read it" she said snatching the scroll off the table and thrusting it at him.

Lord Caton's violet eyes scanned the parchment.

"Unusual, Your Majesty."

"Unusual! I expected something more appropriate for The Lady Annas. Is that all you can say, Lord Caton?"

"If it is the lady's wish, then surely it should be honoured," he said as Queen Tsabani waved him away.

Sar-Mhirian chanted the last mantras for The Lady Annas, as the Maladorian court in exile filed into the temple to pay their respects.

Caedec leading the procession was resplendent in the red cloak of the Idrean Dynasty, the sleeves wound with white ribbon, as a sign of mourning. He wore a gold circlet on his head and a ceremonial sword was fastened to his belt.

Sapphire walked behind the King. Her gown of silver silk rustled under her mantle of blue. Gai and The Crown Prince walked behind her. Several Knights of The Order of the Median were in attendance. Queen Tsabani and Lord Caton were absent.

As the procession filed past the coffin, Sar-Mhirian chanted mantras. Sapphire was distant as she followed Caedec outside. As the courtiers filtered into the courtyard, small groups lingered.

Caedec noticed the snow was melting, exposing patches of earth. "Where are Tsabani and Lord Caton?"

"I haven't seen either of them – perhaps the arrangements don't meet with their approval," said The Crown Prince.

Sapphire and Gai kept their distance, avoiding each other's gaze.

"Take heart, Sapphire. The thaw is upon us," said Caedec putting a protective arm around her and guiding her towards the palace.

Merrick untied the ribbons on Caedec's sleeves. "Sire, you've cold hands," he remarked removing the cloak.

"I daresay we tarried too long in the courtyard after the lying in state."

"I can't recall seeing Queen Tsabani or Lord Caton? Perhaps I'm mistaken," said Merrick.

"No, she was not there."

Merrick was surprised. "I trust she'll attend the funeral ceremony."

"I believe she will," replied Caedec studying his fingernails.

Sapphire sat on the window seat watching several knights in the courtyard. Sunlight was filtering through the clouds, the light falling on their silver mail and white tunics. She noticed Sorrel and thought he looked like his father, Egrinar. She could not bear to think of them wounded or slain in battle. She thought of Annas lying in her coffin, still and cold like a sliver of ice, and shivered. Death was never far away.

Ice on The Whispering Sea had thawed, allowing the funeral ceremony to take place. Sapphire waited by the window, dressed in winter's shade of white.

Courtiers filed past a line of knights as they made their way to the temple. Sapphire stopped as she drew level with Sorrel and touched his face. The Crown Prince felt his heart tighten and Arrkir was transfixed.

Queen Tsabani and Lord Caton were dressed in black. Amongst the courtiers attired in winter's white, they were like ravens caught in a flurry of snowflakes.

"Shall we begin our journey to the shore? I believe the time has come," said Sar-Mhirian.

The courtiers waited as the knights lifted the coffin on to their shoulders and the procession began. Patches of snow lay on the ground and the knights' feet crunched into the frozen remnants as they bore the coffin up the hillside to the inlet where the death ship was moored.

As the procession reached the copse on the hilltop, the courtiers stood looking on as the King's retinue, followed by Queen Tsabani and Lord Caton, made their way to a secluded cove.

A sun shone and rays of white played on the sea. A pair of eagles circled as the knights lowered the open coffin into the vessel. A sail of finely worked lace draped around the mast fluttered in the breeze. The funeral party gathered on the shore watching the waves ebb and flow.

"My end in this world is my beginning in another," said Sar-Mhirian as the ship caught the tide.

"So be it," they said in unison watching as the eagles flew out to sea with their distinctive red and black tipped wings moving gracefully, as they pursued the death ship.

"Where will Lady Annas go?" Janus enquired gazing at the King.

"Only the wind can answer."

Azenia groaned as if in mourning. Captain Oxghar, Hhariann and several members of the ship's crew watched as the death ship passed the harbour walls and sailed into the distance.

"Dear lady, we salute you," said Captain Oxghar bowing his head.

Darthus strolled across Castle Adranabar's courtyard in the pouring rain. In his hand was a scroll, bearing a red seal and addressed to the Prince.

"At last, tidings from my cousin," said Prince Orthon smiling. "This is the second letter I've received today."

Darthus withdrew leaving the Prince reading Caedec's scroll – the other lay opened on the writing table.

Prince Orthon read it again as gusts of wind battered the castle's windows. He wiped a tear from his eye. "Such a shame - dear Lady Annas, how sudden her loss. Poor Sapphire, unwell and so far away…from me," he said to himself.

Prince Orthon drew the other scroll towards him. "At least I have an heir and the matter of succession is secure. That's a weight off my mind."

Darthus returned and Prince Orthon handed him Caedec's letter.

"Read this," said Prince Orthon, warming his hands at the fire as Darthus studied the parchment.

"I am saddened to hear of The Lady Annas's swift demise," said Darthus.

"Yes indeed. She'll be missed. Misfortune and death are never far from the hearth. I'm heartened to hear your lad is faring well," replied Prince Orthon.

"Yes," said Darthus passing the scroll to Prince Orthon with a sad smile on his lips.

"Darthus, you and I have had our differences. I know you would like to bring Janus home, but the fact is I can't spare you at this point in time. You know the lad is safe and happy. That is some comfort is it not?"

"I suppose it is."

"I'm sorry to see you unhappy. You know, Caedec's son, Greylan, vanished from the battlefield. My cousin lives with that loss. He would give anything to know what happened to him. Janus will return to you."

Darthus's face burned and his grip tightened on the arm of the chair.

"I see things are still not settled between us," said Prince Orthon.

116

"With respect, my circumstances are different to the King's - but I too have experienced loss," replied Darthus struggling to control his emotions.

"Your wife's death in childbirth haunts you," said Prince Orthon.

"It does, Loranda's ghost keeps me company. I've no respite from her anguished cries."

"And Janus is the image of her. I've seen it in his features. He has the same eyes like Delvia silver, brilliant yet brooding. And through him she lives. Now I understand why you feel his loss so keenly and for that I'm sorry. Have you thought about marrying again? It might be good for you."

Darthus stared at the floor and did not answer. He was listening to the wind whistling an eerie tune as it whipped around the ancient building.

"With your permission, I'll return to the stables and attend to the horses – this weather disturbs them."

"Of course, you may go."

Darthus withdrew, leaving the Prince with his thoughts.

Jhinn lay on the coverlet listening to the wind screeching and clawing at the window like a demon. His thoughts turned to Saravia. He was longing to see her again. His feelings for her had deepened - their stay at Viarra had sealed his love and he was thinking of betrothal.

He pulled the coverlet around himself, as the wind seeped into the castle's nooks and crannies. Then the rain came down in a gushing torrent. Jhinn heard it lash against the narrow windows of his bedchamber like an angry god.

At nightfall Lord Griann arrived at the sally-port. Yarrow's flanks gleamed, he snorted, steam rising from his nostrils. Summoning a guard, he handed Yarrow's reins to him with orders to find his groom.

Lord Griann made into the castle. "I must see Prince Orthon," he said catching his breath.

Several guards stared at his dishevelled attire, but said nothing.

"Did you not hear me?"

The guards scattered and moments later Darthus appeared, followed by Salmir, the Prince's adviser.

"I must see the Prince," Lord Griann reiterated.

"Pray, what is the matter, why such haste?" Salmir enquired.

"I rode out into the countryside. On my way back I encountered people fleeing Askengarr. They gave me grave tidings, Salmir. Rebels have taken Askengarr Castle. They're raising support in the north. I fear they'll soon be strong enough to make a move on Castle Adranabar."

Salmir grimaced. "Mararuss lives to wreak havoc on this land. You're right, Lord Griann, the Prince must be informed. I'll go to him."

Jhinn, disturbed by the sound of raised voices decided to investigate. "Lord Griann, I see you've been out riding."

Lord Griann gazed at his boots. Darthus felt the tension between the young men.

Darthus broke the uneasy silence. "I'll return to my chamber, I trust I'll be summoned, if I'm needed."

Jhinn studied Griann's mud-splattered attire. "You look as though you have ridden through a forest, my lord."

Salmir approached with a worried look on his face. "Prince Orthon wishes to speak with you Lord Griann. He'll receive you in his chambers, please hurry."

Lord Griann was relieved to get away from Jhinn's awkward questions as he followed Salmir to the Prince's chambers.

Jhinn watched them, wondering why his uncle wanted to see Griann. He returned to his chambers with his mind full of questions. As he lay on the four-poster watching a watery moon dance across the rain swept sky, he searched for the answers.

Prince Orthon was standing by the fire when Lord Griann entered.

"Lord Griann, I see you haven't had time to change your attire."

Lord Griann studied his apparel in the firelight and realized how dirty and dishevelled he was. "Sire, please forgive my appearance. I came immediately to your summons."

Prince Orthon seated himself indicating a chair. Lord Griann sank into it, feeling every bone in his body scream in agony.

"Salmir tells me you rode out into the countryside and encountered travellers from Askengarr. They told you the castle had fallen, stormed by rebel soldiers."

"Yes, they did."

Prince Orthon wore a puzzled expression. "If this is true, why haven't riders brought these tidings? Surely the Marshall of Askengarr would've sent word. Were these people of sound mind?"

Lord Griann gazed at his wet, dirt sodden boots. "I thought so – I don't think they were lying. Why would they? What reason could there be?"

"Where were they going? Would they not come here to warn us?"

"They entrusted me with the message and went to seek shelter with their kin."

Lord Griann could see the Prince remained unconvinced.

"I cannot think the rebels are strong enough to take Askengarr. There's some mistake surely."

"I can't say. If the news be true we should act."

Prince Orthon was tired, his face was lined and grey. "I think you should rest. We'll see what the morrow brings. If there's no word by then we'll send outriders to Askengarr."

Lord Griann bowed and withdrew, feeling disappointed with Prince Orthon's response he returned to his chambers.

Atheil prepared supper and filled a bath with water sprinkled with soothing herbs. Lord Griann ate, draining a goblet of Adras before he discarded his filthy attire and stepped into the bath. He felt the water, warm and scented, easing the pain as he immersed himself. Atheil studied his lord's apparel and frowned.

Candles flickered and guttered as outside the wind continued to screech and rage against the walls of the castle. Lord Griann dozed. He struggled to fight the realm of sleep as he thought of Saravia, the memory of her face vivid in his mind. He wondered if she would be safe. He had believed the tidings of Askengarr. Thoughts crowded his mind like prisoners in an overcrowded dungeon, struggling for breath.

Lord Griann dragged himself out of the bathtub. Atheil wrapped him in a linen towel, dried him and helped him don a nightshirt. Atheil had warmed the bed. Lord Griann sank into it and slept like the dead.

Prince Orthon wished the howling wind would cease. He put his hands over his ears to block out the noise. He thought about his conversation with Lord Griann and wondered whether Askengarr really had fallen. He could not bear to contemplate such a threat to his sovereignty. He hoped the morrow would bring good tidings.

"Griann has brought bad news. He believes Askengarr has fallen," said Salmir.

Darthus grimaced. "Could it be so?"

"Well, he was crestfallen after his audience with the Prince. Perhaps it's true and Orthon can't bring himself to believe it."

"That's understandable. Facing up to the possibility of civil war isn't easy," replied Darthus.

"Is that really what it means?" enquired Salmir.

"I'm afraid so. I can't see Mararuss backing down, unless he's forced to. There must be a war council and outriders sent to Askengarr on the morrow. There can be no further delay," said Darthus, his brow lined with worry.

Several guards were gathered at the main gate. Cries echoed through the courtyard as it opened letting two horses through. Their riders' bodies were lifeless, several arrows were lodged in their flesh.

Darthus went into the courtyard to behold the gruesome sight.

"Dear Crilm preserve us," he said as the horses drew nearer. He strode towards them as an eerie silence descended. He recognized the horses and their riders. An anguished cry escaped from his throat. Jhinn and Griann ran towards him, followed by Prince Orthon. They froze with horror.

"May Crilm have mercy on us," Prince Orthon whispered.

Jhinn and Griann exchanged glances as Darthus sank to his knees and began to sob.

Salmir rushed into the courtyard followed by his daughter, Aramintha, her red hair flowing in the breeze. Salmir was horrified at the sight he beheld.

"In Crilm's name, do something!" said Prince Orthon.

Several guards stepped forward and lifted the bodies off the horses, laying them on the ground as Aramintha went to comfort Darthus.

"It's Darthus's brother and nephew, the Marshall of Askengarr and his son," said Prince Orthon kneeling by the corpses.

He stood up and made towards Darthus. "Those responsible for this will be punished. You have my word."

Darthus nodded.

"See that they're taken to the temple. Then we ride to Askengarr," Prince Orthon commanded.

"Mararuss and his rabble have gone too far, Salmir," said Prince Orthon as they entered the castle.

"Poor Darthus, I fear for his state of mind now he's lost his brother and nephew – butchered by the rebels. May Crilm protect him - the dark gods have looked upon him."

"I meant what I said, Salmir. I mean to ride to Askengarr, to see for myself."

"It could be a trap."

Prince Orthon glanced at Salmir, touching his arm. "Always the sensible one, I value your counsel, but it is time I came out of hiding."

Salmir nodded in agreement. "Then we ride to the gate of Askengarr Castle."

Darthus lay on the bed, staring at the panelled ceiling, consumed by a desire for vengeance.

Several outriders were gathered outside the stables. Their cloaks and boots were black as Phinas tree bark. Their horses were encased in a dark lightweight metal studded with silver. They pawed the thin layer of snow still covering parts of the cobbled ground.

Darthus opened the coffer and took out his sword. He studied the shining blade and the dragon's eyes on the hilt. "No longer can I be a man of peace while vengeance grows like a poisonous flower in my soul. May Crilm have mercy and bless this sword, unused and dormant for so long," he whispered holding the blade aloft and gazing at it with intent.

"Summon the nobles – tell them to gather their troops," commanded Prince Orthon.

"It shall be done," said Salmir.

Prince Orthon sighed. "I wish to speak to the Lords Jhinn and Griann."

Salmir nodded and withdrew.

Salmir showed the young Lords into the Prince's chamber.

"Ah, my Lords Jhinn and Griann – here you are."

"You summoned us, sire," replied Lord Griann.

"I did. I wish to speak to you both as you are like sons to me," he said pausing, his gaze settling on Jhinn. "I hope you'll secure the future of the House of Viarra, as I could not. I may die – this foray to Askengarr may be my last, I'm aware of that. And for that reason you will both remain here – I command it."

Jhinn's eyes widened in amazement, "Uncle, you can't mean to ride to Askengarr without us. Must you go? You could be captured and held to ransom or worse."

"Jhinn, you haven't listened to me. That's why you will remain here to defend the throne of Adranabar, your throne, at all costs."

Lord Griann struggled to regain his composure and gather his thoughts. He studied Jhinn, trying to imagine him as Prince of Adranabar.

"Askengarr beckons – I must face this. If I don't, then all confidence in my position as ruler will be lost. My honour is at stake, surely you can appreciate that," said Prince Orthon.

"Yes, yes of course. You must act as you think fit," said Lord Griann.

"Thank you, Griann. At least you've listened to me," said Prince Orthon noticing a jealous look on Jhinn's face.

Darthus gazed at his reflection in the glass. His armour was finely wrought and chased with the shapes of animals. His tunic of silk, half red and half gold with unicorn motif suited him. He thought he wore the guise of a warrior well as he gripped the hilt of his sword.

Nobles, knights and their retinues gathered in the courtyard - their standards fluttering in the breeze.

Prince Orthon's standard-bearer looked uneasy as the Prince's flag of scarlet, embroidered with a golden unicorn, caught the prevailing wind.

The Palace of Aiianvall's gardens were full of tiny, brightly coloured birds singing their sweet songs.

The Whispering Sea ebbed and flowed freely and a warm breeze drifted over the high white walls of the city. Flowers were in bloom and the trees sighed as their branches, laden with lush green leaves, swayed. The Dance of the Spring Moon had begun. A time of renewal was on its way through the worlds.

Captain Oxghar stood on the deck of *Azenia*. He breathed a sigh of relief as he watched the sparkling water moving in the light of a yellow sun. He looked up watching Hhariann perch himself atop one of the masts. Soon he would be confident enough to try out his healed wing. Captain Oxghar studied the War Kotroi, praying he would not come to grief again. A snow falcon circled the War Kotroi with caution then flew across the sky towards Aiianvall.

The Crown Prince sat by the lake, studying his reflection in the water. He thought The Winter of the Grey Wolf had aged him. He felt his spirit was at a low ebb and sought renewal in the silken water.

"You're as handsome as ever, Vinaii. I believe the lilies floating on the lake are in love with you."

The Crown Prince blushed as he turned to find Queen Tsabani standing behind him, dressed in a gown of golden silk with a wide sash of silver fastened around her waist. Her shoes had heels set with clear Azuriene crystals. Her hair was piled high on her head and set with crystals. The Crown Prince thought she looked like a column of sunlight.

"When I saw you looking at your reflection in the lake I couldn't resist speaking my thoughts."

"I'm flattered, but it's untrue. My brother, Nheve, is the handsome one."

"That's as may be. But you're the lucky one. And to possess good luck can make one a handsome prospect indeed."

The Crown Prince laughed. "Tsabani, how beautiful you are today."

"Now it's your turn to flatter me."

"You seem happy. It suits you."

Queen Tsabani blushed. "The thaw has come, the spring moon dances and I'm going home."

"I'll see your ship is prepared and your progress is as unhindered as it can be."

"I'd be grateful for that kindness. I'm homesick - I've been away from my beloved Azuriene too long. Thank you for your hospitality – it has been appreciated," she replied.

"I wish you safe passage."

"Such a fine day," Caedec remarked.

"Will you be taking a stroll in the gardens?" Merrick enquired.

"I have not decided. I wish to speak with The Crown Prince about the voyage. I am anxious to discuss our plans now that we encounter a more auspicious time."

As Gai strolled, his thoughts were of the coming voyage. He decided to visit the inlet again and say a more private goodbye to The Lady Annas. As he reached the edge of the trees, he looked down at the cove and over the wide expanse of sparkling water that was the Whispering Sea. He noticed a lone figure standing on the shore - a thin man with hair like a silver wolf's fur. He was wearing a cloak of emerald green and leaning on a staff incised with ancient lettering and symbols. His frame cast a long shadow in the sun.

A flicker of recognition crossed Gai's mind as he made towards the beach. He drew nearer, his curiosity overcoming any fear of the stranger.

"I knew one day we would meet again," said the stranger.

Gai was astonished. "Heziale?"

"It is I."

Gai returned his gaze, noticing Heziale's grey beard and slender fingers with nails filed to a deadly point. Gai didn't know what to say to this apparition from his past.

"I see I've startled you. Forgive me, that wasn't my intention," said Heziale.

"What was your intention?" said Gai.

"I can see you're hostile towards me."

"I can still recall you talking to my mother in the Banqueting Hall at home in Eihir, after that I was sent to Maladoria. I didn't see her or my home again," replied Gai with a trace of bitterness in his voice.

"Then it is time you knew the truth of the matter. You see, your mother, dear Countess Gracia, trusted me and I admit I advised her to send you away. But for no other reason than to keep you from harm."

"Didn't you want me out of the way so you could marry her and become Count of Eihir, while my father was still warm in his grave?"

"Certainly not! Gracia was my friend. When your father died I assumed the role of protector to her and you. Your gift is great Gai, but it couldn't flourish in The Delvia States, where evil wanders at will. You'll have to be strong to withstand its influence. And if you hadn't been sent to live with kin near the Palace of Khorec, you wouldn't have fallen into a ravine while out riding. Nor would you have been rescued by the King's son. Needless to say, had you remained in Eihir you wouldn't enjoy the privileged position you hold as the King's confidante," said Heziale stopping to draw breath.

"That may be so. But nor would I have endured years in exile and now my mother is dead. I won't see her again in this world," said Gai his face flushed with anger.

"Your mother and I made a decision we thought best for you and your destiny. It cannot be undone. I'm sorry if it still grieves you. Your mother's passing was a great loss to us all."

Gai's expression softened. "I have waited a long time for an answer to that question."

"And I've waited a long time to give it."

"Tell me, Heziale. What brings you to Ilesh?"

"When your mother died, there was nothing left for me in Eihir. Your brother, Gainen, became Count and as you can imagine had no need or love for me."

Gai nodded. "He has no love or need of anyone, save his wealth and lands."

"I believed my destiny lay in Ilesh, so I left Eihir and sought refuge here and found it. I live by the river that flows to the north and enjoy its peace and quiet."

Gai felt his anger towards Heziale ebb away, feeling compassion for the old man. "I am glad of it."

Heziale's expression darkened. "I've come to warn you of a great evil. Niaa has broken the seal Sapphire placed on the well. She walks free in the worlds and evil follows in her wake. It is as you dreamt."

"Dear Crilm, if the seal is broken, then Sapphire's power is weakened because of it," replied Gai.

"Go well, Gai. I wish you success. I pray we meet again before my time ends," said Heziale staring at the Whispering Sea. "I bid you farewell."

Egrinar and Bhelus studied the treaty.

"A pleasing document, if I say so myself," said Egrinar passing it to Bhelus with a flourish.

"I'm sure this will be acceptable to the Red King and The Crown Prince," Bhelus replied gazing at it with admiration.

"Beautifully executed, the script is exquisite," said Egrinar with enthusiasm.

"It's exquisite," repeated Bhelus.

Caedec studied the treaty. He passed it to The Crown Prince, who then handed it to Erussah. "I'm satisfied with the terms and conditions," he said as he finished reading the document, placing it on the writing table, ready for signature

"Then so am I. That is my answer," said Caedec.

"Well, gentlemen, it seems we're in agreement," said The Crown Prince.

"Shall I arrange the signing?" Egrinar enquired.

Caedec and The Crown Prince nodded in agreement.

Caedec leaned towards The Crown Prince. "Will you be announcing your departure? Are you sure of your intentions?"

"I am and yes, I'm sure," he replied.

Bhelus observed the exchange between the King and The Crown Prince.

The harbour was full of activity, the ships' sails swayed in the spring breeze. Work had begun to get them seaworthy and ready to sail. Queen Tsabani's ship, *Azuronde*, teemed with sailors and tradesmen - it would soon be ready to sail to Azuriene.

Queen Tsabani received Lord Caton with a smile. He was unnerved by this pleasantry.

"I hear *Azuronde* will soon be ready. It's time for me to return to Azuriene," said Queen Tsabani.

"I wish you a safe journey, Your Majesty."

"Thank you. I've arranged for you to join *Azenia* – you'll remain with King Caedec for the foreseeable future."

"Thank you, Your Majesty."

"I expect to be informed of developments, Lord Caton," she said handing him a purse full of coins and a crystal sphere. Lord Caton studied the sphere.

"It will communicate your thoughts to me. All you have to do is look at it. But I'm sure you're familiar with the ways of crystal spheres."

"Indeed, I am, Your Majesty."

Lord Caton bowed low and withdrew. "I'm sure you're familiar with the ways of crystal spheres," he repeated as he tossed it into the air.

Bhelus handed the scroll to Arrkir.

"Good work, Bhelus. I trust this is the final draft of the treaty?"

"It is - approved by The Crown Prince and King Caedec."

Arrkir unfolded the copy of the agreement and began to read it. "Egrinar is to advise Prince Nheve in The Crown Prince's absence! This is outrageous! What about me? This is the work of the Blue Witch. She has poisoned The Crown Prince's mind. What an insult!" he ranted – his face scarlet.

Bhelus smirked as Arrkir paced the floor, holding the copy in his hand.

Captain Oxghar and the crew of *Azenia* stood on deck staring at Hhariann as he flew across the sky. His fur shone like fire as he swooped and circled the ships.

Captain Oxghar grinned. "What a magnificent sight, Thoro. How I've longed to see him well again."

"Aye, captain – but I can't help wondering where the rest of them are."

Captain Oxghar's expression darkened.

"You know something, captain?" he enquired.

"I fear something tragic may have befallen his kin, Thoro. There's such sadness in his eyes."

Thoro stared at the sea. "You don't think Khinart has slaughtered them?"

Captain Oxghar's face betrayed his answer. "Khinart will be well aware of our plans to regain Maladoria. He'll do anything in his power to prevent it."

"May Crilm preserve us," replied Thoro.

"Perhaps I'm wrong."

"If something untoward has befallen them - how are we to secure victory?" pondered Thoro.

"Without War Kotroi to aid us, I don't know. We're at the mercy of the Gods."

"May Crilm preserve us," repeated Thoro.

Adina had gathered most of Queen Tsabani's possessions. Gowns and jewels were piled on the bed ready to be placed in coffers and taken to the ship.

The Crown Prince had made similar arrangements. Like *Azenia and Azuronde, Amalande,* Ilesh's most impressive war ship was almost ready to sail. An air of desertion permeated the palace as the time of departure drew near.

"Merrick, I want you to cut my hair."

"Sire?" he replied with an incredulous expression.

"My hair, Merrick cut it short."

Merrick shrugged his shoulders and began cutting the King's hair – dry grey strands fell away and lay in clumps on the floor. Once it was shorn he looked different. His hair was streaked with gold, making him appear young and vigorous again. Merrick was amazed at the transformation.

Caedec gazed at his reflection in the glass. He was astonished.

"Am I…is that really me?"

"A good haircut that is, even if I say so myself."

The Lords and nobles of Ilesh began to assemble in the palace. The Crown Prince embraced his brother. "Nheve, I trust Mhiria is well and married life is agreeable."

"Thank you and yes, I find it most agreeable."

"I've told you about the terms of the treaty, haven't I?" enquired The Crown Prince.

"Yes, you have."

"Yet I haven't said I mean to join Caedec's campaign. I sail to Maladoria and have appointed Egrinar as your adviser – you will rule in my absence. Should I not return, I name you as heir apparent."

Nheve was startled. "I didn't imagine for one moment you would join the King."

"Neither did I, but I've made my decision and I'm happy."

"Then so am I brother. I wish you well - return to us in one piece," replied Nheve not convinced of his brother's wisdom.

The state apartments were full of chatter. On the writing table lay the treaty. All the nobles were seated as The Crown Prince entered with King Caedec.

As Queen Tsabani and her ambassador arrived, the nobles exchanged glances. A fanfare sounded as the treaty was signed. Caedec rose, smiling as he began his speech.

"When I lost my country I was downcast and without hope. My cousin offered me and those loyal to me, refuge and kindness. Orthon believed in my cause, when I did not. I am forever in his debt. And now I am fortunate to have an ally in Vinaii, Crown Prince of Ilesh, who joins me on this quest. Let word spread throughout the worlds that I am a force to be reckoned with - to Maladoria!"

A rousing cheer resounded through the state apartments. The Crown Prince stood beside Caedec and made a short speech.

"I'm happy to join Caedec, rightful King of Maladoria. My brother, Nheve will rule in my absence. He will be advised in all matters of state by Egrinar - to Maladoria!"

A cheer rose through the palace. Several of Ilesh's aristocracy wore troubled expressions as Arrkir sidled up to Nheve engaging him in conversation. Egrinar watched with concern and a feeling of unease.

Queen Tsabani and Lord Caton wore expressions of complete surprise.

"Were you aware of this, Lord Caton?"

"I was not. This must be a recent development, very recent indeed."

Queen Tsabani eyed him with suspicion. "Of course I intend to help Caedec. I'll send ships to join his war fleet."

"Your Majesty, that's most generous of you."

"Yes, it is," she said with a look of self-satisfaction on her face. "I'm astounded at the change in Caedec's appearance. He looks younger. He's a changed man. Do you think it could be witchcraft, Lord Caton?"

"Your Majesty is most observant. I'm amazed at the change myself, I'm afraid I don't know whether it is of magical origin," he replied.

"You don't know much about anything!" said Queen Tsabani in an exasperated tone.

Aramintha was forlorn as she watched Darthus mount a black war horse she did not recognize. She noticed the straps fastened around the horse's fetlocks were studded with metal spikes. Prince Orthon's war party was well prepared. Salmir put his hand on her shoulder. Aramintha glanced at his face and noticed it was etched with worry. She was glad that Prince Orthon had commanded him to remain at the castle. She felt they would both have need of each other in the days to come.

Aramintha noticed the sun coming out. She thought the Prince's army would reach Askengarr before nightfall and dusk would hide them from the enemy. She thought Mararuss and the rebels would be firmly ensconced within the castle's walls.

She watched the horses thunder through the main gate. Prince Orthon's standard whipped in the wind as his army headed into the countryside bound for Askengarr.

Darthus pondered what they would find there and wondered what Mararuss would do next. He felt uneasy. It was a long time since he had fought in battle, though he prayed it would not come to that. He rode alongside Prince Orthon who was in good spirits. Darthus felt vengeance hung in the air, like a blade of steel.

Jhinn and Griann watched from the battlements as the Prince's army vanished into the distance.

"What are we to do?" said Jhinn.

"I'm not staying here," replied Griann.

"And what would my uncle say if we're caught following him, when he has forbidden us to leave the castle?"

"Your uncle may be glad of our assistance if he's riding into a trap."

Jhinn was thoughtful. He felt torn, pulled in two directions. One held adventure, the other obedience and duty to his uncle.

"Perhaps we could follow at a safe distance?" I'm not happy about leaving the castle."

"Then don't. Obey your uncle. But I'm leaving."

Jhinn said nothing as he gazed at the landscape. He watched as Lord Griann disappeared into the castle.

Lord Griann bid Atheil fetch his mail and armour and ensure his groom saddle Yarrow.

"Forgive me for asking Lord Griann, but are you proposing to ride alone?"

"Lord Jhinn chooses to stay here, so yes, I ride alone."

Atheil grimaced.

"I see that does not please you."

Atheil would not be drawn.

Yarrow pawed the ground as Lord Griann mounted. Horse and rider were discreetly attired for battle. Lord Griann wore a cloak of cloud grey over his armour. Yarrow wore a bridle set with a powerful amulet.

Jhinn watched from the battlements as Lord Griann emerged from the sally-port. He waved as he rode away. Jhinn breathed deeply. From the battlements he felt he could see the worlds. As he stood on the walkway he felt an eerie silence descend over Castle Adranabar.

Darthus gazed at the narrow track stretching in front of him like a taut length of ribbon. A mist lay over the land. They rode in silence - Prince Orthon's gaze was fixed firmly in the distance.

Darthus hoped they would stop to rest soon. He was disturbed by the silence. He longed for the distraction of conversation - even a few stilted sentences would be welcome.

Saravia heard the sound of horses' hooves. Sigamus flicked his tail as he sat by the kitchen door. She opened it a fraction and saw her father talking to two men and a woman.

Saravia could tell by their ashen faces all was not well. One of the grooms emerged from the stables to attend to their horses as her father ushered the strangers towards the house.

"Saravia! Now where is that daughter of mine?" said Erarunde.

Saravia opened the kitchen door.

"Ah, there you are. Come and meet our guests. They bring tidings from Askengarr."

Saravia was intrigued. Travellers from Askengarr did not usually pass through the forest. It was not the easiest route to Castle Adranabar. A feeling of foreboding overwhelmed her.

Jhinn had remained on the battlements longer than he had intended. Lord Griann had not returned and all remained quiet – uneasily so. He felt the castle was vulnerable to attack. There was but a small garrison left - fewer guards and soldiers than usual. He wished his uncle had not taken so many men with him.

Darthus was pleased to dismount. He was thankful Prince Orthon had commanded them to stop and rest awhile. Young squires took turns taking the horses to drink at the large trough by the side of the road. They were not far from Askengarr Castle now. He thought the countryside strangely quiet. There was not a soul in sight. This worried him - he could tell Prince Orthon was anxious, though he was trying not to show it.

They resumed their journey to Askengarr. Darthus felt the air was full of tension when at last the dark outline of the castle came into view. He noticed a plume of smoke rising from the battlements and felt his throat tighten. He glanced at Prince Orthon, but his gaze was fixed on the castle. Buzzards had begun to circle over Askengarr. As they drew nearer, Darthus saw why. Corpses hung over the battlements - remnants of the murdered garrison. Askengarr was sullied by cruelty and murder. Its walls ran red with blood.

Prince Orthon and his standard-bearer rode ahead. Darthus was wary and followed as closely as he could.

"Show yourself, Mararuss! Let there be an end to this bloodshed!" Prince Orthon's voice carried up to the battlements. There was no reply save the cries of the buzzards, preparing to feast. Some of the horses started to sidle. Darthus was filled with foreboding. Several arrows flew through the air. One embedded itself in the standard-bearer's chest and he slid from the saddle, the Prince's standard falling on the ground.

"Surround the Castle!" Darthus commanded drawing his sword he made to shield the Prince.

Prince Orthon grimaced as another arrow found its target - its shaft protruding through his armour. Darthus prayed it had not gone deep. At least there was no sign of blood.

Prince Orthon's army continued to advance. Darthus bade one of the squires attend to the Prince and lead his horse out of danger. They surrounded Askengarr Castle. Darthus gave the order for several soldiers to scale its walls. More soldiers followed, disappearing over the battlements into the heart of Askengarr. As the knights waited the wind turned and the air was cold. Eventually, the doors to Askengarr swung open and an officer appeared. He made towards Darthus to give his report.

"Sir, the castle is deserted – there's no sign of life here."

"How can this be?" said Darthus shaking his head in disbelief.

"Look sir, over there!" A soldier shouted pointing to several horsemen disappearing over the ridge into the countryside beyond.

"Damn! The archers have slipped through our net and live to create more havoc." Darthus cursed.

Prince Orthon was in a foul mood as they made camp for the night on a hillside not far from Askengarr Castle.

"Damn that Mararuss! He's made a complete and utter fool of me," said Prince Orthon pacing the campaign tent.

"Sire, I must remove the arrow," said Arunsar, the Prince's physician as he brushed a lock of hair, the colour of cold ashes, from his face.

"It's nothing – go away!" snapped Prince Orthon.

"Very well," Arunsar replied.

Darthus thought of the standard-bearer and how quickly he had fallen. Death was only a heartbeat away. It could so easily have been Prince Orthon.

Arunsar returned to attend to the arrow still embedded in the Prince's thigh. "Sire, I insist the arrow is drawn. You're in mortal danger."

"If you must - get the damn thing out and let's be done with it."

Arunsar prepared his instruments and removed the arrow. Prince Orthon breathed a sigh of relief. "Raze Askengarr to the ground and make sure there's nothing left of it," he commanded.

Prince Orthon's advisers nodded and withdrew.

"Sire, our forces are exposed camped out here in the open," said Darthus.

"I won't run from my enemies, Darthus."

"Castle Adranabar is vulnerable to attack."

Prince Orthon rubbed his forehead. "Very well, we return to Adranabar. It seems we serve no purpose here."

Darthus breathed a sigh of relief.

Lord Griann rode into the forest. A mist obscured familiar landmarks. Yarrow whinnied and sidled and he patted his neck to soothe him. He rode until he saw a light through the trees. He thought Saravia's house must be near. Darkness was falling and the mist was rising. As he approached he saw several figures in the kitchen and assumed all was well in the household.

Jhinn paced his bedchamber. Lord Griann had not returned and there was no word from Askengarr. He felt anxious and isolated. Darkness had fallen and a mist surrounded Castle Adranabar. Jhinn felt as if he was an animal caught in a trap. He had eaten a sombre meal with Salmir and Aramintha - they had dined meagrely and without mirth. A pall of sadness lingered over the castle.

Lord Griann was greeted warmly by Erarunde. "Well, my lord. What brings you to these parts?"

"I wanted to warn you…" Lord Griann's voice trailed off as he recalled the Marshall of Askengarr's fate.

"About the fate of Askengarr."

"You've heard?"

"Three travellers from Askengarr passed this way. They brought us the grim tidings."

"Prince Orthon has ridden to Askengarr," said Lord Griann.

"That doesn't surprise me, but he'll find nothing there. I've heard the rebels have moved on, further north, some say. Me, I'm just pleased I'm too old for that fighting lark. Nothing good'll come of it – mark my words. We've enough food for a guest. Cook has made so much we'll not be able to eat it all ourselves," said Erarunde tapping his round stomach.

Saravia was sitting at the dining table when her father entered accompanied by Lord Griann.

"My lord, I didn't know you were coming," she said standing to greet him.

"Lord Griann comes with news of Askengarr. He's staying for supper."

Lord Griann smiled shyly, as he seated himself at the table. Erarunde noticed the glances exchanged.

Prince Orthon's leg ached - beads of sweat stood on his brow. His face was drained of colour. "Sapphire!" he cried out in his disturbed slumber.

Darthus went to his side. "Fetch the physician," he barked the order at a squire who ran off like a frightened hare.

Arunsar was puzzled as he gazed at the Prince. "Studying the symptoms, I believe the arrow's tip may have been poisoned. I will try to determine its nature."

Darthus frowned. "He wanted to return to Adranabar. Can he be moved?"

134

Arunsar shrugged his shoulders. "I wouldn't advise it, but the decision doesn't rest with me."

Darthus breathed deeply as Prince Orthon cried out again. He strode out of the tent into a mist. The Mist of Arunsay - a wizard's breath, covering the land. Altering the boundaries of time, when wolves roam, gathering souls of the fallen and guiding them to the Vale. Darthus had seen it before, after the Battle of Eihir Plain.

Lord Griann was sorry to leave, but felt he must go. He wanted to catch up with Prince Orthon's retinue at Askengarr. He saw a mist rising in the depths of the forest and wished he had stayed at Saravia's house, as her father suggested. He heard the howl of a wolf and felt Yarrow shiver. He thought the trees looked sinister. Their branches groaned - the sound echoing through the forest. In the mist all directions seemed the same and perhaps were. He was lost.

Darthus had strayed from the camp. His vision was blurred as he tried to find his way back to Prince Orthon's campaign tent. Darthus had lost his sense of direction and stumbled awkwardly over the rough ground. Shadows of wolves rose from the earth. Their ghostly forms guiding him, eventually he found his way back to the camp. As he approached he heard battle cries. His hand felt instinctively for the hilt of his sword, as he drew the shining blade he felt a crushing blow on the back of his neck and everything turned black.

Stones rolled on the ground of Aiianvall's harbour. Caius was anxious as the symbols formed a pattern. Adranus traced the outlines with a long finger. A crowd of people were standing on the quayside, jostling and elbowing each other, trying to gain a better view.

"I sense fair weather. A settled voyage," Adranus announced to the cheering crowd.

"Though not fair play," he whispered to Caius as he led the seer away.

Caius was troubled. "Treachery?"

"Treachery and deceit."

Caedec stood at the window looking onto the palace gardens. He studied the green shoots coming up through the earth. The spring moon had danced, bringing renewal and his spirit was at one with the energy flowing through the worlds.

Merrick announced Caius and Adranus.

"Adranus, Caius, and how was the reading of the stones?" Caedec enquired.

Caius was downcast. He felt the weight of Caedec's gaze and felt uncomfortable.

"Perhaps the reading did not go well?"

"Sire, the stones tell of fair weather. Yet they foretell treachery," replied Adranus.

Caedec said nothing.

Merrick returned with alphus berry cakes and a flagon of warm Adras, setting them on the table, he poured the clear, bubbling liquid into a goblet, handing it to Adranus. "I know you prefer it warmed. Can I interest you in an alphus berry cake?"

"You may indeed, Merrick. That's kind. You'll be the saviour of us all, I'm sure," he replied clasping Merrick's arm.

Caedec and Caius exchanged glances.

"A lovely cake, Merrick," said Adranus.

Caedec stared at his hands. "Adranus, I seek your advice on another matter."

"I'm happy to give my King advice on anything."

"Should Liviaa and Janus travel with us to Maladoria or remain here in Ilesh?"

Adranus paused. "Darthus's young lad and the orphan girl - I sense their fates are intertwined. They should continue their journey to

Maladoria. Janus is destined to be a warrior - his father would deny him his path, if it was in his power to do so."

Caedec nodded. "My question is answered."

Caius sipped the warm Adras, savouring the taste of crushed meadow flower and woodland herb.

"Treachery, Adranus?" said Caedec.

"That's what the stones foretell - I can't determine the nature of betrayal. A veil is drawn over it."

Sapphire's sleep was disturbed. She was haunted by a vivid dream. She heard Prince Orthon calling her name, feeling a stabbing pain in her thigh - she woke up wiping beads of sweat from her brow. She reached for the amulet, holding it tightly in her hand - she recited a healing spell, watching as a sphere of golden light flew through the air towards Adranabar. "May Crilm bestow blessings on you and your troubled realm," she whispered.

Lucha entered. "Mistress, are you well?" she said approaching the bed where Sapphire lay, limp and spent, the amulet slipping from her hand on to the floor. A look of horror crossed Lucha's face as she ran out into the corridor, colliding with Merrick.

"Lucha!' he cried dropping several goblets.

"I think Mistress Sapphire is dead," she cried scrambling to her feet.

Merrick's eyes widened. "By the will of Crilm it can't be so."

Merrick entered the bedchamber - leaning over Sapphire's inert body he looked for signs of life, holding her wrist he felt the faint rhythm of her pulse. "She's alive."

"Thank Crilm," replied Lucha.

Merrick picked up the amulet, placing it on the bed beside her. "Sapphire needs rest, but she'll be all right – see she's not disturbed for a while, Lucha."

Caedec made to the Far Tower, finding the door ajar he entered to find Gai placing his alchemical instruments in their respective cases.

"I see you are preparing for the voyage," said Caedec.

"I thought it was time."

"Merrick tells me Sapphire is unwell. I believe she has performed some magic, which has drained her. I thought you should know."

"I'll attend to her, if she'll let me. What has Adranus said about the stones?" said Gai.

"He said they foretell fair weather and treachery, a betrayal of some kind. He cannot tell what."

Gai looked troubled. "The stones are seldom wrong. We must be on our guard."

Caedec nodded.

Gai noticed an aura of scarlet around Caedec, smiling he recalled striding through the Palace of Khorec, the corridors bathed in the light reflected from Caedec's eyes.

Sapphire woke, feeling strength returning to her body, like a river flowing into the sea.

"Mistress, are you awake?" enquired Lucha.

Sapphire moaned, rubbing her forehead.

"Lucha, tell the King I wish to speak with him."

"Yes, of course," she replied withdrawing.

Caedec was sitting in the gardens admiring the flowers. He heard the stirring of wings, staring at the trees he saw Kotroi landing on the branches. As got up and made towards them, they came to him, making meowing and chirruping sounds.

"My friends," he said with arms outstretched. As they landed, balancing themselves on the sleeves of his cloak, their furry bodies gleamed in the sunlight. A Kotroi with silver fur landed on his shoulder. It nuzzled its head on his cheek purring, he felt its whiskers brush his skin. "Llorian, you have returned from the seventh world. I am so happy to see you."

Lucha made her way through the palace to the King's apartment.

"Lucha, what business have you here?" Arrkir said blocking her path.

Lucha stopped in her tracks - staring at the floor she said nothing.

"Has Sapphire seen the scroll I gave you?"

"Yes, of course, sir."

"I rather think she hasn't."

Lucha's cheeks flushed, her palms felt damp.

Arrkir moved closer until she felt compelled to take a step back.

"I'm certain she has," she replied.

"Now why do I wonder if you're telling me the truth? Where is the scroll? Return it to me."

Terror gripped Lucha and she struggled to breathe.

"I presume the coins have been spent by now - no matter. I'm disappointed in you, Lucha. However, I'm sure I'll think of some way you can repay me," he said as he strode off down the corridor.

Lucha breathed deeply and leaned against the wall for support. Her mind was full of fear. What was she to do?

Queen Tsabani stood at the window watching Caedec encircled by Kotroi. "Look at that fool. Why is he encouraging those creatures?" she said in disgust.

Lord Caton gave her a cold look as he watched Caedec laughing and smiling as Kotroi flew to him, landing on his arms and shoulders.

Lucha composed herself and continued on her way to the King's apartment. She knocked and the door swung open. "I've a message for the King from my Lady Sapphire," she said as Merrick stood on the threshold.

"Lucha, the King is strolling in the gardens at present – pray seek him there."

Lucha saw the King and ran across the lawn towards him, stopping to stare at the creatures perched on his arms and shoulders.

"Isn't it wonderful? My friends have returned," he said.

Lucha nodded. "Sire, my Lady Sapphire is asking for you."

Gai made his way to Sapphire's apartment, finding the door ajar he tapped and wandered inside. "Lucha! Sapphire!"

Sapphire stirred. "Gai?"

Gai stared at Sapphire's pale countenance. "What's happened, Sapphire? What have you done?"

"I tried to help Orthon, I saw him wounded by an arrow in my dream. I feel there's trouble in Adranabar. I asked Lucha to fetch the King. Where is she?"

"They'll be here soon, you must rest. I'll make up some incense for you."

Sapphire felt her eyelids grow heavy. Gai touched her hand and withdrew, lingering in the chamber, hoping the King was on his way.

Lucha found it difficult to keep up with Caedec's strides. She was glad when they reached the apartment, noticing the door was ajar she realized she had forgotten to close it in her haste to fetch the King.

"How is Sapphire?" Caedec enquired.

Gai frowned. "She's been close to death."

Caedec grimaced.

"She tried to help Prince Orthon," said Gai.

"What has happened to my cousin?"

Gai hesitated. "I gather he lies wounded."

The colour drained from Caedec's face, giving him a deathly pallor. "This is grave news."

The Crown Prince was perplexed. He had watched Lucha and the King return to the palace and felt something was amiss. He was uneasy and doubts began to creep into his mind. He had made the decision to join the King's campaign without giving it enough thought. He had been impulsive, reckless even. In the stillness of the afternoon these thoughts haunted him.

Gai and Caedec sat staring at the fire as Sapphire slept. The smell of incense wafted in from the bedchamber, filling the apartment with the scent of roses in bloom.

"What are we to do, Gai? Have we any warships to send to Adranabar?"

"Alas, to split the fleet might jeopardize our campaign."

Caedec shifted in his chair. "Then we must leave Orthon to his fate."

"I wouldn't put it quite in those terms."

Caedec frowned. "My head is splitting. I could do without the masked ball this evening."

Gai nodded in agreement.

There was a knock and Lucha sauntered in. "Sire, The Crown Prince is here. He enquires after my Lady Sapphire's health."

"Show him in."

"Caedec, my Lord Gai. I didn't realize you were here. I trust you're both well and prepared for the voyage," said The Crown Prince seating himself.

Gai and Caedec were silent. The Crown Prince felt a chill in the atmosphere.

"Is something wrong?"

Caedec sighed, wondering what to say. "Sapphire is indisposed. She has dreamt my cousin lies wounded by an arrow. This dream has disturbed her and naturally, we are concerned."

"May I see her? Why was I not told?"

"She's resting. She will be all right soon," said Caedec.

"An inauspicious dream," replied The Crown Prince.

"We believe it was more than that, Vinaii. Can we spare any warships to send to Adranabar to help my cousin?"

"Perhaps one or more, but I wouldn't advise it – we need all the ships we have. Khinart will be prepared to defend his realm," said The Crown Prince.

"My realm Vinaii, it is my country, not his," replied Caedec in a curt tone.

"My apologies, of course it is."

"Friends we are becoming agitated. And to what end?" said Gai trying to ease the tension.

"Please help them!" cried Sapphire.

Gai, Caedec and The Crown Prince rushed to the bedchamber, followed by Lucha and Merrick, who had brought a flagon of Adras for the King. Sapphire was tossing and turning in her sleep. Lucha grabbed her hand, trying to wake her.

"Stop that!" said Gai pulling her away.

Lucha was distraught as Merrick escorted her out of the bedchamber.

"It's all right, Sapphire," said Gai wafting incense under her nose as The Crown Prince looked on.

Lucha was still crying. Merrick handed her a plate of alphus berry cakes and a goblet of Adras. "Don't concern yourself Lucha, Sapphire will be all right. I've seen this before. It's all part of a witch's life. You'll have to get used to it. Now drink up and have a cake."

Lucha sniffed. She sipped some Adras and started to eat, managing a few mouthfuls before dissolving into tears.

"Whatever is the matter, Lucha?" Are you in some sort of trouble?" Merrick enquired.

Lucha's face was flushed.

"You are aren't you? If it's one of those young knights…"

"No, no it isn't…it's…"

"It's what, Lucha?"

"Arrkir gave me a scroll. It had a drawing and some writing on it – disgusting it was. I couldn't bring myself to show it to Lady Sapphire like he wanted, so I put it on the fire – burned it. He gave me some gold coins as well. I gave them to my brother so he could buy medicine – he's sick you see. Now Arrkir knows she hasn't seen it and wants ..." Lucha's words came out in a torrent.

"Oh dear," said Merrick.

Lucha gulped staring at the floor.

"I'll tell the King – he'll know what's to be done and Sapphire will need someone to look after her now The Lady Annas has gone. We sail to Maladoria and that's far enough away from Arrkir."

Laderine was pleased with the fruits of her labour - the ballroom was exquisitely decorated with flowers. A masked ball was held to celebrate The Dance of the Spring Moon and on this occasion it would also celebrate the voyage to Maladoria.

Nobles, knights and their ladies were the first to arrive, sumptuously attired with elaborate masks. Days were lengthening and guests strolled in the gardens waiting for the dancing to begin.

Gai, Caedec and The Crown Prince arrived wearing their masks, attired in costumes of black and gold in the style of the Alchemists of Emonand in The Delvia States. Sapphire was absent - she would need all her strength for the voyage.

Caedec noticed Arrkir and Bhelus deep in conversation by the entrance to the gardens. He saw Queen Tsabani and Lord Caton enter, stopping to admire the flowers. Queen Tsabani was dressed in a gown of black velvet. She wore a headdress in the same hue, framing her face, with a band of net encrusted with Azuriene crystals across her eyes.

Lord Caton was also dressed in black. His mask shaped like a cat's head. Caedec observed them conversing with Laderine of Gyle.

The Crown Prince said a few words of welcome then the music started. The orchestra's melodic strains drifted into the palace gardens. Dancing began as the candles were lit and a moon rose in the sky, casting shadows on the lawns.

Caedec was in sombre mood and declined invitations to dance. He noticed Queen Tsabani and Lord Caton leaving as the ball drew to a close.

The Crown Prince watched Mhiria and Nheve dancing, he felt a twinge of jealously – they looked so happy together. As people gathered around him offering their good wishes and saying their farewells, he was pensive.

Queen Tsabani and Lord Caton travelled to the harbour by carriage, followed by The Crown Prince's and several others. All the coaches and teams of horses were as black as night. Carriage lamps were the only lights in the darkness as the horses thundered along like phantoms in flight.

Lord Caton watched a crowd gathering on the quayside. Torches on the harbour walls burned, flooding the area with light, as the carriages parked in a line. Footmen opened doors and the illustrious occupants alighted.

Queen Tsabani stepped out of her coach followed by Lord Caton and The Crown Prince, she waved to the cheering crowd as Caedec, Gai, Laderine, Nheve and Mhiria gathered to say their farewells. She noticed Egrinar, absent from the masked ball, was standing on the quayside accompanied by Bhelus and a sulking Arrkir.

"Well, Tsabani, this is goodbye," said The Crown Prince embracing her.

Queen Tsabani wore a sad expression, the corners of her mouth turned down. "Perhaps in another life we'll be together."

The Crown Prince gave her a sad smile and kissed her. "Farewell, my Queen."

Queen Tsabani waved and a barrage of fireworks exploded over the harbour as she went aboard *Azuronde*.

Lord Caton turned to the King. "I am at your service."

Sorrel walked along the sun filled colonnade, his armour making a clinking sound with the movement of his body, interrupting the silence. In the distance a snow falcon cried.

The young knight noticed the lush gardens and the brilliant colours of the flowers. Sorrel saw the colonnade stretch before him, as if into infinity.

Egrinar stood beside one of the pillars. Sorrel saw him, he was partly hidden by the ancient stone, wearing a cloak of blue and bathed in the light of the sun. Egrinar smiled as he approached. He stepped forward, embracing his son.

"Hello Father."

"How well you look. Come walk with me."

They strolled in silence. As the end of the colonnade came into view Egrinar stopped. "The Crown Prince sails for Maladoria on the morrow, as do you, my dear son."

Egrinar put his hand into the folds of his cloak. A silence as deep as the grave settled between them, as his hand emerged, his fist clenched tightly around something. Sorrel was curious, wondering what it was. Egrinar's fingers unfurled and resting in the palm of his hand was a small gold coin and a key set with an emerald. Sorrel gazed at them as Egrinar's hand moved towards him.

"My father gave them to me and now I'm giving them to you."

Sorrel took them, he recognized the key - he had seen his father unlock the secret drawer in his writing table with it. He studied the coin briefly before putting them in the pocket of his tunic.

"Thank you, Father."

Egrinar embraced him again. "May Crilm protect you - may we meet again, in this world or another."

Sorrel watched his father walk back along the colonnade, feeling his heart tearing. He felt lost and alone as he made his way to the knights' quarters.

Captain Oxghar and Thoro admired the battle fleet moored in the harbour. Captain Oxghar thought the white and silver sails of the Ileshian warships were a sharp contrast for the Adranabar warships whose sails were now blood red with the black symbol of the Idrean dynasty in the centre. He unfurled the scroll in his hand and read the document bearing Lord Fhinn's seal aloud.

'On the recommendation of my good friend, Caedec, King of Maladoria, I hereby bestow the rank of Admiral upon Lhimm Oxghar'.

"I command a battle fleet, Thoro."

"Congratulations Captain … I mean Admiral. It's a great honour for you, sir. If I may say so, it seems an odd destiny for a poet."

Thoro and Admiral Oxghar laughed.

Sunlight played on the water like a mischievous nymph as Admiral Oxghar gazed at the sea thinking of Queen Irmardia. He breathed deeply and felt the air in his lungs. Another adventure at sea was about to begin and the atmosphere was charged with anticipation.

Merrick approached the King. "Sire, may I speak with you?"

"Certainly, Merrick."

"It's about Lucha."

Caedec wore a puzzled expression. "Lucha?"

"Yes, you see she's fallen foul of Arrkir."

Caedec raised an eyebrow. "Has she indeed and how has this come about?"

"Arrkir gave her a scroll to deliver to the Lady Sapphire. I haven't seen it myself, but by all accounts its contents were unpleasant."

"I see."

"Lucha didn't show it to Lady Sapphire – she disposed of it and Arrkir has, shall we say, noticed she hasn't fulfilled her obligation to him."

"What am I to do about this?"

"Could she sail with us, as Lady Sapphire's maid?"

Caedec smiled. "I see no reason why not. I'm sure Sapphire would be glad of her company. I expect Lucha's sudden departure will upset Arrkir, losing a victim always does."

Lord Caton studied his attire, which was more suited to the life of a courtier than a voyage at sea. "They will have to do. There isn't time to visit the tailors of Aiianvall," he said, a note of disappointment in his voice. "Well, perhaps another time?"

"You look much better today," said Caedec noticing Sapphire was dressed and ready for the voyage.

"I believe I've recovered."

"And not before time, you've caused me a great deal of worry," said Caedec smiling.

"Thank you, I'm quite well."

"I am glad to hear it and you are prepared for the journey?" enquired Caedec.

"Yes, I believe so."

"Will you take Lucha with you?"

"I hadn't thought about it."

"You have need of a maid, now that …," Caedec's words trailed off, wondering if he should mention The Lady Annas.

"Yes, I'll ask her."

"Good… have you any news?" Caedec enquired.

"Of Orthon and Adranabar – I've seen nothing more."

Lord Caton watched as coffers holding his possessions were taken from his apartment. He studied the purse Queen Tsabani had given him, threw it into a box, inlaid with his initials, turned the key and placed it in one of the remaining coffers. "The spoils of war," he said aloud.

Caedec strolled through the palace thinking of the voyage. "May Crilm help me liberate my country from that blackguard," he said aloud, his pace quickening.

The Crown Prince was alone in the Hall of the Written Word, with its vaulted ceiling painted a glacial white and walls lined with books. He gazed at the spines, pausing before taking a handful. He chose several volumes of Lhimm Oxghar's poetry, Fables from the Whispering Sea and a History of the Witches of Azuriene. Opening a volume of poetry - he noticed an inscription on the flyleaf:

> *For my dearest Vinaii*
> *with all my love*
> *Tsabani*

Sadness clouded his features. "How could I forget?" he said aloud.

For a fleeting moment he recalled the day she had given it to him. "I'm sorry I didn't love you, as you loved me," he whispered.

Admiral Oxghar boarded his ship, anxious to set sail. He was happy as *Azenia* cast off and put out to sea with *Amalande*, pride of the Ileshian fleet, following. His ears rang with the sound of cheering on the quayside. A salty breeze brushed his face and felt like the touch of

146

Queen Irmardia's hand. He was overcome by the smell of the Whispering Sea, the scent of his love.

"Look!" shouted Thoro as Kotroi, smaller than their relatives the War Kotroi, but as quick in flight, flew over the Walls of Aiianvall and across the Whispering Sea, disappearing like specks of sand scattered across parchment.

"Safe passage to Maladoria," said Admiral Oxghar.

Sapphire stood on the deck of *Azenia*, feeling it roll beneath her feet as it gained speed, heading into the open sea. She wondered how The Crown Prince was faring, thinking it seemed an age since she last saw him, holding the amulet to the sky, she kissed it. "Safe journey Kotroi, bring good tidings from Maladoria," she whispered.

Caedec and Admiral Oxghar pored over the map.

"We are here," said the Admiral pointing to an area of the Whispering Sea.

Caedec nodded.

"If the weather conditions remain as they are, we'll make good progress," Admiral Oxghar continued.

"And the Aizan ships when will they join us?" Caedec enquired.

"On the morrow, at this point," said the Admiral pointing to another area of the Whispering Sea.

Arrkir sat brooding, his hands steepled. He stared at the writing table made from Phinas wood with a patina of aubergine. A snow falcon's head on each corner carved with his initials, AV, Arrkir Vermian, Lord of the Vermian Plain, east of Aiianvall. Consumed by ambition, he plotted how to wrest power from Egrinar and win Laderine's heart, taking the minature looking glass from the folds of his cloak, he gazed at his reflection. "I'll order new attire - appearance is all important in matters of state."

Dusk was settling over the Whispering Sea, clothing the ships in a mantle of grey. *Azenia* slowed as the wind dropped. Below deck Merrick prepared dinner for the King and his guests, Admiral Oxghar, Gai, Sapphire, Caius and Adranus. Merrick tried to complete several tasks at once as Janus and Liviaa chattered.

Admiral Oxghar was inspecting the guns. "Well, Thoro, everything is in order."

147

"Thank you, sir - Adranabar's finest cannon."

"Indeed, Thoro. We'll see how they perform no doubt."

"Aye sir, we will."

Caedec put a napkin to his lips. "Merrick has excelled himself this evening. Now let us make a toast," he said holding his goblet aloft. "To good friends, victory and Maladoria."

"To good friends, victory and Maladoria," they repeated.

Merrick heard the sound of goblets clinking as he sat in the galley kitchen adjoining the dining room. A tear trickled down his face. He missed the companionship he had found in the palace kitchens and Laderine of Gyle's welcoming smile. He gazed at the copper pans she had given him as a present. "The King's party is going well, by the sound of it. If the fates allow, when all this is over I'll visit Ilesh and see Laderine again," he said aloud.

Caius and Adranus were enjoying themselves telling stories and jokes. Sapphire's smile lit up the cabin, as Gai watched her he felt a pang of regret. Before long the King and his guests began to feel sleepy and retired to their quarters.

"Why, Merrick, what troubles you?" Caedec enquired, noticing his cheerless manner.

"Oh nothing, I'm a little homesick, that's all," he replied clearing the table.

Admiral Oxghar stood on deck. Night was falling, as black as raven's wing. The lights on the ships reminded him of stars floating on the water. He noticed the scent of the Whispering Sea as a white hand with blue fingernails caressed his cheek.

"You look so handsome in your new uniform," said Queen Irmardia – her voice a silken whisper.

Admiral Oxghar smiled taking her hand. "May I look upon you?"

"Only for a moment, I cannot stay."

"How beautiful you are. Your attire is at least worthy of a poem," he said admiring her gown and noticing her hair set with an ornament of crystals, fashioned like *Azenia*. Her skin glowed with a silvery sheen. He kissed her, brushing her face with his lips.

"Why Admiral, your new position has made you bold."

"Forgive me, I couldn't help myself."

Queen Irmardia laughed, and then vanished, leaving him alone, wondering what the future might hold.

Admiral Oxghar was alarmed as circles of red light were reflected on the water. Hairs on the back of his neck started to rise and he felt nauseous. He heard the sound of paws on deck. Admiral Oxghar stroked Hhariann's broad head and he purred gazing at the Whispering Sea, as *Azenia* ploughed through the water. Suddenly, Hhariann growled, baring his teeth, as more red lights appeared. "Acelphidi, may Crilm protect us from the scourge of the seas," said Admiral Oxghar.

Below deck, Adranus was uneasy. He rose from his bed and opened the door of his cabin. "Caius, come quickly," he called.

Caius appeared, looking sleepy. "Adranus, what troubles you? Are you unwell?"

"I sense danger. I must tell Admiral Oxghar," Adranus replied in an anxious tone.

"Wait here, I'll speak to him."

Caius ran along the galley and met Thoro, making a tour of the ship.

"Where's Admiral Oxghar?"

"He's up on deck," replied Thoro. Is anything amiss, Caius?" he enquired, intrigued.

"Adranus wishes to see the Admiral."

"I'll fetch him. I was going up on deck anyway. And you're not dressed for a cold night on the deck of a ship," said Thoro with a look of disapproval on his face.

Caius realized the cloak he had donned hastily over his night attire was not appropriate for the weather conditions.

Thoro noticed Admiral Oxghar and Hhariann near the prow and made towards them. "Admiral, I've a message for you."

"A message?"

Thoro noticed a concerned expression on the Admiral's face. "Is everything in order, sir?" enquired Thoro following the the direction of his gaze.

"May Crilm preserve us!" Thoro cried as his eyes fixed on the red lights in the distance. "This cannot be. Acelphidi aren't usually seen in these parts," he continued, struggling to convince himself he was not hallucinating.

149

"Then I'm not mistaken, Thoro. And your message, what is it, pray?"

"Adranus wishes to speak to you, sir."

Admiral Oxghar frowned. "I'll go to him – it must be urgent. He wouldn't ask if it wasn't. Stay here, Hhariann. Guard the ship well while I'm below deck," he commanded.

On the ships' prows, figureheads of dragons and wolves woke from their slumber. They yawned, noticing the reflection of red lights on the sea, they murmured the warning *'Acelphidi'* to each other – their chant floating across the Whispering Sea.

Caius reassured Adranus the Admiral was on his way. Adranus remained anxious and Caius was relieved when he appeared.

"Admiral, good of you to come so quickly," said Caius ushering him into the seer's cabin.

"What troubles you, Adranus?" enquired Admiral Oxghar.

"I sense danger, a great danger," replied Adranus.

"I've seen red lights in the distance. Is that the danger you speak of?" enquired Admiral Oxghar.

"Yes, Acelphidi."

Admiral Oxghar felt his heart race. He took a deep breath, calming himself. "I fail to understand why they're sailing in these waters."

"Perhaps they've been asked to," Adranus replied.

A look of grim realization crossed Admiral Oxghar's face. "Could this be the work of Khinart?"

Adranus nodded. "It could."

"I will inform the King and prepare for attack," said Admiral Oxghar.

"You must ask Sapphire to summon a mist to hide our ships. It may be our only hope of avoiding conflict with those evil barbarians."

"Of course Adranus, I'll attend to it."

"Good man - may Crilm protect you."

Darthus saw a burst of golden light in the sky.

"We vanquished them," said the squire helping him to his feet.

Darthus swayed, feeling the back of his neck. He removed his hand, noticing his palm was smeared with blood. "What happened? Where's our Prince?" he enquired.

"We were attacked, sir, by the rebels. Most likely those horsemen we saw galloping away from Askengarr. They must have joined more of Mararuss's followers before they set upon us. We made sure we protected the Prince and killed as many rebels as we could," explained the squire.

"Good, what's your name?" Darthus enquired.

"I'm Mathuen, sir."

"Of course you're Ethuen's son. I knew him well."

"Indeed, sir. I'm at your service."

Darthus studied the young squire. His face and hair were streaked with sweat and blood. His tunic was torn and his sword hand bore a deep gash. It must have been a bloody fight, he thought. He could see the rebels were well trained in the art of combat. "I must see Prince Orthon."

"Certainly, follow me, sir."

Mathuen led Darthus to the Prince's tent, its flaps fluttered in the breeze. He was greeted by Arunsar. "Darthus, you are alive. Are you hurt? We have many wounded."

"It's nothing. How's Prince Orthon?"

"He lies between this world and the Vale of Wolves. I've tried, but I can't reach him."

Darthus stared at Prince Orthon's inert body. "Is there nothing we can do for him?"

Arunsar shook his head. Darthus noticed how tired he looked. There were deep shadows under his eyes.

"Prince Orthon will either come back to us or wander beyond the Vale of Wolves, never to return. I cannot predict what transpires."

"I see." Darthus seated himself on the couch near the Prince's bed, holding his head in his hands. "What's left of our army?"

"We've lost a great number of soldiers and Knights of the Realm. I'm sorry to be the bearer of such tidings."

"It's not your fault."

Arunsar noticed Darthus's bloodstained hand. "Let me tend your wound, less it fester, causing you distress."

"Of course, thank you. I feel wretched – I've been of no assistance to my sovereign."

"Don't reproach yourself. We couldn't prevent what's happened. Prince Orthon won't think ill of you."

Darthus remained unconvinced, feeling powerless and wracked with guilt - he thought it better to be dead than dishonoured.

Arunsar examined the wound. "You're fortunate - the blow to your head could've killed you. It's a deep gash," he said covering it with herbs.

"Perhaps I've been spared for some purpose?"

"There's a reason for everything, if we have the wisdom to see it."

Darthus pondered Arunsar's words, feeling the herbs on his skin.

Darthus woke thinking he heard Prince Orthon speak - looking at his motionless body he realized he was mistaken. "We must leave for Castle Adranabar," he said as he lay down, waiting for the morrow.

Prince Orthon could not feel the weight of his limbs. His body felt light, a white mist hung over the countryside. He saw a forest on a hillside - the trees were unusual and unlike those in Adranabar. He felt himself float over the ground, shrouded in white mist, noticing a river he made towards it, hoping it would lead to Adranabar.

Then he saw her, a woman in winter, clothed in white, crossing the river in a longboat. Frost crackled on her marble skin. Her face framed by a hood, edged with white fur. "Varcia!" he cried.

As the longboat passed a settlement, he heard a wolf howl - following the longboat as it drifted downstream, he was sure the woman in white was Varcia. If it was, it meant he had crossed into the Vale of Wolves, bound for the worlds beyond. And yet if that was so why had she not heard him call out to her?

Prince Orthon felt the cold air as he studied the landscape. He watched the river disappear into the distance. He noticed something dark jutting out from the bank. It was made from wide planks of wood, forming a platform over the river. The structure was supported by several tall posts, each one carved with the masks of wolves. He saw the longboat drift silently towards it.

He watched as it drew alongside. A man clothed in grey, like an evening shadow lashed the longboat to a wolf pole, he offered his hand to the woman in white. She took it, stepping gracefully on to the platform. Her cloak trailed as she glided towards a sleigh pulled by four wolves. He saw the gleam of their eyes, their breath hanging in the air.

Prince Orthon was drawn to the woman in white, watching as she sat in the sleigh - Grey Shadowman standing behind her. As the wolves started to run the sleigh moved swiftly. He saw a castle and watched as the drawbridge was lowered and the sleigh glided over it. He stared at its white stone walls and towers partially covered in snow. It reminded him of the Palace of Aiianvall, as he remembered it, from a state visit made with his father many moons ago.

Prince Orthon passed through the entrance unnoticed. He wandered through silent halls and corridors. At the end of a winding passage he came upon a large chamber. He saw the woman in white sitting on a chair. Grey Shadowman was standing behind her and a wolf lay at her feet.

He could see a roaring fire at the end, yet the air was cold. "Varcia," he called.

The wolf stirred. She followed its gaze. He could see her face clearly. He was certain it was his late wife, who so resembled his sister, Oriahh.

"Varcia, can you not see me? It is I, Orthon."

"Orthon? You are but a wraith. Go back - you should not be here."

"Are you not pleased I have come? Can we not be together again?"

She sighed and the wolf shifted. "This is not the time."

"Why, Varcia? Can't I stay here with you?"

Grey Shadowman stepped forward and the wolf bared its teeth.

"As I have said, it's not time. I cannot give you the key. Your life isn't over yet. There are those in the worlds who have need of you. You'll take another wife and have a child."

A tear froze on her cheek.

"The border will still be open. Wolf shadow hasn't fallen across the vale. There's still time before night comes, follow me," said Varcia rising from her wolf throne.

Prince Orthon and Grey Shadowman obeyed her command and boarded the longboat. It glided through the silent water. Nothing stirred in the cold, white Vale of Wolves.

"Our daughter, Ormia is she with you?" he enquired.

"No, she is not."

Prince Orthon felt his body grow heavy as a line of trees came in to view.

"We're approaching the border. I can't go any further. You must continue alone. Take the path into the woods. You'll see a statue of Carvenn, the wolf god, tap three times on his right paw and you'll have safe passage. Now go, and may Crilm protect you until we meet again," said Varcia.

Prince Orthon watched from the riverbank as the longboat drifted back towards the vale. His heart lurched when he saw Grey Shadowman embrace Varcia. Then she was gone and he was left standing among the trees. He saw the statue of Carvenn, the image of the wolf god dominated the forest. Carvenn's head and ears were almost level with the treetops.

Prince Orthon hesitated then tapped Carvenn's paw three times, as Varcia had instructed. He felt the weight of his bones and stirred, feeling disorientated.

"Thank Crilm, our Prince lives," said Arunsar.

"We are blessed," said Darthus.

Prince Orthon studied their faces. As he breathed, he felt his limbs whole and without pain.

Arunsar felt the Prince's pulse. "You're still with us and regaining your strength, I might add."

"How soon can he be moved, Arunsar?" enquired Darthus.

"He's out of danger and may be able to ride in a day or so."

"We should be gone by then. I believe we must ride to Adranabar on the morrow. It will not be safe to tarry," said Darthus.

"Then let us hope the Prince makes a swift recovery."

Prince Orthon leaned back on several pillows and cushions covered in scarlet silk. "Fetch my horse, lad," he commanded.

The young squire was startled and went in search of Darthus. "Sir, the Prince is asking for his horse."

Darthus was surprised. "Well, that's a better sign. I'll speak to Arunsar. I believe his counsel is needed."

Darthus went in search of Arunsar, finding him tending the wounded. "Prince Orthon has asked for his horse."

Arunsar smiled. "Then he's stronger than we think, or more stubborn than we anticipated."

"How are they? Can any of them be moved?"

"Some are well enough to travel. Others…" Arunsar stopped in mid sentence, his expression betraying his thoughts.

"I see. We must break camp."

Arunsar sighed. "I am in agreement. I will do what I can."

Lord Griann gazed at the clouds, the mist had not lifted and he felt it would be sensible to remain in the forest. He would spend the night sheltering amongst the trees. "Damn that girl, Saravia, she'll be the undoing of me," he said aloud.

As the forest was plunged into darkness, he could smell the scent of wolf on the wind. Yarrow shifted. A great weariness came over him and he lay down at the foot of a Phinas tree, its gnarled roots protruding from the ground and fell into a deep sleep.

He woke to the sound of birds singing, the mist had cleared leaving filmy traces over the ground. He yawned, stretched his aching body and looked around. Yarrow pulled a few blades of thinly sown grass from the black earth. He realized how hungry he was. "How foolish am I, to find myself lost and alone without food in the depths of a forest. I'm a poor master, am I not, Yarrow?" he said as his horse continued to feed on what grass he could find.

Lord Griann took the saddlecloth he had used to sleep on, shaking the remnants of soil and leaves from it. He studied the blue and gold material, embroidered with his family's coat of arms, a bear holding a spear, sewn by his mother. He smoothed the fabric before putting it on Yarrow. Then placed the saddle on it, deciding he would try to find his way to Castle Adranabar while the light was good. "Walk on, Yarrow, it's time we were on our way," he said, settling himself into the saddle as the war horse shook its head.

"Where's my horse?" Prince Orthon roared like a lion with a thorn in its paw, stopping the camp in its tracks. Mathuen's blood froze in his veins and Darthus made towards the sovereign's tent.

"Darthus, fetch my horse."

"Sire, your horse is being saddled, as we speak."

Prince Orthon flopped back on the pillows, angry and exasperated, fidgeting with the coverlet.

Arunsar entered wearing a worried expression. "Let me examine your wound before you ride to Adranabar."

Prince Orthon gave him a withering look.

"I'm amazed – it's healed. There's not even a mark where the arrow was lodged. How can this be?"

"Witchcraft probably, now fetch my horse or I'll execute the lot of you!"

Stifling a grin, Darthus helped Prince Orthon put his foot in the stirrup.

"A good day for our journey,"said Prince Orthon watching as Darthus swung himself into the saddle, manoeuvring his horse to draw level with his.

"It is. I pray we make good progress."

Prince Orthon placed his hand on Darthus's arm. "You're a good man. You'll be rewarded for your bravery at Askengarr."

An expression of surprise crossed Darthus's face. "It was nothing."

"You'll be rewarded. Don't argue with me. I'm not in the mood. Have you sent outriders to Adranabar?"

"Yes, they left a while ago."

"Good."

Darthus was apprehensive - the road to Adranabar was quiet. Far too quiet he thought as his eyes darted back and forth, fearing an ambush.

Mathuen's head was full of images of Askengarr. He tried to cast them aside, but found it difficult thinking of anything else. He hoped they would not find such gruesome scenes at Castle Adranabar.

Elthann, the court jeweller, arrived at the castle with his assistant, a scrawny lad with lank, brown hair.

"I have business with Lord Jhinn," he announced.

A guard eyed Elthann's sturdy build, sharp features and wiry, grey hair. He exuded confidence - his apparel was fashionably styled.

Another was dispatched to obtain permission from Lord Jhinn. Elthann tapped his foot as the guard returned with a note addressed to the commander of the garrison.

Eventually, they let him pass and Elthann made his way to Jhinn's chambers, without his assistant.

Jhinn stared at the ring.

"Made of sylverine and set with the Stone of Korothon, as you desired," said Elthann with aplomb.

"It's beautiful. Your craftsmanship is unsurpassed."

"Praise indeed from you, my Lord Jhinn."

He gave the court jeweller a smile. "Are my demands so exacting?"

Elthann did not reply as he bowed low and withdrew.

"Saravia will love this. It's almost as beautiful as she," Jhinn said aloud.

He put the ring back into the silk pouch the jeweller had brought and went to the window, gazing longingly in the direction of the Imperial Forest.

Prince Orthon was in good spirits as they rode to Adranabar. Darthus remained at his side, as they galloped to the castle. Heavy clouds scudded across the sky and it started to rain. Darthus saw the outline of Castle Adranabar in the fading light.

Jhinn thought he heard a noise, like the sally-port opening, followed by the sound of running feet. He wondered if his uncle's army had returned. But dismissed the thought - they would enter through the main gate, not the sally-port. He was alarmed, watching the courtyard. He saw several shadows move quickly. Jhinn held his breath as the garrison fell one by one, overrun by rebel soldiers. He saw Mararuss ride through the main gate astride a black horse.

He reached for his sword and tucked a dagger into the sash fastened around his waist.

Jhinn locked the door, sliding the bookcase back to reveal a staircase leading down to the stables – once on the first step - he slid it back into place behind him. The stairwell was pitch black, damp and musty. He slipped several times as he made a hasty descent, gripping the rough stone sides to steady himself. He found the door at the bottom was locked. He could hear the sound of feet above him - the rebels must have broken into his chamber. He was sure they would find the secret staircase if they looked hard enough.

He felt frantically for the key. His hands grappled for the recess in the wall. It must be here, he thought, hearing a clink of iron as it landed on the ground. He knew he had dislodged it from its hiding place, crouching he used his fingers to search the floor. Suddenly, he felt cold metal, with deft fingers he picked it up, thrusting it into the lock as fast as he could. He felt the key turn, but the lock would not budge. Beads of sweat formed on his brow and he began to despair. He made several more attempts, without success, then finally the lock freed, pushing the door open cautiously, he tried to determine whether there were any soldiers in the stables.

Jhinn saw nothing and thought the rebels must be concentrating on the castle itself. He saw Atheil hiding near the entrance observing activity in the courtyard, his hand gripping the hilt of his sword. Jhinn ran towards Atheil, but as he broke cover,

Mararuss charged into the stables, bearing down on him with such speed he had no time to escape. Mararuss threw himself from his horse, pinning Jhinn to the ground. Atheil tried to overpower Mararuss, but he was set upon by rebel soldiers and thrown down.

Mararuss pulled Jhinn from the ground, holding a knife to his son's throat.

"Prince Orthon and his army are outside the castle walls!" a rebel soldier cried.

"Well, it's about time Orthon showed up. A pretty hostage you'll make," said Mararuss.

Jhinn struggled against his father but to no avail.

"What shall we do with this one?" a rebel soldier enquired.

Mararuss glanced at Atheil. "He's Lord Griann's man. He might fetch a hefty ransom. We'll parade the hostages along the battlements and give Orthon something to think about," he replied with a grin.

As Jhinn was led up the steps he saw a rebel soldier hand a purse to the jeweller's assistant.

Salmir, Aramintha and Atheil were paraded along the battlements. Jhinn felt sorry for Aramintha, she was shivering and frightened. He felt embarrassed listening to his father and uncle trade insults.

Darthus stared at Aramintha. He was concerned for her safety at the hands of the rebels. He watched the Prince vent his fury as Mararuss goaded and taunted him.

"And your sister was a whore," Mararuss cried.

Jhinn was appalled and all fell silent.

Prince Orthon turned to Darthus. "Lay siege to the castle," he commanded.

The Whispering Sea shone black. These were uncharted waters for the Acelphidi, the air smelt strange to them and their direction was uncertain.

Rharll stood on the deck of the pirate ship, the surface awash with sea water. He reached out to steady himself as the vessel rocked, staring into the darkness, he saw tiny lights in the distance and was not sure whether they were from ships or reflections of the moon. He was almost invisible. His hair was the colour of night. Black markings on his face blended into the darkness. A broad ring of sylverine on the third finger of his left hand was the only visible part of him. His tall, slender frame swayed, as he felt for the dagger in his belt.

He gave the order to sail towards the lights in a quiet, rasping voice - a hallmark of Acelphidi. The ship moved to port as the breeze filled black linen sails, emblazoned with a silver circle.

Caius was at a loss. He could not remember a time when Adranus had been so agitated and upset. He felt the ship pitch in the water, a wind was getting up. A sense of foreboding washed over him as the realization of approaching battle came to him.

Sapphire made towards the deck of *Azenia* to recite the incantation. She saw Hhariann at the prow and heard him growling. She gazed at the Whispering Sea, thinking how dark the water was and noticed the red lights of the Acelphidi in the distance. Then she saw something else. A sequence of lights reflected on the water shone in the direction of the pirate ships. Below deck someone was signalling to the Acelphidi.

Sapphire felt hot and weak, wondering whether someone on board was in league with them. She shuddered at the thought.

Hhariann's ears twitched, seeming to sense her unsettled state of mind. He padded towards her, his paws pounding the deck. Suddenly, the signalling stopped. Hhariann's wings flexed as if he wanted to fly. But he remained at her side, resting his broad chin on the rail of the ship - his whiskers quivering in the breeze.

Admiral Oxghar was concerned Sapphire might fall overboard if she grew weak whilst summoning the mist. When he reached the deck he saw Sapphire and Hhariann looking over the side and made towards them.

"Admiral, someone is signalling the Acelphidi from their cabin. I saw lights reflected on the water," said Sapphire in an anxious tone.

"Look!" Sapphire cried.

Admiral Oxghar watched - a startled expression on his face. "I'm going to investigate."

Sapphire took the amulet from its pouch and began falling into a trance. She started to recite a mantra and strands of vapour rose from the Whispering Sea. Hhariann was transfixed as it enfolded the ship.

Admiral Oxghar's feet echoed below deck, bursting through the cabin door he thought was nearest the reflection of light, he was confronted by Gille, Lord Caton's servant, wearing a contemptuous expression. He strode past him to find Lord Caton standing by the cabin window holding a crystal goblet to a candle flame. Refracted light played on the sea.

"Stop that!" said Admiral Oxghar snatching the goblet from Lord Caton's hand.

"Well really, that's most uncalled for, Admiral. Most uncalled for."

Niaa smiled, The Black Witch's lair was cold and smelt of evil. Khinart was a generous patron, giving her jewels and a wing of the Palace of Khorec, in return for her help defeating Caedec and his allies. She was only too pleased by the pact she had struck with Maladoria's ruler and self-proclaimed King.

Niaa gazed at the crystal. She could see the dark water of the Whispering Sea and the fleet of Acelphidi. She saw no other ships, only a rising mist.

She sighed, wondering if the Red King was planning to invade Maladoria and thinking it might be just a rumour. By all accounts his life in exile had left him a broken man, a shadow of his former self and what chance would an invasion have? Khinart had all but wiped out the War Kotroi, Niaa thought admiring a pelt lying on the floor. She heard the door opening and footsteps. Her patron had arrived.

Rharll was uneasy. He could see a mist rising, as his ship made towards it. Sea water splashed over the side, white spray clung to the blackened bones and sinew covering the pirate ship, souvenirs of bloody forays across the seas beyond The Delvia States. He had a bad feeling about this voyage and nothing had happened to dispel it. Rharll watched the other ships draw alongside.

Lord Caton stared at Admiral Oxghar as he placed the goblet on the table.

"Were you signalling to another ship, Lord Caton?"

"Of course not, how dare you say such a thing."

"I accept it's a serious accusation. However, a sequence of signals was seen coming from the vicinity of your cabin."

"I was merely inspecting the crystal ware. Why, it might have been damaged coming on board. I fail to see what you're upset about."

"Lord Caton, I believe there are Acelphidi in these waters and your inspection of crystal by candlelight may have drawn attention to our presence here."

"Acelphidi, you say – those barbarians who think it good sport to rip out their victims' hearts while they're still alive?" he enquired flopping down on the nearest chair.

"I believe so," said Admiral Oxghar.

Lord Caton was ashen. "This is Khinart's doing. He has offered them generous terms to venture out of their territory. I expect Niaa has some involvement in luring them here."

Admiral Oxghar was surprised. You think they have formed an alliance?"

"Quite likely, all too likely, I'm sorry to say."

"Forgive me, Lord Caton, I must leave you. I believe I'm needed on deck."

Admiral Oxghar found Sapphire slumped on deck. He saw the mist was steadily rising, though it was not dense enough to obscure the ship. "Sapphire! Wake up!"

She stirred, opening her eyes. "I'm so tired, Admiral."

"You must raise the mist or we're lost."

Sapphire nodded, gripping the rail. Gai appeared through the swirling, vapour.

"Admiral! What in Crilm's name is happening here?" he said, rushing towards Sapphire.

"Lord Gai, I was assisting Sapphire in her magical endeavours - the mist must rise or we're lost to the Acelphidi."

"And at what cost to Sapphire. Can't you see how ill it has made her? Give me the amulet, Sapphire - let me finish this," said Gai.

"Never!"

A sound of clinking bones on the pirate ships drifted over the Whispering Sea. A shot was fired across *Azenia's* bows and the air resounded with cannon fire.

"Too late," stated Admiral Oxghar.

Sapphire continued to recite the incantation. Admiral Oxghar, Gai and Hhariann stared at the pirate ships as they gained on the Maladorian fleet. Gai was transfixed with horror at the sight of them.

"May Crilm shield us from them," he uttered as they drew nearer.

Admiral Oxghar was silent as the Acelphidi fired a volley of cannon. Gai saw The Crown Prince's ship take a broadside.

Thoro rushed to the Admiral's side. "I await your orders - the guns are primed and ready to fire."

"Thank you, Thoro. I was hoping to conserve as much ammunition as possible for the main onslaught. I don't want to waste it on shadowy targets."

Thoro was disappointed. He was longing to take a shot at the Acelphidi.

A mist rose dense as a warrior's shield. A strong wind filled the warships' sails and at last the pirate ships fell behind.

A look of horror crossed Rharll's face as his vessel sailed into the mist. His mind frantically sought a means of escape, but he knew his fate was sealed. He prayed to the dark gods – asking them to spare him.

Admiral Oxghar saw legions of hands rise from beneath the Whispering Sea.

"Irmardia," he murmured.

As *Azenia* gained speed and just before the mist obscured the Acelphidi completely, he watched the pirate ships sink, pulled down into the depths by outstretched hands.

Strands of smoke rose from *Amalande,* The Crown Prince's warship, into a pale sky. Remnants of mist lingered above the water - the ships were on course for Maladoria. *Amalande* had sustained damage to its hull, but otherwise the fleet was sound and ready for battle.

Admiral Oxghar was slumped over his writing table. His sleeping head resting on crumpled maps. He stirred hearing the sound of wet footsteps on polished floorboards. He felt a cold hand stroke his hair. Queen Irmardia was standing by his side. "My love, you're here," he said.

Queen Irmardia sat in a chair by the writing table - the hem of her silver gown was covered in strands of seaweed. "The Acelphidi have gone. My people sank the pride of their fleet and drove them out of these waters."

"I'm eternally grateful, Irmardia."

"I am pleased of it."

Admiral Oxghar's hand reached for hers. He clasped it tightly in his own. Their rings fused together with a frisson of energy.

"So we have an understanding, Lhimm?"

He gazed at her in rapture. "We have, my love."

She smiled. A smile so radiant it filled the cabin with light. He grinned, tightening his grip on her hand. He glanced at the unfinished poem on the table with a sad expression.

"A King may write poetry. There are halls of writing in our cities."

Admiral Oxghar nodded. "But there are no forests like those of Aizan."

Queen Irmardia was irritated - pulling her hand away their rings came apart with a blue flash of energy. "I thought we had an understanding. Now I'm not so sure."

"Am I not allowed to miss my homeland?"

"Of course you are. I've seen the forests of Aizan. They're magnificent."

"Then we understand each other?"

"Indeed we do. I must go, Lhimm. My ministers are expecting me. There's much to do."

"Of course you are needed elsewhere."

"Be careful, Lhimm. The battle for Maladoria will not be easy - I'll help if I can."

Admiral Oxghar's expression darkened. "Let us hope victory is ours."

Sapphire was resting when Caedec entered. "I have come to thank you for risking your life, Sapphire. Your noble efforts saved us from the barbarous Acelphidi, and for that I am forever in your debt."

"Then it has been worthwhile"

"Indeed," replied Caedec with a look of admiration.

The seer did not stir. As the sun rose his spirit departed for the Vale of Wolves. Caius shed a tear.

Merrick was carrying a tray filled with goblets, when he heard the sound of sobbing coming from Adranus's quarters. He stopped to listen and decided to enquire further. He tapped on the cabin door with one hand, balancing the tray on the other. There was no answer. He was concerned as he nudged the door open, placing the tray on the nearest table. He found Caius kneeling by Adranus's bed. He saw the seer's hand hanging over the side like a withered root.

"My dear Caius, my poor dear Caius," he uttered.

Caius seemed oblivious to Merrick's presence.

"I'll send for the King's physician."

Merrick withdrew in search of help. He came upon Thoro patrolling the ship.

"Something awful has happened. Would you fetch the King's physician, Adranus has need of him - I pray it's not too late. I'll tell the King," said Merrick all a fluster.

Hhannon followed Thoro to Adranus's cabin, his steps falling lightly on the boards. He carried a black wooden box decorated with a dragon. Thoro offered to carry it for him several times, but on each occasion he politely refused, as if it was too precious to entrust to anyone other than himself.

Merrick found Caedec in Sapphire's cabin, talking to Gai as Sapphire slept.

"Sire, Adranus is unwell."

Gai and Caedec wore startled expressions.

"I've taken the liberty of sending for your physician. I could think of no other action. Please forgive me."

"There's nothing to forgive, Merrick. I presume the situation is serious."

"I would say so."

"Then we must go to Adranus. Perhaps we can be of some assistance. How is Caius?" enquired Caedec.

"He's rather quiet."

Caius watched as the King's physician examined Adranus. He hoped he was mistaken and Adranus was sleeping - Hhannon's expression was impassive. Caius could not read his thoughts. Hhannon shook his head and let go of the seer's hand. In his heart Caius knew Adranus had begun his journey to the Vale of Wolves.

With a handkerchief he wiped his tears away and rose to his feet, knowing the King would come to pay his respects to his beloved seer of the unseen.

Adranus lay lifeless and cold, as dignified in death as in life. He had not lived to see Maladoria again. Caius thought the fates could be cruel.

Caedec's presence lifted the atmosphere. He stood erect and dignified as Caius and the physician bowed to him. Caedec sensed Adranus had gone and was consumed by sadness. "We have lost a dear friend."

"His spirit followed the wolf - its mark is upon him. It was his time," said Hhannon.

Lucha wiped Sapphire's brow with a damp cloth. She pulled herself up as Lucha adjusted the pillows. "How long have I slept, Lucha?" she enquired with a dazed expression.

"A while my lady."

"Where is Gai? I thought he was here," she said.

"He has gone, my lady. He attends the King."

"I see. I expect they have much to discuss."

"Yes, poor Adranus. Such a shame to hear..." said Lucha, stopping as she realized Sapphire was unaware of his passing.

"Adranus has not left us? Has he Lucha?"

"I'm afraid so, my lady."

Caius stood on deck. He felt empty, his emotions spent as he read his friend's Will of Wishes. Adranus wanted to be buried in Maladoria near the Palace of Khorec. His body an offering to the woodland God, his bones would feed the trees and he would live on through them.

Night had passed and the dawn heralded a new day. Rosy strips of light streaked the sky as Thoro gazed into the distance.

"That's Maladoria all right," he said aloud as he went below to tell the Admiral the good news.

Admiral Oxghar was sitting at his writing table when he entered the cabin. Thoro noticed wet spots on the maps spread out in front of him and wondered what to say.

"Sad news, Thoro - Adranus has gone."

"Gone, sir?"

"Yes, he has departed to the Vale of Wolves."

Thoro's expression changed to one of sadness. "Poor soul and he was almost home."

"Now, have you anything to report?" enquired the Admiral, changing the subject and composing himself.

"Yes, we're on course and on schedule," he said, noticing wet marks on the floorboards and a trail of seaweed as he waited for a reply.

"Keep me informed, Thoro."

Gai and Caedec were on deck. Sorrow was etched on their faces. Their hands gripped the rail as *Azenia* ploughed through the sea. A spray of water covered the King's cloak.

"Our voyage has been tinged with sadness, Gai."

"It has and now we must continue without our seer's sage advice. A great blow to our campaign and a personal loss for us all, especially Caius."

"It is as you say, Gai. I hope Caius will not fare too badly. His loss is greater than we can imagine. He has no other kin in the worlds."

Gai stared at the sea as Admiral Oxghar joined them.

"We're travelling at a steady rate," he said.

"Ship ahoy!" a cry came from aloft.

Admiral Oxghar looked through his telescope.

"Khinart's fleet, I assume?" Caedec replied.

Admiral Oxghar nodded in agreement.

"Then he is prepared for battle," Gai stated.

"That would seem to be the case," said the Admiral.

"How is *Amalande* faring?" enquired Caedec.

"Well enough, the damage isn't serious," Admiral Oxghar replied.

"Then we must prepare to face the enemy," said Caedec.

Caius sat by the coffin, the ship's carpenters had worked quickly and made the best one they could, given the materials to hand. He stared at his friend's waxen features for the last time, then closed the lid and bound it with three white silk ribbons. "Farewell," he said putting the last one in place.

Khinart stood at the prow. He was a tall man, with handsome features, olive skin and eyes like a raven. "Take no prisoners," he commanded, addressing the captain.

Niaa smiled. She bit her lip, tasting the blood as she gazed at Khinart. "And the King?" she enquired. "We want him taken alive. We'll send him to the gallows with his Queen. I'll use his hide as a rug, like that hapless Kotroi," she enthused.

"Enough! The Queen will be spared," Khinart replied.

"Spared...? Has she bewitched you with her beauty and good nature? Are you in love with her?" she enquired, her eyes wide with amazement.

Niaa sidled up to him. "What of Tsabani. You promised her the King and Queen would die in return for her support. She's our friend," she hissed.

"What do I care for promises," he retorted.

"Hah! You want Caedec's wife for yourself. Ruling his country must be an added privilege."

"The Queen will be spared – I have my reasons," said Khinart, giving her a black look. "We wait for battle to commence."

Azenia sailed the Whispering Sea, a strong wind behind her - a lion wind, wild and unruly. Khinart's fleet was clustered along the coastline. There would be no element of surprise to help the Maladorians.

Admiral Oxghar and Thoro studied Khinart's ships and decided on a battle plan. They thought the fleet should be split into two with each group taking a formation line astern. In this way they hoped to draw Khinart's vessels out to sea, breaking their line. *Azenia* would lead the first group. *Amalande* would lead the other. Caedec was in agreement and the order was signalled to the war fleet.

Gai and Caedec watched as *Amalande* drew alongside followed by several warships manoeuvring to take their positions behind The Crown Prince's vessel.

Sorrel gazed nervously at the Whispering Sea. The Knights of the Order of the Median wore the attire of battle. The Crown Prince's men lined the ship's rail ready to face the enemy. The Crown Prince drew his sword gazing at its blade as he held it aloft. "May Crilm and his sisters bless us and protect us as we sail into battle. So be it."

"So be it," echoed *Amalande's* crew.

Several ships of the fleet positioned themselves behind *Azenia* - the lines of battle were complete. Admiral Oxghar looked through his telescope. Khinart's fleet was sailing towards them. He could see their sails embroidered with gold gryphons. Caedec felt his chest tighten as the Admiral passed the telescope to him and he saw the enemy through the lens. Khinart's vessels were much bigger than *Azenia* and *Amalande*. Caedec lowered the telescope and gave the Admiral a grave look.

"Gentlemen, don your battle attire. We haven't much time," said Caedec.

Merrick helped him dress. Caedec studied his sword before placing it in its scabbard. "Action is imminent, Merrick. Take Liviaa and Janus to Sapphire's cabin and stay there. Lock the door and let us pray we are not boarded."

"Of course, may Crilm be with you, sire."

"And you."

Caedec smiled as Liviaa and Janus ran to him.

"Is there going to be a battle?" Janus enquired.

"Yes, Janus, there is. I want you to look after Merrick, Liviaa, Sapphire and Lucha while I'm gone."

Janus's expression changed, his excitement dampened. "Yes, sire."

"That's a good lad. Keep them safe and you will be rewarded."

Janus's face lit up.

Gai sheathed his sword, as he made to the deck he saw it was swarming with soldiers and crew taking up their places. Admiral Oxghar and Thoro were deep in conversation with the King. Khinart's fleet was drawing nearer. Battle was about to commence.

Khinart's attire was as black as his expression. He hungered for combat and death. Niaa stood beside him. She too was dressed for war. She laughed - a sound like shards of glass blown on to a mountainside.

Caius sat by Adranus's coffin with a dagger poised at his chest.

"Let me follow you," he said, his hand gripping the hilt as he prepared to plunge the blade into his heart.

"Don't be such a fool," Caius heard Adranus's voice loud in his ears.

"Why? There's nothing for me here."

"The Vale of Wolves is barred to you, Caius - it's not your time."

Caius was crestfallen, his hold on the dagger's handle loosened. "Where are you?"

"I am near - I have yet to enter the vale. I trust Carvenn will meet me at the gates. I'm sorry there was no time to say farewell. Forgive me, Caius. I'll help you when I can. Now take heart and protect the King. He has need of you - go!"

As Adranus's voice drifted away Caius listened to the silence as the dagger slipped from his hand on to the rug. Adranus's favourite – of all his possessions he had favoured this one most, woven with the shapes of animals from the forests of Maladoria.

Azenia shuddered. Caius heard the sound of cannon. He opened the cabin door, listening he heard the sound of cannon fire again.

He made his way up to the deck, hoping Crilm would guide and protect him.

Khinart's fleet was within range though there was no sign that either *Azenia* or *Amalande* had returned any fire. They were waiting until the ships drew nearer in the hope of exacting extensive damage to the enemy. A cloud of smoke drifted over the Whispering Sea. Caius breathed the acrid air.

Admiral Oxghar gazed at the dolphin swimming alongside *Azenia* and took comfort from its presence.

Khinart's fleet continued to bombard the Maladorian ships with cannon as the sky darkened and billowing clouds of smoke clung to the vessels like shrouds of the dead.

Admiral Oxghar looked through his telescope. He was alarmed at the sight of so many enemy ships. Khinart's fleet far outnumbered the Maladorian's. He gave the order to return fire with heated shot - the noise was deafening. One of Khinart's ship's masts was shot away - the burning sails fell in sheets of fire. And so the battle raged.

"Any sign of Tsabani's ships, Admiral?" Caedec enquired.

"I haven't seen them. Lord Fhinn's are bringing up the rear."

"Khinart has more ships than we anticipated, is that not so, Admiral?"

"I'm afraid it is."

An enemy shot cut into *Amalande* and she began to take in water. Another razed the mast and sails - the rigging caught fire and rapidly started to burn. Gai and Caedec stared at *Amalande* in horror. *Azenia's* crew lowered rowing boats into the water as it became obvious The Crown Prince's ship was sinking.

Hhariann made several attempts to attack the enemy fleet. He circled and swooped at their sails but the cannon fire and a hail of burning arrows drove him off and he returned to *Azenia,* where Caedec forbade him to make any more forays, knowing he could easily be mortally wounded.

The Crown Prince, Sorrel and several knights clambered into the boats. Others were not as fortunate – *Amalande's* loss was a severe blow.

"I see Queen Tsabani's ships," said Admiral Oxghar with a degree of optimism as several sailed into view. Admiral Oxghar saw their golden sails with the emblem of a serpent in the centre. He breathed deeply, wondering if their fortunes would change.

Sapphire felt uneasy. "I'm going to help," she announced.

Merrick was horrified. "The King will not be pleased if you put yourself and others in danger."

Lucha gazed at Sapphire. "Please don't leave us."

Sapphire ignored their pleas and went up on deck. She noticed Admiral Oxghar, Gai and Caedec clustered around The Crown Prince's body. She saw blood seeping from a wound in his shoulder. He had been hit by a piece of shot. She smelt fear and suffering as clouds of smoke drifted across the sky.

"Take The Crown Prince below, my physician will see to him."

Sapphire rushed to where The Crown Prince lay. She gazed at his pale countenance and held his hand. Several of *Azenia's* crew made towards them. The Crown Prince had lost consciousness and was oblivious to his surroundings. Gai gently prized her away.

Admiral Oxghar held his telescope to his eye and then passed it to the King. Queen Tsabani's ships were travelling at a steady rate.

Khinart's ships continued to bombard the Maladorian fleet with cannon. Admiral Oxghar was concerned. They had lost several ships including *Amalande* - one they could ill afford to lose.

Caedec watched Queen Tsabani's ships. Some of the crew were busy ferrying the wounded below. Their cries were pitiful. Those gravely injured and dying were left where they lay as the battle took its toll. He passed the telescope back to the Admiral and went to comfort the dying.

Admiral Oxghar looked through the telescope. He watched Queen Tsabani's ships knowing they could make all the difference to the battle. Praying they would join the King's fleet, but to his dismay he saw the golden sails merge with those of Khinart's fleet. She had broken her promise and was siding with the King's enemy.

Thoro read the Admiral's expression. Defeat was etched on his features. Caedec watched their exchange and knew what the Admiral would say.

"I fear the battle is lost. I suggest we retreat and sail for Aizan."

"Is he gravely injured?" Sapphire enquired.

"The physician will determine that. Come, Sapphire – this is no place for the wounded. The Crown Prince must be moved below deck," said Gai.

Hhannon came scurrying to Sapphire's cabin. Merrick ushered Liviaa and Janus away from the door as they brought The Crown Prince into the cabin and laid him in one of the state rooms.

Hhannon put his hand on The Crown Prince's pulse, nodding his head as he counted the beats. He addressed Merrick, Sapphire and Lucha who were standing around the bed gazing at him with expectation. "I need some boiled water."

Merrick disappeared in the direction of the galley and Lucha went to fetch some linen to use as dressings. Sapphire remained transfixed, frozen with shock at the sight of the gaping wound.

"Do you think...?" she began and then stopped, the words dying in her throat, as if she did not really want to hear the physician's reply.

"I've seen worse wounds than this one," he said, anticipating her question.

"Yes, I expect so," she replied.

Admiral Oxghar sighed at the view of his homeland, Aizan. The craggy coastline was a welcome sight and the forests beyond were lush with leaves of yellow and verdant green.

The ships were moored in a secluded cove, well hidden from the Whispering Sea. Caedec and his retinue were ready to travel inland as soon as the horses were guided safely on to the shore.

Lord Fhinn lived deep in the forests. It would be a ride through rugged terrain to ask for his help and sanctuary. Admiral Oxghar breathed the Aizan air, a scent of wood and grasses filling his lungs. He felt he had been away from his homeland too long as he walked up the hill. When he reached the top he stopped to look at the valley below and the forests on either side. He heard a rustling in the grass followed by a loud voice.

"Well, my good friend, Lhimm Oxghar, you are home at last."

Admiral Oxghar turned to find Lord Fhinn of Aizan smiling at him.

"My Lord Fhinn, I cannot tell you how good it is to see you," he said, kneeling before his sovereign.

"And I, you, Admiral," he replied with a broad grin.

Lord Fhinn stood tall and straight. His eyes shone with good humour. His hair fell onto his shoulders in a golden cascade. He was accompanied by two Karatroi, large cat-like animals - distant relatives of Kotroi.

"My Lord Fhinn, may I speak with candour as your loyal subject?"

"Of course, I'm surprised to find you here in Aizan."

"My lord, I am afraid all has not gone well with our voyage to Maladoria."

"Ah, so it's true the battle is over, Khinart is victorious and you've come here seeking sanctuary."

"My sovereign is very perceptive."

Lord Fhinn was thoughtful. "Consider it granted. I care nothing for that upstart, Khinart and his Black Witch. Is the Red King safe?"

"He is, my lord."

"Then let us thank Crilm for that mercy."

"My lord, I cannot thank you enough. We have lost ships, men, our seer, Adranus and The Crown Prince of Ilesh lies wounded."

"I'm sorry to hear it. You've had an eventful voyage, if an unfortunate one. Perhaps the time has come to rest and contemplate the journey."

"Come, Lhimm let us not be sad. We must give thanks for our meeting here at this time. All is as it should be in the worlds. I believe that. I'll send my men to help you. You shall have everything you require."

"Thank you, my lord. I will speak to the King of your great kindness."

Lord Fhinn clasped the Admiral's shoulder.

"It's good to see you, Lhimm. I go to prepare my lodge for your arrival."

The Lord of Aizan set off in the direction of the forests, flanked by his faithful Karatroi. A cold wind swirled up through the valley as the Admiral watched him go.

When Admiral Oxghar returned the horses were grazing on the hillside.

Caius walked among them patting them as he went. He was pleased they were in good spirits.

Gai and Caedec paced the shore.

"The Crown Prince's wound concerns me, Gai. More than I can say."

"He has the best care we can offer. Your physician attends him day and night and Sapphire sits by his bed. What more can we do for him?"

"And if he dies what then?"

Gai paused, noticing Admiral Oxghar approach. "Let us pray he has some good news for us."

"Sire, my Lord Gai. I bring tidings," said the Admiral bowing. "I encountered Lord Fhinn while strolling on the hillside. He has granted us sanctuary."

"Admiral, I applaud you. That is good news," replied Caedec.

As promised, Lord Fhinn's men arrived to help the King and his retinue unload their chattels. The Crown Prince and the wounded were transported in litters and in a short time they were on their way to meet Aizan's ruler. Hhariann circled overhead as the ships were left with skeleton crews to guard them.

Their progress was slow as Lord Fhinn's men led the horses down on to a grassy plateau. A forest lay beyond - the scent of the trees was heady and sweet.

Queen Tsabani watched the rain as it poured down the mullioned windows of her palace in Azuriene. She held her hand to the glass. Gold rings coiled around her fingers. A necklace of pearls glistened in the yellow light. Her hair was plaited around her head, another string of pearls woven through it. Her complexion was like polished marble, reflected in the glass. She heard a light knock. "Come," she commanded, turning to face the door, watching as her Chief Minister Marial, Duke of Azur, entered.

He doffed his black, pearl encrusted hat with a flourish. He was a handsome man, older than QueenTsabani, yet he retained a youthful air. His hair was a shining mass of black curls. His eyes were a startling hue of emerald. He was a man who kept his own counsel. He had no confidantes at court.

Duke Marial of Azur's hands clasped a letter bearing a black seal. "Your Majesty, this has arrived for you."

Queen Tsabani took the letter from the Duke's bejewelled hand. As she read it a tear fell from her eye, falling on to the faded rug. She faced the window again, hiding her tears from him. A Golden Hare sat on the palace lawn. She gazed at its coat of liquid gold and shuddered, thinking it a bad omen.

"What troubles you, Tsabani? We know each other well. I can tell when you're upset. Has the content of the letter displeased you? Was it not the news you hoped for? What of Lord Caton?"

Queen Tsabani gathered her thoughts, trying to compose herself. "It seems Lord Caton has betrayed me. He signalled the Acelphidi, but his message caused confusion and their attack was thwarted. They suffered substantial losses - Rharll went down with his ship. How stupid of me to trust him. See to it his lands are forfeit – there's no place for him in Azuriene!"

Duke Marial nodded in agreement.

"Khinart has won the battle. He has defeated the Maladorian fleet. *Amalande* is sunk and The Crown Prince is presumed drowned," she said, her voice cracking with emotion. "I pray my niece still lives."

A look of confusion crossed the Duke's face. "Forgive me, but is that not the news you desired? Your fleet has ..." he said stopping in mid sentence.

Marial was no fool and quickly realized the Queen had hopes of being reconciled with The Crown Prince and now they were dashed and she was vulnerable. He wondered if this could be the opportunity he had waited for. He decided to seize the moment. "My dear Tsabani, you mustn't reproach yourself. Such events could not be foreseen."

Queen Tsabani's face flushed. "Of course they could. Niaa saw it as it would be. I have been tricked by flattery and promises - now Khinart has killed the only man I ever loved or wanted for a husband."

Duke Marial drew closer, putting his arm around her waist. He touched her face, gazing at her with adoration. "Tsabani, don't despair. This is a great victory. At last you have revenge on your brother-in-law for casting you aside. And The Crown Prince cruelly neglected you before breaking your betrothal. As for a husband, there's someone here, who wouldn't refuse you and has always loved you. Why he would be the happiest of men if your gaze and affections should settle upon him."

Queen Tsabani, blushed as she studied the Duke's handsome features. "Then that is something I shall consider."

Gai and Caedec gazed at the structure with amazement.

The Lodge, as Lord Fhinn called his residence, was made of wood, black with age and so tall its roof almost reached the sky.

"I've heard of the Legend of Zansarial. Apparently, the Aizan's called a tree after the god who climbed its trunk, taking refuge from a blizzard amongst its branches. If you find it and touch its bark, your dreams will come true. Look, the carving depicts the legend," said Gai pointing to the outline of a tree incised on Lord Fhinn's abode.

"Remarkable," replied Caedec.

Two immense doors opened and Lord Fhinn, dressed in a cloak of green, descended several steps to greet his guests. "Caedec, what a pleasure to see you again," he said ushering him inside.

Lord Fhinn engaged Caedec in conversation as they walked through the hall lit by candles set in silver circles hanging from a vaulted ceiling and lined with paintings of wolves and dragons. Lord Fhinn had been as good as his word. A feast had been prepared. As they reached the Banqueting Hall, Caedec could see tables covered with plates piled with food.

Merrick gasped at the sight of so many alphus berry cakes.

"I have a little supper for us, my good King," said Lord Fhinn.

Caedec smiled. "Thank you, my Lord of Aizan. My gratitude is beyond words."

"Then I'm pleased," he replied indicating a table at the end of the Banqueting Hall.

A turn of fate seated Admiral Oxghar next to Lord Caton. Admiral Oxghar felt uncomfortable in such close proximity to him. Music played as they ate and drank and the Banqueting Hall rang with laughter.

Lord Fhinn filled Caedec's goblet with Adras. "A good vintage -here's to Adras - a wonderful wine and a great source of income for my friend, Griann," said Lord Fhinn as their goblets clinked. "How are things in Adranabar, Caedec?" he enquired in a serious tone.

Caedec grimaced.

"I've heard rumours of rebellion in your cousin's realm. Pity, I like Orthon, but he's a headstrong fellow and his rule is absolute – it doesn't suit everyone," said Lord Fhinn.

"You're right, my lord. All is not well in Orthon's realm. He is a good man and Adranabar is not an easy country to govern, the Lords of the Northern Isles, grow richer and more powerful – they do not like to be controlled."

Lord Fhinn nodded in agreement. "Tell me about your quest, Caedec. How goes it?"

"Alas, not as well as I had hoped - Tsabani sided with Khinart and our ships were outnumbered. We lost *Amalande* and The Crown Prince was wounded."

Lord Fhinn wore a serious expression. "A sad business, *Amalande* was a good ship. I remember when she was built. How is The Crown Prince?"

"He is resting and his wound is healing, I confess I feared the worst for him."

"He's a strong lad. He'll be all right," said Lord Fhinn in a reassuring tone. "What are your plans now? Have you contemplated your next move?"

Caedec fell silent, shaking his head.

"Then might I suggest an offensive from here in Aizan?"

Caedec raised an eyebrow. "I'm listening – what do you propose?"

"Why not make to the border, head towards Sarhynel and strike at the heart of Maladoria - the seat of Khinart's power. Your people will help you overthrow him. He's not fit to rule. He treats them with contempt - they care nothing for him, so I've heard. You're their King and they love you, my friend."

Caedec was thoughtful.

"You won't fail. I'll send my men with you and at the same time a fleet will sail to Maladoria. Khinart will think you come again by sea. He'll be full of arrogance from his victory and overconfident – he may be careless and make a mistake," Lord Fhinn continued with enthusiasm.

"And what do you want in return?"

"Peace along my borders again and a neighbouring ruler I can trust."

"Then we have an agreement."

Their goblets clinked again and more Adras was drunk than was wise. And no one seemed to care.

Sapphire sat by The Crown Prince's bed reading from a volume of Admiral Oxghar's poetry.

The Crown Prince was awake but still pale and listless. He looked dejected, haunted by the memory of drowning men and the demise of *Amalande*, knowing Arrkir would use its loss to cause dissent.

Admiral Oxghar gazed in awe at the craftsmen, noticing several vessels in various stages of construction, on the shore beyond the forest. Walking up the hill, he stopped to look at the view of the village where he grew up.

Catching sight of the graveyard beside Crilm's Temple he felt a crushing sadness. He thought of his family sleeping in the earth and longed for their comforting presence, wondering why he had been left to wander the worlds alone.

Admiral Oxghar stood in front of the house and thought it changed. As he gazed at its square paned windows he heard children playing in the gardens, as he had done. He saw his mother's face at the window and turned away, disturbed by ghosts and knowing he would never return.

Lord Fhinn laid several maps on a table in the Banqueting Hall. Gai and Caedec stared at them with furrowed brows.

"Here is a way," said Lord Fhinn, his broad fingers tracing a line on the parchment.

Gai and Caedec exchanged glances.

"It will not be easy – the road to Sarhynel will be guarded by Khinart's men," replied Caedec scratching his head.

"We've come so far, we can't turn back now. Where would we go?" Gai replied in an earnest tone.

Caedec nodded. "Gentlemen, we have a new plan - to Maladoria!" he said in a rousing tone.

Chapter 27 – Siege

The siege of Castle Adranabar was dragging on and Darthus was weary of Prince Orthon's impatience. Mararuss was in no hurry to surrender.

Jhinn was standing at the window, staring at the courtyard. He felt dizzy and weak from hunger as he watched the rebels with their grimy faces full of discontent. He heard them grumbling about their conditions and meagre pay. Several complained that the families they had left behind had little to eat and they had nothing to send them to alleviate their suffering. "Father's popularity seems to be waning," he said aloud, observing the general dissatisfaction prevalent in the ranks.

Aramintha wandered the corridors, searching for Mararuss. She had decided to plead for her father's release - the siege had weakened his constitution and she was worried about him. She hoped Mararuss would show mercy and release him.

"What do you want?" said one of the rebels, as she approached the apartments usually occupied by Prince Orthon.

"I would like to speak to your leader, Mararuss."

"Wait here," the rebel growled.

Aramintha waited for the rebel soldier to return.

"Mararuss will see you. Follow me."

Aramintha was announced. Mararuss was sitting in Prince Orthon's favourite chair with his feet resting on the side of the fireplace. She was shocked by his appearance. His face was gaunt as he stared at a portrait minature with hollow eyes.

"I loved her, you know. They say I didn't, but that isn't true. In the end it was her brother who drove us apart. Orthon thought I wasn't good enough for his sister," he said.

Aramintha sensed his sadness as she watched him continue gazing at the portrait miniature.

"Mararuss please let my father go. He's ailing and too proud to plead for himself."

He stirred, as if from a dream, fixing his gaze on her. "I wish your father no ill, Aramintha - he will be released. Have you any other requests?"

Aramintha was amazed. "No, but thank you, your kindness is appreciated."

"I will tell the guards to release him. And in return he will negotiate with Orthon for me."

Aramintha's eyes widened. "You want him to negotiate with Prince Orthon?" she enquired, repeating the words in disbelief.

"That's what I said. He will deliver a letter for me."

A rebel soldier grabbed Salmir's arm, waking him from a deep sleep. "Mararuss says you can go. I'll take you to the gate."

"Go?" Where's my daughter? Has Mararuss released her too?" Salmir enquired.

"I've got orders to take you to the gate."

"I'm not going without my daughter."

"If I were you, I'd do as Mararuss says. Come on, before he changes his mind. You've to deliver this letter to the Prince for him," said the rebel handing him a scroll.

Salmir went through the gate, feeling disorientated he made towards Darthus, who guided him towards Prince Orthon.

"Salmir, how are you? Is Aramintha well? What news from within the castle walls? We've noticed little movement for a while now – are the rebels preparing to surrender?" enquired Darthus.

"What a terrible time, Darthus – we've had meagre rations and little water. But you're right something is amiss – the courtyard is too quiet. I noticed that on my way out."

Salmir handed the letter to Prince Orthon. "Mararuss commanded I deliver this in return for my freedom."

"What is the meaning of this?" Prince Orthon roared, shaking the scroll with fury. "Salmir, do you know what he has written?"

Salmir shook his head. "I do not."

"Then I'll read an extract from it,"

'Orthon, when you receive this, I will be far away from Castle Adranabar. Don't bother looking for Jhinn, Griann's man and Aramintha - I've taken them with me to ensure the safety of my person."

"Gone! How can this be?" Prince Orthon bellowed - his face flushed with anger.

Mararuss read the faded words on the tattered parchment, studying the plan, drawn in ink. "This way!" he commanded riding into a hidden tunnel at the rear of the stables, accompanied by several rebel soldiers carrying torches.

Jhinn was anxious, finding it hard to breathe. He found the noise of horses' hooves deafening. He hoped they would soon reach the end and be released from the nightmare that was the tunnel.

"Ram the gate!" yelled Prince Orthon.

Several soldiers were sent scurrying through the camp. They came back with reinforcements carrying the battering ram.

Darthus watched as the soldiers prepared to charge the main gate. After several attempts they broke through, the wood shattering in a hail of splinters. He was sad to see good craftsmanship destroyed.

Prince Orthon rode towards it with Darthus following in his wake. Castle Adranabar was silent as a tomb – they encountered no resistance from the rebels. Prince Orthon dismounted, making to the main building. Darthus tried to keep up with him, cursing his foolhardiness under his breath. He saw the Prince enter his apartment, hearing him curse in several languages, as he approached. Prince Orthon leaned over his writing table, sliding his hand back and forth underneath it. Darthus heard a click and Prince Orthon's hand emerged, holding a torn piece of parchment, with a detailed plan of the castle drawn on it.

Jhinn wondered if he was dead and being taken to the Vale of Wolves, as he gasped for air, struggling to breathe. His fingers gripped the reins as the noise made by the horses' hooves reached a crescendo.

He noticed the tunnel narrowing, sensing they were coming to the end. He heard shouting and scraping noises as a door opened and light poured in, dazzling the horses as they galloped into a clearing.

Jhinn's eyes smarted from the light, breathing the forest air he felt exhausted, his limbs racked with pain. He stared at his new environment, catching his breath as he came upon Mararuss engaged in conversation with Saravia's father. He pressed his mount forward a little, deciding he would try to eavesdrop on their conversation.

"No hard feelings then, Erarunde?" said Mararuss.

"I thought I'd seen the last of you," replied Erarunde scowling.

"Now that's no way to think of your old friend," said Mararuss laughing.

"I don't know how you can be merry at a time like this. Prince Orthon will scour this country until he finds you and hangs your hide out to dry. Don't ask me for any more favours – I've committed treason opening that tunnel for you."

Mararuss smiled. "It's not such a secret now is it?"

"If I were you I wouldn't tarry. It won't be long before Prince Orthon knows how you escaped and he'll come for you. There's more than one map."

"Perhaps he will. But I, my friend, will be gone. There's a ship moored off the coast and safe passage to The Delvia States, by virtue of the Emperor himself. My son will guarantee my safety," Mararuss boasted.

"Your son?" Erarunde uttered in disbelief. "You would hold the Prince's nephew to ransom - take him with you to the court of his uncle's enemy. He'll be slain by the Emperor's murderous emissaries. Have you no thought for him, Mararuss? Is there nothing you won't do to further your own gain?"

Erarunde was appalled. "My daughter will be looking for me. I bid you farewell."

"Ah yes, poor Saravia. I expect she'll be distraught when she hears her dear Jhinn has been spirited away," said Mararuss.

"What are you talking about?"

"Your daughter, my son and their secret trysts in the forest."

"What!"

"I have my spies, Erarunde."

"My daughter hasn't time for secret trysts."

"I see you don't want to lose her, my friend. But you will, if not to my son or Lord Griann, then to the Prince. If he sees her, he'll want to marry her - she looks so like his dead wife and sister."

"You talk in riddles, Mararuss. Again, I bid you farewell."

"May Crilm protect you, Lord Jhinn, I pray you come to no harm," said Erarunde as he marched past with a face like thunder.

Prince Orthon and Darthus approached the panel in the stable. Darthus stared at the painted scene. He gazed at Varmarah's face, hoping the rebels were treating her well. Prince Orthon rubbed the space between her eyes and the panel rolled to the side. Darthus was amazed when he saw the entrance to the tunnel.

"Guard this secret with your life, Darthus. To speak of it is treason. A crime I do not look kindly upon."

"You have my word."

Prince Orthon's expression was grave. "This is how the rebels escaped - we ride to the Imperial Forest, that's where it leads. We must make haste if we're to catch our quarry."

Lord Griann felt as if he had been travelling for eternity. And still was not sure where he was. He was confused as he tried to find his way through the trees. He recognized Saravia's father strolling along a path. "Erarunde," he shouted.

Erarunde's pace quickened when he saw Yarrow's golden form.

"Lord Griann! You're safe."

"I am, and pleased to see a friendly face."

Lord Griann dismounted, studying his features. "I see you're troubled."

"Not I, in fact I'm on my way home. I've finished my rounds of the forest and Saravia will wonder where I am. Much has happened since you disappeared, Lord Griann. Mararuss captured Castle Adranabar and Prince Orthon has laid siege to it. Come, Saravia's waiting."

"I see there have been developments since I was lost, wandering in the mist."

Sigamus ran to the door and Saravia knew someone was coming. She heard voices as it opened, gasping when she saw her father with Lord Griann.

"Thank Crilm you're safe," said Saravia.

"Aye lass, I found Lord Griann in the forest."

"Are you well, Lord Griann?" Saravia enquired, her cheeks flushed.

"I'm well, thank you, but hungry."

"Of course, I'll ask Cook to prepare something," she said making to the kitchen.

Erarunde showed Lord Griann into a chamber, while a meal was prepared for him.

"Make yourself comfortable, my lord. I expect you'd like a bath and a change of clothes."

"Griann, please address me as Griann."

"Of course, if you insist."

"A bath and a change of clothes would be most welcome, Erarunde. I would like to speak to you… about Saravia."

"Pray what of her?"

"I want to ask you for her hand in marriage."

Erarunde was astonished.

"I see you have not anticipated my request."

Erarunde scratched his head, his mind in a spin.

"I believe I have much to offer your daughter, position and influence in the worlds, which you of course will also benefit from. I love her and intend to dedicate my life to her happiness."

"I'll consider your proposal. Forgive me if I don't give you an answer. I've had a trying day."

Lord Griann was downcast and making his excuses withdrew to gather his thoughts, trying to hide his disappointment at Erarunde's reaction.

"Father! Come quickly, Prince Orthon is here," Saravia shouted, running down the hall.

Erarunde was startled. "Prince…here. Oh my word," he said, rushing to the window.

Erarunde was anxious at the sight of Prince Orthon's standard. He felt beads of sweat forming on his brow.

"Erarunde!" Prince Orthon bellowed as he strode towards the house.

"Sire, welcome."

Prince Orthon gave him a withering glance. "I'll rest here awhile. The horses are tiring."

"I'll see you've everything you need."

"Yes, I expect you shall."

Erarunde bowed as the Prince stepped over the threshold, taking off his gauntlets and throwing them on a table. Saravia appeared and Prince Orthon stopped in his tracks, believing he had seen a ghost. She curtsied. Prince Orthon was transfixed as Darthus looked on in amazement.

"My daughter, Saravia, sire."

"Of course you were a child when I saw you last. Have I not seen you since then? I have a feeling I …," said Prince Orthon, realizing she was the girl he had seen with Jhinn. "Ah, no matter."

Saravia gazed at his countenance, remembering his visit to the house and thinking him still handsome.

Darthus noted the striking resemblance she bore to the Prince's sister and late wife. He wondered if Prince Orthon's attitude to Erarunde would change, now he had seen his daughter.

Prince Orthon strode into a chamber, seating himself in a chair. Darthus sat near him watching the servants as they trouped in carrying serving dishes, a jug of Adras and several drinking vessels.

"I expect Erarunde will be looking for a husband for his daughter," said Prince Orthon, lacing his fingers.

"I expect so – I don't know."

Prince Orthon was thoughtful. "I think not, Darthus. I will have a say in the matter."

Darthus was unsure how to reply.

Saravia's father entered. "Sire, the horses are ready."

"Then we'll be on our way. Your hospitality is as good as ever, Erarunde. Now, I hope to catch up with Mararuss Laboute."

Erarunde felt uncomfortable.

"I expect you've heard the siege is over. Mararuss has escaped, with help I imagine," said Prince Orthon, draining his goblet.

Erarunde's mouth felt dry.

"You were friends at one time, were you not? Perhaps you're still loyal to him?"

"Sire, my loyalty lies with you."

Prince Orthon studied Erarunde's expression. Darthus observed them in silence as time began to slow. He felt sleepy - feeling the Adras taking effect.

Soldiers' voices were heard. An officer ran into the house in search of Prince Orthon.

"Sire, the outriders have sent word."

Prince Orthon turned his attention to the young man. "What news, pray?"

The officer presented a scroll to the Prince.

"Mararuss is heading for the coast," said Prince Orthon, his eyes narrowing.

Dismissing the officer, Prince Orthon strode into the hall, stopping to admire the clocks.

"I trust everything is to your satisfaction, sire?" Erarunde enquired.

Prince Orthon glared at him. "I believe you opened the tunnel."

Erarunde was caught off guard. "I..."

"Don't lie to me. I know Mararuss and his men were here. Why did you do it, Erarunde? You have betrayed me - I could have you hung, drawn and quartered for this,"

Saravia could not help overhearing their conversation.

Erarunde gazed at the floor. "Forgive me, I'm a foolish man, frightened of a rogue I once called a friend."

"He threatened to take Saravia, didn't he?"

Erarunde nodded.

Prince Orthon's expression softened. "She should enjoy the protection of a husband. I believe Saravia would enjoy life as Princess of Adranabar."

Saravia was shocked.

Darthus stirred, hearing the Prince's words.

"We'll speak again, Erarunde."

Lord Griann returned, entering the kitchen he noticed Saravia was upset. "What's happened? Why are you sad?"

Saravia started to sob. Sigamus jumped on to the table, putting his paw on her wrist. She scooped up the furry bundle - her tears falling on to his fur.

Erarunde tried to comfort her, but she pushed him away.

Lord Griann felt awkward, not knowing what to do for the best. "Will someone tell me what has happened?" he said, addressing the servants. He received no reply as Darthus made towards him.

"Poor Saravia – she seems unhappy about the Prince's proposal," said Darthus.

Lord Griann was astonished.

"Are you riding with us to the coast, Griann? he enquired. We hope to ambush the rebels at Ilepo Pass. Pray Crilm we do and Aramintha and Lord Jhinn are delivered safely back to us."

Lord Griann felt guilty. He had disobeyed the Prince's orders and left Jhinn and Aramintha to their fate, he wondered what had happened to his manservant, Atheil.

Saravia's sobs grew louder when Jhinn's name was mentioned. Lord Griann was aware the kitchen was crowded and Cook was irritated with the interlopers in her domain. Erarunde noticed her rising colour and withdrew. Darthus took the hint and followed him. Lord Griann remained.

"Saravia, come away with me. We can leave – go north – far away from here. You must know how I feel?"

Saravia gave him a weak smile. "And incur the wrath of your sovereign and live in exile?"

"Yes, if it meant we would be together."

She shook her head.

"I have loved you from the first moment I saw you."

Saravia blushed. "I am flattered, Lord Griann. But how could I leave my father to his fate. Prince Orthon knows he helped Mararuss. He might be imprisoned and tried for treason. My lord, your affection is returned, do not think otherwise."

Lord Griann wore a sad expression. "Then I'm destined to be unlucky in love. I must take my leave. I'm called to battle," he said withdrawing, his heart aching with the pain of loss.

A tear rolled down Saravia's cheek. "How sad I feel. What am I to do?" she whispered.

"Here, drink this and dry your eyes," said Cook, wiping her hands on her apron.

Saravia stared at the pink vapour rising from the goblet. As she took a sip of the hot, soothing liquid her eyelids felt as heavy as tombstones as she was drawn beyond the frontier of sleep.

"Maladoria seems a long way off," said Caedec.

"Perhaps it's not as far as you imagine, Caedec. Take heart you'll soon be home again," Lord Fhinn replied.

Caedec smiled. "Have the ships sailed?"

"They sail on the morning tide."

"Let us hope Khinart is deceived."

Lord Fhinn grinned. "He'll rise to the bait."

Caedec sighed. "Nevertheless, I see a long road before us. I pray that all goes well."

Admiral Oxghar strolled along the shore. His heart leapt when he saw the warships. He caught his breath - they were a magnificent sight, with the Aizan flag fluttering atop their masts. He watched the rippling surface of the Whispering Sea, hoping for a glimpse of Queen Irmardia.

He contemplated the journey inland to Maladoria, knowing it would take him farther away from the Whispering Sea. He knew he wanted to continue sailing on his beloved *Azenia* and decided he must tell Caedec how he felt and ask his leave. He knew his place was with the sea offensive.

Admiral Oxghar watched as a wave made to the shore. He took several deep breaths, closing his eyes as he did so. When he opened them, he saw Queen Irmardia. She took his hand and he found her touch comforting.

"I sense your troubled thoughts, Lhimm."

Admiral Oxghar nodded in agreement. "I cannot accompany Caedec. My home is The Whispering Sea and I cannot bear to leave it, or you. I must find a way to tell him, without causing offence. I'm fond of him and I'll miss his company," he answered with sadness in his voice.

"Then tell him what you've told me. He'll understand."

"How wise you are, my Queen. That's what I'll do."

"Our time is coming, Lhimm. We'll be together soon. I can sense it. Do you?"

Admiral Oxghar was thoughtful. "I do, the time approaches."

Queen Irmardia moved closer to him. "Then you're truly mine. I can't tell you how happy this makes me."

Admiral Oxghar blinked slowly and she was gone.

Lord Fhinn stroked the Karatroi, as his guests prepared to leave, disguised as travellers and merchants making for Sarhynel to sell their wares.

"Sire, please stand still. I must ensure your disguise is at least well fitting," said Merrick.

Caedec stopped fidgeting.

"That's it all done. I'll have your new attire sewn in no time at all."

Sapphire handed The Crown Prince an infusion of herbs. A golden vapour rose from the cup as he sipped its contents.

"Why must I drink this foul tasting liquid?"

Sapphire smiled. "It will heal your troubled mind."

"I'm well enough to travel. I *am* better," he replied in an irritated tone.

Sapphire took his hand, studying the lines on his palm.

"What do you see, Sapphire? Tell me."

"I see you have a stubborn streak, Your Majesty," she said, smiling as she closed his outstretched palm.

The Crown Prince grinned. "Is that all you can tell me of my future in the worlds?"

Sapphire stared into the distance. "That's all I will tell you, at least for the moment."

Admiral Oxghar bowed as Caedec approached. "Sire, have you a moment? May I speak with you?"

"Of course you may, come hither," said Caedec indicating an antechamber housing several comfortable chairs. "You have an air of sadness about you, my friend."

Admiral Oxghar attempted a smile. "I confess my heart is heavy."

"Then open your heart and speak of what lies within."

Admiral Oxghar took a deep breath. "I cannot accompany you to Maladoria. I'm afraid the Whispering Sea consumes my spirit."

Caedec nodded. "Understandable, perhaps I was wrong to suggest you accompany me - selfishness on my part.

"No, please don't think that."

Caedec stared at a painting of a unicorn hung above the fireplace.

"Your life is changing, Lhimm. I hope you will be happy with Irmardia."

Admiral Oxghar wore an expression of surprise. "I haven't mentioned it to a living soul."

Caedec smiled and spread his hands. "It is written on your very being."

"Are my thoughts so transparent?"

"I'm afraid they are, to those who know you well enough."

Admiral Oxghar fell silent.

"You have found love, my friend. Something rare and precious, many search for, and some are destined never to find. Hold on to it. That is my advice. I trust you will obey me and follow it?" said Caedec grinning.

"I will do my utmost."

"Then you can do no more than that. I wish you well and if Crilm wills it, we will meet again."

Admiral Oxghar fought back the tears as he withdrew from his audience.

The ships put out to sea, with a strong wind behind them. They were soon in full sail as they left Aizan. Sapphire watched from the shore as a sphere of light flew across the Whispering Sea, exploding over the ships, showering them with light as she cast a Luck Spell. She heard a sharp intake of breath from the crowd gathered in a circle around her. They stared with upturned faces at the silver sky, basking in the reflection of pure, shining light.

Sar-Mhirian turned to Caedec. "I pray Crilm is with those brave souls on the sea."

Caius knelt by the body of Adranus. "I know this is not Maladoria, but it is the best I can offer. Our country is still a long way off."

Tears flowed down his cheeks as it was lowered into the freshly dug earth of the hillside and Sar-Mhirian recited Crilm's mantra for those destined not to return to the worlds.

Caedec's court in exile wore expressions of sadness. Adranus had possessed a gift they had valued. His advice and guidance would be missed, especially at this crucial stage in their journey.

Caedec pressed his hand against Caius's face. "Adranus will return with us to Maladoria in spirit, my friend. His body is but a shell now. He has left it behind. But his spirit has not left us - he will be with us always. You must believe that, Caius, and take strength from it and your suffering will ease."

Caius considered Caedec's words and took comfort from them.

Erussah approached.   He touched Caius's arm.   "My condolences - Adranus will be missed. I have some papers he left with me a while ago. I'll give them to you at a more appropriate time."

"Yes, of course."

Erussah nodded and withdrew.

Caius remained by the grave, saying a last farewell, returning to The Lodge with the other mourners to prepare for the journey.

Lord Fhinn watched Gai and Caedec disappear into the forest. Kotroi were gathering in the trees, their numbers increasing as time passed. He heard their voices echo through the valley. "I pray they have brought good tidings for their sovereign," he said aloud as he watched their dark forms in flight.

Caedec wore a broad grin when he saw Llorian fly towards him in greeting. "What tidings do you bring?"

Llorian stared at Gai. Their eyes locked – an energy passing between them.

"Good tidings, the people await their King. Our cause enjoys a great deal of support amongst them. They're oppressed by Khinart and want to see him overthrown," said Gai with cheer.

"That is good news indeed," Caedec replied with enthusiasm.

Gai thanked them for their journey to Maladoria and for the good tidings they had brought back with them, as the forest came alive with the sound of their wings rustling amongst the branches.

"Sire, try these on for size," said Merrick.

Caedec donned the brown, woollen traveller's cloak, tunic and breeches handed to him. They fitted well in spite of the haste in which they had been sewn. "I think these will do. You've done a good job, Merrick, thank you."

Merrick beamed. "I am pleased to be of service."

Janus and Liviaa laughed at Caedec.

"You don't look like a King wearing that," Janus observed.

"That is the idea. I am wearing a disguise."

"Why don't you want to look like a King anymore?" Liviaa enquired.

"Because I am going on a journey and this is more appropriate attire."

"Are we going too?" Janus and Liviaa enquired in unison.

"I want you to remain here with Lord Fhinn. You will be safe in Aizan."

Janus was downcast. "We want to come," he said in a sad, little voice.

"I know you do. We'll be together again soon."

Janus said nothing, wearing an expression of resignation.

"It is a good day for travelling, sire," said Merrick.

Caedec fixed his gaze on the horizon. "I think you may be right. A settled sky and a warm breeze bode well."

Lord Fhinn nodded his head in agreement. "The weather couldn't be better for the start of your journey. I wish you all the luck in the worlds, Red King. Go home and claim what is yours."

"My thanks, Lord Fhinn - I hope we shall be peaceful neighbours once again," said Caedec smiling.

Lord Fhinn of Aizan beamed. "I'm sure we shall and I look forward to the dawn of that day. Go well, dear friend. My men will assist you on your way to the border and beyond."

Caedec mounted Aylvian the Grey, his courtiers followed suit and they rode down the hill flanked by Lord Fhinn's men, who were also disguised.

Caedec felt the cool air on his face as the horses picked their way down through scattered rocks and undergrowth - he felt the blood pound in his veins. He felt he could almost smell the forests of Maladoria. Every stride the horses took brought him nearer to his beloved country. Even if he failed to regain his homeland and his crown, he would surely die in Maladoria and if his blood was spilled on Maladorian soil, then it had all been worth it. All the years spent in exile, waiting and plotting to return had come to fruition.

Gai surveyed the countryside - its wild beauty stirred his soul. He looked across at Sapphire riding alongside The Crown Prince. He noticed something sparkling on one of the fingers of her left hand - the marriage hand.

Caedec glanced at Gai's expression knowing he had seen Sapphire's ring. He would have to pick the right moment to tell him of her betrothal to The Crown Prince. He thought he would not take the news well.

A solitary eagle circled, then flew off into the forests beyond. Merrick stopped to look at the view from the hillside. He gazed at the endless sky and hills that gave on to mountains, stretching up to the sky like arrows in flight. He noticed the hills were cloaked in trees and waterfalls. He remembered stories told by travellers about the beauty of Aizan, but he had not believed there was such a land in the worlds. Now he knew the tales were true. Aizan's splendour was almost beyond words and he felt privileged to have seen it for himself.

Lord Fhinn had arranged for them to stay at an inn by the foot of the hillside, so they would have time to rest before continuing to the border.

Copper pans clanked together in Merrick's saddlebags as his horse negotiated its way down the slope.

The building looked as old as the hills and mountains themselves. It was constructed of forest timber, weathered by storms and touched by the hand of time. Caedec's retinue stopped, tethered the horses outside and entered. The floor was bare, the walls were hung with a few paintings and several wooden tables and chairs filled the main room.

Caedec sat at a table by a window. He noticed the panes of glass were clean and the floor had been swept. He wondered whether it had been cleaned and tidied in anticipation of their arrival and smiled. He gazed at the window and the magnificent view of the hills and mountains. He thought Lord Fhinn fortunate to rule such a beautiful realm. As he continued to gaze at the view he noticed the light was fading. Night was drawing near and darkness would soon clothe the land.

The innkeeper and his wife were a jovial couple. They welcomed Caedec's retinue warmly and soon trays of goblets brimming with warmed Adras appeared. Rulf, Lord Fhinn's adviser, was engaged in conversation with the innkeeper. Rulf was a tall man with a regal bearing. His hair was white as a summer cloud - his skin was tanned from a life spent outdoors. He spoke with a voice as clear and crisp as a mountain stream.

"Sire, may I sit here and speak with you?" Rulf enquired.

"Please do."

"The innkeeper tells me the border is rife with Khinart's spies at the moment. We must be vigilant. There is a man the innkeeper suspects is not all he seems. He is given to frequenting this place and the innkeeper has heard he will be here before nightfall.

"Then we must be on our guard," Caedec replied with a thoughtful look on his face.

"I expect he may be curious about the number of travellers here," said Rulf.

"I believe it is not unusual."

"That is so, sire. There are vast numbers of merchants and travellers in the worlds and Maladoria needs trade, or so I hear."

"Then his visit may be a routine one. Perhaps we are unduly anxious," Caedec replied with optimism.

Rulf stared at the gathering darkness as the candles were lit one by one and the yellow flames were reflected in the window panes.

Caedec stared at the vapour rising from his goblet, as the innkeeper and his wife received a steady stream of visitors looking for somewhere to tarry for the night.

Rulf studied them as he raised a goblet to his lips. He lingered a moment, savouring the aroma.

"Welcome! Good to see you again," said the innkeeper in a loud voice.

All attention turned to the young man. He cut a striking figure with his lean frame and dark hair shining in the candlelight. His eyes burned with the intensity of a dark star. He wore riding boots that shone like glass and his travelling cloak and apparel were the colour of smoke from a forest fire.

Caedec recognized him instantly. He grabbed Rulf's arm. "That's Mordain, Khinart's younger brother - if he sees me, we are undone," he whispered.

"Quickly, pull your hood up and follow me," said Rulf in an anxious tone.

Caedec did as Rulf suggested - but before they had time to leave their table, Mordain appeared next to them, as if by magic.

"The hostelry is busy this night, gentlemen," said Mordain as an opening gambit.

"Indeed, it is quite crowded," Rulf replied.

"Unusually so, I would say," said Mordain, surveying the company with a chilling gaze.

Rulf did not reply. He hoped he would move on to another table so he could steer Caedec safely away from him. But Mordain did not budge. He stared at the hooded figure of Caedec.

"And your friend, does he not speak?" he enquired, placing his hand on Caedec's hood as a look of horror crossed Rulf's face and silence settled over the occupants of the inn.

"Ah, there you are," Merrick called as he approached the table.

Mordain was distracted by the intrusion.

"Is this gentleman interested in our wares?" Merrick enquired of Mordain.

Mordain relinquished his hold on Caedec's hood, turning to Merrick.

"Sir, can I interest you in our copper pans? I assure you the craftsmanship is second to none," said Merrick, producing a selection of pans from a tapestry-covered bag and placing them on the table.

Mordain was mesmerized as he examined them. Such wares were scarce in the worlds and usually reserved for royalty and the aristocracy. His eyes locked on to their gleaming surface and Merrick could tell he admired good craftsmanship. Whilst Merrick engaged Mordain in conversation he managed to nudge one of the pans towards the edge of the table until it was situated directly above Mordain's foot. Merrick gave it a final push and it fell onto Mordain's riding boot, making him howl and curse while Merrick apologized profusely - creating a diversion and enabling Rulf and Caedec to withdraw without undue attention.

Rulf breathed a sigh of relief. "Sire, if Mordain had recognized you I shudder to think what might have happened to us. But we are not out of danger yet," he whispered as they climbed the stairs to their chambers situated away from those of the other travellers.

Rulf opened the door to a chamber and ushered Caedec inside. "Let us pray Mordain is gone by the time we leave on the morrow."

"I expect Merrick may have talked him to death by now," he replied, grinning as Rulf laughed.

By the morrow, Mordain and his men had gone, called to Sarhynel on urgent business according to the innkeeper.

Merrick was in good spirits, having sold a number of pans in one fell swoop and with relatively little effort.

Saravia woke feeling light-headed and drowsy, the taste of Cook's drink lingered. She wondered what the powerful concoction was made from to have such a strange effect. She noticed her chamber looked bare and some of the paintings were missing from the walls. There was a small coffer by the door with her favourite travelling cloak draped over it. She began to feel alarmed. Something was afoot.

The door opened and Cook scuttled in. "Mistress Saravia, the horses are saddled. You must get ready to ride north."

"Why? This is ridiculous, I'm not going anywhere."

"Yes you are my girl."

"Cook, stop this nonsense at once. I tell you I'm not going. My place is here in this house. Have you taken leave of your senses?"

Cook gave Saravia a cold, hard stare.

"Your place is with the man you love and he does not dwell here in this house," she replied.

Saravia could scarcely believe such impertinence.

Cook's expression softened. "Your late mother once told me of a prophecy. It's time you knew of it. When you were an infant, not one season old, she travelled into the mountains to consult Gunhildran the Wise, as is the custom in these parts. He told her of a prophecy."

Saravia listened. "Please, tell me more of this."

Cook sighed and seemed lost in thought. "Gunhildran told your mother that three men would vie for your affection. But the man who would bring true happiness to her daughter would state his intentions with the phrase 'I have loved you since I first saw you'. Until I heard Lord Griann utter those very words I wasn't sure whether he was indeed the man mentioned in the prophecy – now I'm sure he is the one Gunhildran the Wise spoke of. That is the first part of the prophecy."

"I see," Saravia said, slightly puzzled by this sudden revelation.

"Now you know why I'm so anxious for you to go. Seize this chance. I know your mother would have wished it so."

Saravia wore a serious expression. She felt her heart jump at the thought of eloping with Lord Griann, yet this joy was tinged with the sadness of leaving behind all she held dear. She glanced at the sleeping bundle of ginger fur at the foot of her bed.

"Take Sigamus - he won't be happy without you."

"And father, what will become of him?"

"Speak to him. He's aware of the prophecy. Go quickly – don't tarry. There's not much time."

Saravia went in search of her father, finding him standing by the stable door in deep contemplation.

"And now you're leaving," he said.

Saravia felt uncomfortable, not knowing what to say.

"I knew this day would come. I've dreaded it, more than you'll ever know. And yet I believe it to be right. I pray you'll be happy and that one day you'll return," Erarunde continued.

"I'm sad, father. My heart's torn."

"Don't be dear daughter. Gunhildran's prophecy has come true. Though for my own selfish reasons, I hoped it wouldn't. Forgive me, you have my blessing. Ride north, Griann will meet you on the other side of the forest," he said embracing her.

Lord Griann waited for his chance. He had deliberately fallen behind Prince Orthon's retinue. When he felt sure no one was watching he broke away and slipped into the forest.

He was on tenterhooks, waiting for Saravia. He scoured the trees for signs of movement. Yarrow was uneasy, sensing wolves nearby. He patted the war horse's muscular neck. As he was about to give up hope and thinking she would not come, he saw her riding a brown mare and leading a packhorse. As she approached, he noticed two furry, ears protruding from a saddlebag and found himself grinning.

"So, my Lord Griann, which way is north?"

Prince Orthon was in a dark mood and Darthus was doing his best to placate him.

Darthus saw the road to Ilepo Pass in the distance. As they drew nearer the coast the temperature dropped. He shivered, knowing the pass was treacherous with a sheer drop down the mountainside into the Whispering Sea.

Atheil sought a means of escape as the rebel soldiers forged ahead towards Ilepo Pass. He could just see Jhinn and Aramintha at the forefront of the army alongside Mararuss. Atheil sensed he was of little importance to the rebel leader. As the rebel army skirted the edge of the forest, he hoped his chance would come.

Mararuss's commander barked an order. "Keep up you lot!"

197

The rear guard quickened their pace. Atheil moved to the edge of the column. He saw a horse and cart approaching from the opposite direction and knew this was the moment he had been waiting for. As the cart drew nearer, the bulk of it taking up most of the already narrow track, a line of soldiers surged past it. Atheil paused, throwing himself under it. He rolled clear, falling into a ditch on the other side. He covered himself with fallen branches and waited. Silence followed. He got up, brushing the debris from his stained attire and set off into the trees, not knowing what he would find.

As the rebels reached Ilepo Pass rain began to fall. In the distance Mararuss noticed a solitary patch of blue sky. He was jubilant when he saw the outline of the Emperor's ship moored in the Whispering Sea. Deliverance was at hand and there was no sign of an army in pursuit. He felt confident that all was going to plan.

"Hah! I've reached safe harbour," he gloated.

Jhinn noticed the rebel soldiers were exhausted. His father was pushing them to their limit. He realized they were heading for Ilepo Pass. He had heard tales of unwary travellers perishing as they tried to negotiate the ribbon of stony track, with only a few stone markers to guide them away from the edge and the sheer drop offering nothing but certain death. He watched as the rebels surged forward to the lowest point of the pass where there was a path leading down to the shore.

As Prince Orthon gave the command, the army stopped and the soldiers split into two forces. One half disappearing into the forest to lie in wait for the rebel forces at the head of the pass, while he led the remainder in the enemy's wake. Prince Orthon was laying a trap.

Darthus knew it would be a massacre, rather than a battle and prayed Jhinn and Aramintha would be unharmed. He doubted whether Mararuss would negotiate with Prince Orthon, their natures and positions were as entrenched and immovable as the land itself. Prince Orthon's army pressed on to Ilepo Pass.

Prince Orthon turned to Darthus. "Let's quicken our pace - I want this over and done with."

An order was given and the army gathered momentum. Prince Orthon's standard-bearer leading the way as the horses broke into a gallop. Darthus could not bring himself to look at the sheer drop. He noticed the tops of the mountains on either side of the pass still had a scant covering of snow. He could see the rear guard of the rebel army straight ahead, thinking they were also gathering speed. As he glanced over the edge he saw the reason. A ship was moored not far from the shore.

"Sire, look there's a ship down there," he said pointing to the sea.

Prince Orthon's gaze followed the direction of Darthus's finger.

"Damn! I thought that blackguard would have something up his sleeve," he replied drawing his sword.

Mararuss saw the path to the shore. His heart leapt in his chest as he prepared to dismount. Then he saw them. Soldiers wearing Prince Orthon's colours were riding towards him.

"Jhinn! Get off your horse now! You're coming with me."

Jhinn was paralyzed with fear.

Mararuss realized he was all but surrounded. He was cornered, like a wild animal, watching as Prince Orthon's army moved closer and the rebels broke rank. Some standing firm, while others fled. Suddenly Prince Orthon and Darthus charged, cutting down all in their way.

Aramintha was horrified, struggling to compose herself as her horse sidled, drifting perilously close to the edge. She shuddered staring at the drop, watching as several rebel soldiers went over the edge to their deaths. She saw their bodies broken on the shore below. A red stain crept over the rocks.

Darthus dismounted and after several attempts managed to catch Aramintha's horse. He held on to the bridle, coaxing it towards him. He patted its nose as he handed the reins to Mathuen. "You will be safe now. I'll follow the Prince," he said as he mounted and rode away.

Aramintha watched until he was out of sight.

Darthus dismounted, looking at the uneven path slippery from the rain. He saw Prince Orthon riding towards Mararuss, noticing the rebel leader had dismounted, pulled Jhinn from his horse and was dragging him along the path down to the shore.

Mararuss thought he must be at least halfway down the mountainside. He longed to be on the Emperor's ship. He felt Jhinn struggle and try to break free.

"Let me go!" Jhinn's cry rang in his ears.

"Stop it! You young fool," he replied tightening his grip.

Prince Orthon was gaining on them with Darthus bringing up the rear.

"Leave the lad alone, Mararuss. This is between you and me. Don't be a coward – stand your ground and fight man," said Prince Orthon.

Mararuss spun round, holding a dagger to Jhinn's throat. "Save your breath. Any closer and there's no telling what'll become of your precious nephew."

Prince Orthon hesitated. "Let him go. He's your son, for Crilm's sake show him some mercy."

Mararuss sneered. "Mercy – hah! I'd be dead if you had your way."

"I'll offer you a full pardon if you release him."

Mararuss grinned. "Will you now? A full pardon you say."

"A full pardon will be granted if you go abroad never to return to Adranabar."

"Ah – there's always a condition isn't there, Orthon?"

"That's my offer – do you accept?"

Silence prevailed over the Prince and his mortal enemy.

Atheil ran through the forest as if the Dark Gods were chasing him. He noticed he was not alone, as he watched rebel soldiers running through the trees. He wondered if they were pursuing him, but as they ran past he saw their eyes were wide with fear. They were fleeing for their lives.

Lord Griann and Saravia heard the sound of twigs breaking underfoot then several rebel soldiers brushed past the flanks of their horses. Lord Griann watched them disappear from view. "We can't be far from the battle," he said.

"My Lord Griann!"

"Atheil!"

Atheil ran towards his lord and his companion. Lord Griann dismounted.

"How are you? I trust you're well, despite your ordeal."

"I am, my lord. Why aren't you with Prince Orthon's army?"

Lord Griann wore a sheepish expression. "Saravia and I are eloping."

Atheil was astounded. "My lord, the Prince needs the help of every able-bodied man in order to vanquish his enemy."

Lord Griann looked to Saravia. She nodded her head.

"Let us join the fray," he said.

Atheil leapt on to Yarrow's back and the three of them rode towards the edge of the forest. From there they would find their way to the coast.

Darthus feared for Jhinn's life. He hoped Mararuss would accept the pardon offered to him, but he had not answered Prince Orthon and he was edging his way down the path.

"Atheil, stay here with Saravia," Lord Griann commanded.

"My lord," he replied, his voice tinged with disappointment.

Lord Griann drew his sword as he rode through the line of trees. Through the swaying branches he saw two figures on horseback. He was sure it was Mathuen and Aramintha.

"Lord Griann. Have you killed many of the fleeing rebels?" Mathuen enquired.

Lord Griann formed an answer. "I believe I've slain several," he said trying to make the lie sound convincing.

"My lord, you're too modest. Prince Orthon will be happy you've driven his enemies into the forest and cut them down."

"Aramintha, I'm pleased you're safe," said Lord Griann.

Aramintha nodded. "I thank Crilm for that mercy and my Lord Darthus."

"How goes the battle? Where is Prince Orthon?" he enquired.

Mathuen pointed to the path. "Prince Orthon and my Lord Darthus have pursued Mararuss down the mountainside."

Lord Griann rode to the edge of the pass, looking down he saw the moored ship, Prince Orthon and Darthus. He noticed Mararuss and Jhinn a little further down. He dismounted, sending Yarrow over to Mathuen, who was only too pleased to be given the honour of guarding the war horse. Lord Griann sheathed his sword, quietly making his way with the stealth of a fox. As long as Mararuss was preoccupied with Prince Orthon and Darthus he knew he would have the opportunity to join the path lower down. Then he would be able to cut Mararuss off from the shore, thwarting his means of escape.

As Lord Griann moved closer, Prince Orthon saw him, guessing the nature of his plan - he began taunting the rebel leader, trying to gain his full attention.

Lord Griann crept forward and lunged at Mararuss, taken by surprise his guard dropped and Jhinn managed to break free, though the dagger's blade slashed his neck and a stream of blood fell onto the earth. Lord Griann had Mararuss by the throat. Mararuss gathered all his strength and struggled violently, thrusting the dagger into Griann's side. He cried out, falling onto the path, while Jhinn looked on helpless, his face contorted in horror.

Prince Orthon was furious. He stepped forward and swung his sword, but Mararuss was ready for him. As Darthus approached with his sword drawn, the sound of clashing blades was deafening.

"Get back! Mararuss is mine," Prince Orthon commanded, as the fight continued down the path and on to the shore.

Darthus sheathed his sword - ripping his tunic into broad strips he bound the young lords' wounds.

Jhinn watched his father and uncle with morbid fascination, as the sound of clashing metal carried on the wind and shades of darkness gathered. He saw Prince Orthon's blade slash into Mararuss's arm. He recoiled - his arm covered in blood. Mararuss assailed Prince Orthon, knocking him sideways and slashing his tunic. Prince Orthon regained his composure, rounding on Mararuss, by now they had reached the edge of the shore. Water lapped around their feet as Prince Orthon pushed him into the water, bearing down on Mararuss as he sank beneath the waves. Jhinn did not see his father surface, as Prince Orthon waded out of the sea. Jhinn thought his uncle was certain his enemy was dead.

Prince Orthon was weary, the weight of his armour was crippling, as he sank to his knees. He felt the sand, inhaling the salty air.

Jhinn stood on the shore before him. "Are you wounded?"

"No, Jhinn I'm not, but if I'm mistaken, then I'm oblivious to the pain. I pray now I can sleep in my own bed in peace. I yearn for the hearth of home more than I can say."

Jhinn nodded.

"How's Lord Griann?" Prince Orthon enquired.

"Darthus has bound his wound. I don't think he's in mortal danger."

"He'll be rewarded for his valour," he said rising from his knees and making back to the mountain path to the sound of his army cheering "Long live our Prince!"

A mass of bubbles rose to the surface as the Emperor's ship drifted out to sea.

Chapter 30 – The Road to Sarhynel

A sun rose high over the mountains of Aizan, bathing the valley in a crimson glow. A solitary bird circled overhead, as clouds in abstract patterns drifted by. A winding tract stretched out like a snake travelling through the rough terrain. Here the way was narrow and the sound of moving water permeated the otherwise silent landscape.

Lord Caton paused, thinking of Greylan, his childhood friend, the king's warrior son and heir apparent. Lord Caton thought he heard his voice carried on the wind "Look after my father," he had said as he waved and rode off on his favourite war horse, Armian, into the heart of that terrible battle. Shedding a tear he watched it fall, spreading over the ground as still and clear as a looking glass. "Well upon my soul," he remarked studying his own reflection and noticing that of another staring back at him. He gazed at the dragon in miniature form, its face round and set with eyes of brilliant blue. He turned his face towards his new companion, finding it also had immense paws and a tail, which was curled around him.

Lord Caton thought the creature's form pleasing and unusual, unlike any other dragon he had seen. He watched as it flicked its paw, the movement unsheathing one golden claw amongst four black ones. He was amazed and certain that standing beside him was none other than Mai, the golden-clawed one, guardian of the dragons of Sarhynel, often mentioned in the ancient legends of Maladoria, but seldom seen. Lord Caton recalled the legend that foretold the little dragon would become the protector of a great queen.

"Sire, I'm sure that's Mai the golden-clawed one, over there with Lord Caton, the dragons of Sarhynel must be near. He will take us to them," said Gai.

"It is a good omen," said Caedec dismounting and making towards the dragon.

"Mai?" enquired Caedec.

Mai flicked his tail as wisps of smoke rose from his nostrils.

Caedec nodded in greeting. "Lead me to the dragons of Sarhynel. I have need of them."

Mai trotted along with Caedec following, the forests of Aizan had given way to desert-like terrain.

Caedec struggled to keep pace with Mai as he made towards the mountains. He continued to follow with Gai not far behind.

Gai and Caedec watched as Mai slipped through an opening in the rock, finding themselves inside the mountain. Mai paused to allow them to catch up. When he was sure they were near he continued on his way. As they walked further along they saw cracks letting in shafts of light. They followed Mai into the heart of the mountain. Caedec pulled the folds of his cloak around him to stop it trailing over the ground, whilst Gai felt a rising tide of anticipation mingled with excitement ebb and flow within himself.

Mai stopped abruptly. As they approached they heard a sound louder than thunder, making the mountain shake. Dust fell showering their travelling cloaks in a powdery film of stone.

"They're snoring," said Gai.

"Well, I'm amazed the mountain is still intact," replied Caedec.

Mai watched the sleeping dragons.

"Poor soul, he must be lonely," Gai remarked.

"Aye, he has kept a vigil over them long enough."

Mai withdrew and Caedec studied the sleeping dragons. He had forgotten how powerful they were. He touched one of them and it stirred. A plume of smoke emanated from one large nostril as he passed between them. One by one he stroked their heads and they woke from their sleep.

"Your family are rising from their slumber. You are released from your lonely vigil, Mai. I pray we all return to Sarhynel and live to see our King regain his throne," said Gai.

Mai flicked his tail as he watched his family greet their King and the cavern filled with smoke.

Gai and Caedec inhaled the vapour, which smelt sweet and tasted of burnt leaves.

"They'll return to Sarhynel, now their King is here," said Gai.

As the dragons roared, breathing fire. Gai and Caedec withdrew, using their hands to shield their faces from the heat of the encroaching flames. They watched the dragons stretch. One of them flapped its wings, circling the cavern and soon they were all flying.

Gai stared at them in wonder. Their scales of vibrant scarlet and gold fascinated him.

"Such beauty," said Caedec watching their graceful movements.

"Breathtaking," Gai replied his voice tinged with awe.

Mai's tail flicked back and forth, his eyes shining like a glittering sea. Gai thought he looked happy.

As they rose higher, Caedec noticed they were drifting towards an opening in the rock - one by one they passed through the aperture and disappeared from view.

Lord Caton was amazed as he watched several dragons flying above the mountain.

Riders from Aizan crossed the bridge. Sparks from their horses' shoes flew off the surface of the cobbles. People living in the houses below heard the noise, followed by loud cries of "The King is coming! Take heart and gather your weapons!" A statue of a lion, holding a torch, lit their way as they went up on to the bridge leading to the Palace of Khorec, for the first time since the King's departure and Khinart's curfew in the capital city.

The Bridge People watched them as they disappeared into the darkness on the other side. As the riders vanished like ghosts into the night, they caught a brief glimpse of the King's flag. The battle for Sarhynel had begun.

Night was upon the land, as the King's retinue reached the border.

Caedec listened to the silence - all was quiet, disturbingly so, he thought.

"Sire, I think we should cross here. There are some guards further along. I doubt very much whether they will bother us," said Rulf with a conspiratorial air.

"How can you be sure they will not?" enquired Caedec with a puzzled expression.

"I've bribed them with a substantial sum of gold coin."

Caedec smiled. "Rulf it seems you have thought of every eventuality."

"I try to."

They slipped through the trees, forming the border between Aizan and Maladoria and made their way towards fields edged by high hedges.

Caedec had finally returned to his homeland. He inhaled the cold air of Maladoria. He picked a blade of grass, holding it between his fingers, savouring its texture. "There are no words to describe how I feel," he said.

Rulf smiled. "We should make haste while it's dark. Lord Fhinn has arranged for us to seek refuge at a house near the lowland villages before we travel to Sarhynel."

Caedec nodded, urging Aylvian forward. The war horse cantered, breaking into a gallop as they crossed the open fields, their way lit by a sphere of silver light.

They approached the village with caution, noticing the houses were in darkness.

Caedec peered at the windows - some of the shutters were closed. He saw the mark of the wolf on one of them.

"What has happened to this village?"

Rulf's expression changed. "I've heard tales of fever, I wondered if they were true. I believe the wolves have gathered many spirits here. We mustn't tarry, the disease may linger."

Caedec was distraught.

Sapphire gazed at the mark of the wolf.

Merrick shivered, pleased to leave the village behind, looking back to make sure there were no ghosts following.

As dawn broke, Caedec was beginning to tire. It had been a long night's ride, without any stops to rest the horses. Rulf had pushed them hard. They had travelled far from the border. Mai and the dragons of Sarhynel had flown ahead. Caedec thought they would be resting in the hills and forests above the capital by now.

"Sire, we have reached our safe house," said Rulf, pointing to an imposing building with towering gates.

As Caedec and his retinue approached, the gates swung open and they entered a courtyard.

"Sire, I am your obedient servant," said the owner with a sweeping bow.

"Mir, how good it is to see you again."

Sir Atalamir Iboreal embraced Caedec. "Forgive me, sire. I know it's forbidden for a person of my rank to touch the royal person, but I couldn't help myself."

Merrick was overcome with excitement at the prospect of meeting Sir Atalamir Iboreal, discoverer and grower of Alphus Berries, renowned in the worlds for their flavour and health giving properties.

Caedec watched with amusement. Sir Atalamir was adept at receiving visitors and thrilled to meet The Crown Prince of Ilesh.

Merrick stepped forward to shake hands, gazing at him in wonder, noticing his round face, small eyes and straight nose with an ornate pair of spectacles perched on the bridge. Although his features were not handsomely arranged, his charm compensated for this. His attire was flamboyant and Merrick was so in awe of him he could not speak in his presence.

Rulf and Sir Atalamir Iboreal were closeted in a chamber, while Caedec and his retinue ate and rested.

"I have done my best, Rulf. What's left of the nobility and the able bodied are preparing to join the King. They'll be here by nightfall with all the weapons and armour they can muster."

"Thank you, Mir. You'll be awarded a good position at court when the King regains power."

Sir Atalamir waved his hand in a dismissive gesture. "You must rest, Rulf. Night will come sooner than you imagine."

As night drew near Caedec heard voices in the courtyard, rising from his bed he made to the window. Riders and men on foot were pouring through the entrance. He was overjoyed at the sight of them rallying to his cause.

"Sire, it's time for us to leave," said Merrick.

Caedec and his retinue made themselves ready while Rulf and Sir Atalamir attended to the throng.

"Sire, a messenger from Aizan wishes to see you," said Rulf.

Caedec withdrew from the chamber to receive the messenger.

"Sire, I have a letter bearing urgent news from my Lord Fhinn," he said, kneeling with head bowed.

Caedec's expression was thoughtful as he read it, while the messenger waited for his reply. "Give my thanks to Lord Fhinn for this communication. His kindness is appreciated."

As the messenger withdrew, Caedec returned to a sea of expectant faces. "Lord Fhinn sends tidings of a battle at sea. Aizan warships have all but annihilated Khinart's fleet. There are reports that his ship is on the run. Without his presence in Maladoria, the way to Sarhynel is clear for us. My Lord Fhinn sends us his commanders and troops for the coming battle."

"That is good news," said Gai.

Caedec fell silent and Sapphire sensed all was not well.

"Alas, Admiral Oxghar is feared lost at sea," he continued, withdrawing to address his supporters.

Caedec made a speech and the hall rang with cheers of "Long live the King!" Caedec returned to the chamber to find Sapphire and

Merrick in floods of tears, whilst the others sat in silence. A pall of sadness hung in the air.

"Sire, we must leave now. It may be dangerous to tarry," said Rulf.

The road to Sarhynel stretched out before them like endless night.

"We must win Sarhynel, sire. It would serve as a fitting tribute to the Admiral's memory," said Gai.

An expression of determination crossed Caedec's features. He drew his sword, holding it aloft, the blade shining in the light of the moon. "To Sarhynel!"

Gai held the flag aloft. "May all who see this, the King's flag, rally to our cause."

A rousing cheer was carried on the breeze and the King's army started to gather pace. The atmosphere changed from one of sadness to vengeance and the pursuit of victory. As the army passed through villages and towns people ran to join them swelling the ranks. Deafening cries of "Long live the King!" echoed through Maladoria.

Caedec was overcome, not anticipating such a welcome, as women and children rushed forward to greet him, festooning Aylvian the Grey's bridle with flowers and bursting into tears if he acknowledged them. Any attacks from Khinart's supporters were put down. The road to Sarhynel belonged to the King.

A sun was rising as the King's army arrived at Khorec's Ridge above the city of Sarhynel. Lord Caton was anxious when he saw the dragons circling overhead, ready to strike at the heart of the capital.

Caedec stared at Sarhynel and the countryside beyond. "There were times when I thought I would not see this city again," he remarked to Gai.

"I thank Crilm we're here at last," he replied with a broad grin.

They watched in silence as Rulf rode to the top of the ridge.

"Sire, a battle has raged throughout the night. There's been an uprising. Your people are fighting Khinart's army and I'm told it goes well. The enemy is all but vanquished. But the palace is yet to fall."

"Perhaps we have arrived at an auspicious moment, Rulf?" remarked Caedec.

"If we strike now with the dragons to aid us we can roust Khinart's army and reclaim the throne in your name," Rulf offered.

"What say you, Gai, Sapphire?" Caedec enquired.

Gai exchanged glances with Sapphire who in turn gazed at The Crown Prince. They all nodded in agreement.

"Rulf offers wise counsel, sire. We should act upon it," said Gai in a purposeful tone.

Sar-Mhirian rode to the King's side. "May I recite a blessing for the battle?"

"Of course, by all means do so."

"Crilm, bestow your blessings upon us, protect and guide us to a swift victory … so be it."

After the prayer for victory in battle was said the King drew his sword. Aylvian galloped down the ridge into the mayhem below. Sapphire remained on Khorec's Ridge, holding the amulet in the palm of her hand. Merrick glanced at Lord Caton.

"My lord, you and I are cut out for more homely pursuits than this."

Lord Caton smiled, drawing his sword. "Merrick, I believe that is an astute observation. I pray to Crilm I don't have to use this weapon."

Caius stared at the letter and deed Erussah had given him. Adranus's swirling script seemed alive as he read it again. "I pray I survive this battle and live to enjoy my inheritance," he said as he prepared to join the fray.

Sapphire saw dragons flying over the city. Sarhynel was dressed in a pall of flame and smoke as buildings burned with raging intensity. It was difficult to determine friend from foe in the heat of battle. She watched Gai, Rulf, The Crown Prince and several Knights of the Order of the Median close ranks around the King, as he careered into a battalion of Khinart's soldiers. Aylvian reared and trampled all in his way. Rulf and The Crown Prince cut down all around them, whilst Caius, Erussah, Lord Caton and Merrick brought up the rear to protect them from any onslaught from behind.

Caedec thought his enemy's army must be near defeat. He saw row upon row of bodies, wearing Khinart's colours, piled up by the side of the road and on the bridge leading to the Palace of Khorec. No army could sustain such heavy losses without reinforcements, yet none had appeared. He watched as his army finished off the remnants of the battalion as they tried to retreat and blood ran down the gulleys at an alarming rate. He felt now was the time to attack the palace, purported to be the last stronghold of Khinart's army.

"To the palace!" Caedec commanded as Aylvian galloped across the bridge. He noticed the river below was tinged with red. He longed to see Ahrisa and hoped she was safe. Caedec saw his army join a throng of Maladorians trying to storm the palace. He watched as they surged forward, whilst the remnants of Khinart's guard tried to keep them at bay. He noticed Mordain in a window high up in the palace, watching as he stepped on to the balcony, forcing the woman with him towards the balustrade. Caedec heard the crowd gasp – Mordain's captive was Ahrisa, his Queen.

"Ah so Caedec the Red has returned from exile," said Mordain noticing the King.

Caedec said nothing as Rulf left his side, gathering Gai and a few of his men to him as he went.

Mordain pushed Ahrisa against the balustrade. "Your wife does not favour heights."

Gai, Rulf and his men weaved their way through the crowd. Until, like deft assassins, they were near enough to strike at the guards. As the crowd surged forward, the guards' nerve began to falter. Rulf's men struck them mortal blows and they fell where they stood. Up on the balcony Mordain could not see what was happening below. Gai and

Rulf broke into the palace. Gai leading the way as they ran up the staircase towards the Queen's Chambers.

Mordain was faltering. Caedec's silence and his refusal to rise to his bait unnerved him. Ahrisa's remarkable composure began to irritate him. He had expected a heated exchange with the King and a hysterical reaction from the Queen. Mordain was perplexed. He had achieved neither. He felt his strategy had failed and was not sure what he should do next. Ahrisa sensed his unease. Mordain was rattled and she suspected he would soon look for a means of escape for himself. She waited for a chance to turn on him, gripping the hilt of the slight but deadly, silver dagger hidden in the folds of her skirt.

Gai tried the door to the Queen's Chamber. It was locked. They decided it was too dangerous to break it down, fearing the noise would alert Mordain, putting the Queen in even greater danger. Gai searched his memory of the palace. He remembered duplicate keys to the chambers had been kept in the servants' quarters and wondered if they were still there. While Gai went in search of a key, Rulf tried the other doors on the landing. They were all locked.

Outside the crowd was uneasy. Mordain had ceased goading the King. A tense silence descended as he held her in a tight grip.

Gai returned empty handed. "I can't find any. We'll have to break the door down and hope all ends well."
        "Very well, Gai. Crilm protect us all."

Sapphire pushed her way through the crowd. She was horrified when she saw the Queen held prisoner on the balcony. She reached inside her cloak, holding the amulet fastened around her neck.

Mordain looked up in horror to find a War Kotroi circling with teeth bared and claws exposed. Queen Ahrisa took her chance, plunging the dagger into Mordain's thigh. Rulf and Gai heaved against the door but it held fast.
        Queen Ahrisa climbed over the balustrade.
        Caedec thought his heart was about to explode as he watched her teeter on the ledge.
        Sapphire uttered an incantation with her eyes closed.
        Mordain lunged at Queen Ahrisa, and she lost her footing, plummeting towards those gathered below.

Caedec urged Aylvian forward. "Save the Queen!" he cried out in a voice full of despair.

Hhariann was carried along by a ferocious wind, swirling around the palace, he swooped catching Queen Ahrisa with his powerful claws, tearing the sleeves of her gown and slashing the flesh beneath as he did so.

Sapphire opened one eye.

Finally, the door to the Queen's Chamber finally gave way. Rulf and Gai rushed towards the balcony to find Mordain there alone with one hand pressed to his thigh, a stream of blood escaping between his fingers.

Thoro was saddened by the Admiral's loss. He was downcast as *Azenia* sailed towards Maladoria. He stared at the sea and the remnants of Khinart's ships floating on the surface. Then he spotted two dolphins following in *Azenia's* wake and wondered if Admiral Oxghar was still keeping a watchful eye on his ship.

"We've been duped," hissed Niaa as she gazed across the Whispering Sea. Khinart gave her a cold look. "It's your place to thwart these things."

"I can't understand what's happened. Have my powers deserted me?" she wailed.

"Stop it! Our ships have been shot to pieces and Maladoria is overrun with Caedec and his admirers. What has my brother, Mordain, been thinking of? How could he let such a thing happen? He has failed me beyond measure and for that he will pay," said Khinart, slamming his clenched fist down on the table.

Niaa winced at the noise. "We can sail to Azuriene. Tsabani is our friend."

"Our ship is letting in water by the gallon, witch! Have your powers not determined that?"

The Queen lay limp in Caedec's arms.

"Where's my physician?" he barked.

Hhannon emerged from the crowd followed by Merrick and Lord Caton.

"Oh my word," Lord Caton exclaimed.

Caedec carried Queen Ahrisa into the palace. He looked at her face, thinking how little she had changed since he last saw her. He felt the time he had spent in exile melting away as he entered the palace, climbing the staircase to the Queen's Chambers. As he reached the landing he saw Gai and Rulf grappling with Mordain, who was trying to extricate himself from Rulf's iron grip.

"What shall we do with him?" Gai enquired.

"Have someone attend to his wound and do *not* under any circumstances let him escape," Caedec commanded.

Mordain stared at Caedec with contempt as he watched him carry Queen Ahrisa into her chambers.

Merrick wandered into the palace kitchens. He was worried they might have changed, but he found they were as he remembered them, but not as clean as he would have liked to see them. He touched the doors of the ovens, the copper kettles and his beloved copper pans. They felt like old friends to him. After taking stock of his surroundings he began to clean and tidy.

"Hello, Merrick."

Merrick stopped polishing a copper kettle to find Janus and Liviaa running towards him. With a broad grin on his face he swept them up in his arms.

"When Lord Fhinn heard Sarhynel had fallen he packed these two rascals off and gave my men instructions to deliver them safely to you. It seems they have been quite impossible in your absence," said Rulf noticing Merrick's jubilant expression.

Lord Caton pondered the future as he strolled in the palace gardens. He studied the towers built by Khorec, first King of Maladoria and founder of the Idrean Dynasty. Azuriene and the demands of Queen Tsabani seemed distant. He began to wonder whether the King might offer him a position at court in return for services rendered during the battle of Sarhynel, thinking he might not be welcome at Queen Tsabani's court. He saw Mai wandering in the rose gardens and guessed that the dragons had returned to their abode in the hills above Khorec's ridge.

Sapphire gazed at the plumes of smoke, rising from the heart of the city.

"Fair Sarhynel still burns," The Crown Prince remarked as they strolled through the palace gates.

"And there is fever. I've seen souls in the city shadowed by the wolf. His mark will soon be upon them."

"Yes and I imagine you would like to help them, is that not so?" he enquired in a tone of one who is resigned to such matters.

"Yes I would."

"Then we shall stay awhile. I believe we may spare the King a little more of our time."

Sapphire was overjoyed as she took The Crown Prince's hand.

Caius gazed at the horses, grazing in the paddocks adjacent to the palace. He felt a deep sense of contentment watching them, sensing Adranus's presence.

Sar-Mhirian had ventured into Sarhynel. An eerie silence had descended on the buildings and the cobbled streets that had been bloodstained and dirty were being washed as the dead were lifted into carts. He watched as the last traces of red disappeared from the stone and felt compassion for those who had lost their lives in the battle. He stared at the Temple of Crilm, with its blackened stone walls and still smouldering roof. He felt sure someone close to Crilm would be needed to ensure his wishes were adhered to during the renovations. Sar-Mhirian thought of the blessings he would bestow on the city to ensure its protection from the attentions of the dark gods and their emissaries.

Queen Ahrisa woke to find her husband standing at the window staring at two dolphins swimming in the Whispering Sea.

"Caedec," she murmured.

As he sat on the edge of the bed Caedec smiled, gazing at her with love and admiration. Her golden hair was spread over the pillow. Her beauty still captivated him, just as it had the first time he saw her. "How are you?"

"I'm well enough."

"We have much to do, you and I, our life together is just beginning," he said taking her hand in his.

Castle Adranabar was a welcome sight to Prince Orthon. He saw joiners and craftsmen working hard to repair it in the aftermath of the siege. He noticed the main gates had been replaced and thought they looked well.

Darthus watched as Varmarah and her foal trotted into the courtyard. He glanced at Aramintha, thinking her place was at his side.

Jhinn was less contented, as he thought of Lord Griann's reward for his bravery at the Battle of Ilepo Pass - Saravia's hand in marriage. Lord Griann's request was a bitter blow to him, as it was to Prince Orthon. He had begged his uncle to refuse it, but to no avail. He would not renege on a point of honour and his dislike of Griann festered in its wake. He was rankled the wedding would take place in the Temple of Crilm within Castle Adranabar's walls. They would be guests at the castle until the ceremony and then they would ride north to Lord Griann's estates.

Aramintha had noticed the tension between the young lords. She watched the way Jhinn gazed at Saravia and realized the source of it.

Prince Orthon dismounted. He greeted Salmir as he waited by the main building.

Salmir's heart surged in his chest as he caught sight of his daughter and the rest of Prince Orthon's retinue.

Aramintha almost threw herself from her mount in her haste to greet her father.

"Aramintha! Thank Crilm you're safe," he said, embracing her as Darthus looked on, feeling awkward.

Darthus felt only emptiness inside himself. There was no one to greet him and give thanks for his safe return. He turned his horse in the direction of the stables. As he dismounted and made to Varmarah's stall, she made towards him, nudging his shoulder as he patted her head.

Prince Orthon brushed past his advisers on the way to his apartment. They shuffled along behind him, but he waved them away, intent on his bed and undisturbed sleep. They would have to wait, feeling the morrow would be soon enough to receive them.

Lord Griann was overjoyed at the thought of his coming marriage to Saravia, though he knew it had come at a price. It was unlikely he would enjoy any semblance of a good relationship with Jhinn or Prince Orthon now. But it was a price he had willingly paid and if Jhinn succeeded Prince Orthon, he knew he held sufficient power to withstand such a turn of events.

Although Saravia was happy about her betrothal, she was aware of the upset it had caused, casting a pall over the impending celebrations. She wanted to leave Castle Adranabar and longed for her wedding day. There was another reason for wishing her wedding day near. She had felt unwell of late and suspected she was with child.

As he left the stables Darthus saw the prisoners being led to the dungeons, the captured rebels were thin and dirty. Many were not much older than Janus. He felt Prince Orthon's victory at Ilepo Pass was a hollow one and hoped he would find it in his heart to show them mercy. But he was not convinced of it. He hated the thought of executions carried out as retribution for the uprising, but suspected they would come soon enough.

Jhinn paced the floor of his chamber. He was restless and miserable as the eve of Saravia's wedding dawned. He had asked his uncle's permission to leave Castle Adranabar, but it had been refused. As Lord Griann had saved his life at Ilepo Pass, he must remain and attend his wedding. He was furious with his uncle, but not surprised at his command.

As Jhinn stared at the ring he had intended for Saravia, he decided he would speak to her.

Saravia stood alone on the quayside. She had slipped away from her chambers and the endless fittings for her wedding gown. Visits from friends and family had left her drained. Her father, sister, brother-in-law and noisy nephews and nieces had arrived for the ceremony.

She took a last, lingering look at the Whispering Sea then made her way back to her chambers. As she crossed the busy courtyard she pulled up the hood of her cloak, hoping to pass unnoticed.

"Saravia, I must speak with you," Jhinn's voice was almost a whisper as he took her arm, guiding her to a secluded part of the gardens.

"Jhinn, I'm to be married on the morrow. I can't be seen with you. Please let go of me," she said.

216

"No one will see us. Please Saravia, when you're married you'll live far away from here. Our paths may not cross again," he replied in a coaxing tone of voice.

Saravia relented, allowing herself to be led.

Jhinn produced a key and opened the door of a tower at the edge of the gardens, which seemed empty and falling into ruin.

As Saravia stepped through the door she was surprised to find the interior intact.

"I asked the craftsmen from Adran to restore it. I thought it would be a comfortable place to house my family on visits here. It has wonderful views of the Whispering Sea. I hoped you would like it," he explained.

Saravia was confused, watching him produce a small pouch from the folds of his cloak.

"I intended to ask you to marry me," said Jhinn, handing it to her.

Saravia opened it and looked at the ring inside. "Jhinn why tell me this on the eve of my wedding?"

"I couldn't keep it to myself any longer. Take it, it was intended for you and it's not too late. We could leave, never to return and we'd be together."

Saravia's heart was torn, her mind full of confusion. Her head felt as if it might explode and she felt faint, feeling herself slide down to the floor.

Jhinn was aghast. "Saravia!" he cradled her in his arms thinking the shock had been too much for her, knowing his actions had put them both in a dangerous position. "You need some air. We'll go out into the garden."

Saravia heard his voice, nodding as she tried to stand. Slowly she walked out of the tower.

Atheil noticed them as he cut across the gardens. Fascinated, he hid behind a rose bush to watch the scene unfolding before him. He saw Saravia turn to Jhinn, watching as she whispered in his ear and kissed him lightly on the cheek. He feared for his lord's happiness, wondering if she was really in love with her husband-to-be. Her involvement with Jhinn worried him. He knew Lord Griann possessed a jealous nature where matters of the heart were concerned.

Saravia's head was swimming as she made her way back to her chambers. She passed through the courtyard in a dream, barely acknowledging Darthus and scarcely noticing the disappointed look on his face at her lack of recognition.

A clock chimed as Saravia entered her chamber and sank into a chair, exhausted. She studied the ring of betrothal sparkling on her finger and felt tears welling up inside her. As darkness approached, she fell into despair, dreading the dawn of her wedding day.

As Saravia was dressed in her gown, she was still and pale. She said nothing - her face was expressionless as the maids arranged her hair and fastened a necklace around her throat.

Erarunde fidgeted as he waited for his daughter. He adjusted his attire and paced, until at last he heard the door of her chamber open. He watched with admiration as she came down the stairs, meeting her at the bottom step, he clasped her hand in his. He gazed at her countenance and realized she was troubled. "You've been crying lass. Are you sure about this – do you want to go through with it?"

Saravia fought back the tears and gave a half smile, knowing it was too late to change her mind. She was aware the carriage had arrived and there were guests waiting for her. A cheer rose as she stepped into the coach followed by her father. As the carriage drew up at the temple doors and she alighted, dark clouds obscured the sun and a bitter wind was blowing.

Prince Orthon thought Saravia a vision as she walked down the aisle escorted by her father. Her flowing gown of gold silk, set with Azuriene crystals and tied with a broad sash of blue, was most becoming. Her hair, studded with crystals, caught the light as it filtered through the arched windows. Flowers adorning the altar complemented her wedding gown and from their portraits, Crilm's sisters smiled on those assembled in their brother's temple.

Saravia caught a glimpse of Jhinn and felt a lump in her throat.

Standing at the altar, Erarunde offered his daughter's hand to Lord Griann. He looked at her and smiled. Saravia felt the touch of his skin and was reassured by the warmth of it. She hoped all would be well between them as Crilm's mantras were recited.

As the couple were bathed in golden light, Prince Orthon noticed Jhinn's forlorn expression and felt sorry for him, it was obvious he was in love with Saravia and now she was wed to another. Life had not been easy for his nephew and he hoped the lad's fortunes would change.

Anything was possible in the worlds.